C000010135

THE LEGION OF NOTHING
REBIRTH

© 2012 Jim Zoetewey
ISBN 978-1-926959-26-9

Editor-in-Chief: AM Harte
Copy editor: Terra Whiteman
Cover art: Natasha Dichpan
Book design: Tim Sevenhuysen
Cover art design: MCM

Published by 1889 Labs Ltd.
Visit our website for free books and other fun stuff:
http://1889.ca

To my wife and children, who I've ignored more than I'd like to admit while writing this.

To the readers of inmydaydreams.com, who saw all of this before anyone else, and whose interest kept me writing.

The Legion of Nothing
Rebirth

by Jim Zoetewey

Chapter One

"I'm going out on patrol," Cassie said.

We—and by we, I meant Daniel, Cassie, and I—were in the headquarters of the Heroes League, the 1950's and 60's premiere superhero team. Our grandparents had used it as a secret bunker against evil forces. We were using it to play Rock Band on the PlayStation. Every video game is better on a twenty foot screen.

Except for the musty smell, concrete walls and olive green carpet, it was an impressive place.

Daniel paused the PlayStation, silencing the middle riffs of 'Enter Sandman'. Cassie was standing on the threshold of the bathroom, chin lifted in defiance.

She'd changed.

She wore a costume that was an exact match for her father's—light blue with the red, white and blue of the US flag covering her chest. I recognized the material: my grandfather had designed it for her father. It was resistant to bullets and most physical attacks, but nowhere near as effective as the Rocket suit—my grandfather's powered armor. Captain Commando had preferred mobility over protection. You can do that when you regenerate.

Cap's costume had also been skintight, but I'd never thought about it.

I noticed one other thing. She'd cut off her hair. It was a short, blond brush cut instead of shoulder length.

"Your hair?" I asked.

"Oh," she said, "it wasn't comfortable under the mask and it moved around a lot. So I cut it off back in August."

"You had hair five minutes ago."

She pulled a blond wig out of her duffel bag.

"Now that we've got the *important* stuff out of the way," she said, "why don't we get back to the original point. I'm going out on patrol. Anyone want to go with me?"

Daniel nodded like he'd expected her to say that. He probably had. His grandfather, the Mentalist, was the best known telepath to come out of World War II. His father, Mindstryke was just as well known.

He put down the guitar and stood up. When we were standing, he was half a head taller than me. He was also better looking—literally tall, dark, and handsome. Think black hair, skin a little darker than tan, and a face that reminded me a little of Leonardo DiCaprio in Titanic.

Seriously, girls swooned.

With an easy grin, he said, "Sure. I'll go get into

costume. It's in my car."

"You guys go," I said. "I'll be here."

"Why?" Cassie said. Whether her tone had an accusatory edge to it or not, I believed I heard one.

I tried to think of a reason. I couldn't put it into words. Grandpa had taught me everything he could about how the Rocket suit worked, how all of his inventions worked. He'd arranged for a friend to teach me how to fight. I'd learned a lot from both of them, but how was I supposed to live up to what he'd done?

Still, I didn't say that. I said, "I'd just like to stay here."

"Okay," she said. "Well, do that then."

Daniel said, "Don't worry about it, Nick. It's no big deal."

"Let's just drop it," she said. "You go change, I've got to find something."

As he walked toward the elevator, he grinned at me and I heard his voice in my head. *Don't worry about it. She's just nervous. First time out on the streets at night. And by the way, if you do know where her dad's sword is, tell her. It might be a while before she asks.*

Well, a telepath would know. On the other hand, I thought to myself, I could just let her search.

Not worth it.

Cassie was already looking irritated. The League's meeting room was the size of a basketball court and filled with file cabinets, obscure curios, small monuments and awards.

More than one sword hung on the wall.

"Cassie," I said, "I know where your dad's sword is."

"Really?" Her eyes swept across the room. "That's great, because I don't want to sort through all this crap right now."

I got it for her. It was in the storage area reserved for powered equipment just off the meeting room, along with my grandpa's spare suits, all of them standing at attention, shining golden in the light and waiting for action.

It's been called the Freedom Sword and the Eagle Sword but that's just by the press. Captain Commando simply called it the sword and occasionally "the goddamn oversized can-opener." From what I'd heard, he'd never had any strong attachment to it. It was associated with him in the public imagination because it was the only piece of equipment Grandpa made for him that had lasted more than a couple months. Well, that, and the fact that he'd died with it in his hand.

It wasn't really meant for sword fighting. It was more for chopping through things like tanks, walls and bridges.

Cassie strapped the sword on her back, "Thanks."

"No problem."

"Not to spoil the gesture," she said, "but the only reason you knew what I was looking for is because Daniel pulled it out of my head and told you, right?"

"Yeah."

"He has to stop doing that. Even when it helps, it's still creepy."

"You'll get no argument from me," I said.

They left soon after.

I tried playing Guitar Hero for a little while, but found I wasn't in the mood. I thought about going home and going to bed, but it was only nine.

I got up and walked into the lab. I could almost see Grandpa Vander Sloot there, scribbling on the plans for the next version of his suit, mumbling about what an idiot he'd been when he designed the last version and telling me how much better the next version would be.

He wasn't, of course.

The tools, the tables and the fabrication machines… They were there. The computers we'd used to design the last version of the suit were there too.

He'd included me in the process, justifying it by saying he needed a young mind to help him with the CAD software. By the end, I knew every piece of the suit, the materials, the systems and subsystems, his design philosophy and the experiences behind some of the quirkier design choices he'd made.

The suit stood in the corner like medieval armor— assuming that armor had been designed in an Art Deco style. It was golden with black detailing. Streamlined. Slim.

I stared at the helmet.

Would it kill me, I asked myself, if I took to the streets for one night?

*   *   *

The League's HQ had a lot of exits. The one I shot out of opened up just above water level on Grand Lake itself. It used to pour sewage into the lake, but was abandoned by the city in the 1960's.

It had been Grandpa's favorite way to exit the complex.

I could see why. There's something about bursting out of a tunnel, flying briefly over dark water and then turning to see the lights of the city, the public beach, and the harbor.

I'm not sure what it is.

By the time I crossed the highway that runs next to the lake, I'd formulated a few rules for what I would and would not do that evening. I was not going to go find Cassie and Daniel. I was not going to turn on the police band and listen for crimes.

What I was going to do was get out of League HQ, get out of my parents' house and do something that nobody had told me to do.

If it so happened that I saw a crime being committed, I would stop it, but I wasn't going to seek out trouble.

I landed on a lawn just on the other side of the highway, next to a collection of hotels and high-rise apartment buildings. Running, I crossed the sidewalk and merged into traffic.

With a name like The Rocket, you might have expected Grandpa to have flown everywhere, but he hadn't. He'd only had an hour of fuel to work with, so he'd spent most of his patrols on the ground.

Even though the new version of the suit was better than the original, making that one hour of fuel last three, I liked running. For one thing it charged the suit's battery. For another, if you really wanted to appreciate the physical power the suit made available to you, you could keep up with traffic—provided traffic was moving below forty miles per hour.

Not that I had much traffic to deal with. I'd deliberately chosen an empty street. This evening's exercise was less about fighting crime than sorting things out in my head.

I got into the run, settling on a good thirty mile per hour pace and began to think about what had driven me out for the night.

Grandpa had never asked me if I'd wanted his suit.

He'd just given it to me in a secret clause of his will. He'd also never asked me if I'd wanted his lab or the League's HQ beneath it.

Or if I needed eleven million dollars in a Swiss bank account earmarked for 'fighting evil'—all of which would be donated to the Superhero Legal Defense Fund should I choose not to bother.

So yeah, no pressure.

The SUV ahead of me stopped. I hadn't even noticed it was there.

Not having the space to slow down, I jumped up, shooting over the SUV and landing just short of people smoking on the sidewalk in front of Willy's Bar (or so said the sign in the window). The guy nearest to me dropped his cigarette, shouting, "Holy shit! You trying to kill me?"

I gave a little wave and said, "Sorry." Thanks to the fact that I'd been showing Daniel the suit's ability to imitate sounds, this came out less reassuring than I'd thought it would—we're talking a 100% dead-on imitation of Darth Vader.

On the bright side, the landing had killed my momentum.

Deciding to stop trying to salvage the situation, I ignored them and started walking. The SUV wasn't the only stopped car. From what I could see, the line of cars went to the end of the block.

It wasn't a block that I would choose to be stuck on. This part of Fourth Street seemed to be heavy on bars, liquor stores, seedy shops and boarded-up buildings.

I reached the end of the block to find two cars in the middle of the intersection. A rusty, blue pickup had hit an Audi convertible from behind, smashing the trunk in.

A crowd of people stood on the corners and watched while the owners yelled at each other. In one corner was a thirty-ish, blond guy who looked like he went to the gym several times a week. In the other (next to the truck with the broken headlight) stood a pot-bellied, forty-something with a stringy beard and a Metallica t-shirt.

I stopped at the back of the crowd, wondering if I would have to open up the rockets and fly over. "Excuse me," I said, "coming through…"

No one turned to look at me. No one moved.

It occurred to me that switching the voice mechanism to a lightly modified version of my own voice and away from Darth Vader's might have been a bad idea.

I tapped the guy ahead of me on the shoulder. He wore a Grand Lake University sweatshirt and was standing at the back of a group of guys.

He turned around, beginning to say, "What do you want," when he suddenly noticed the armor.

"Please move," I said, turning up the volume on the PA a little.

"No problem," he said. "Uh… guys?"

They parted like the Red Sea.

The man in the Metallica t-shirt had the passenger door open and seemed to be going through the glove compartment. "Gimme a second," he muttered.

"A second? I've given you twenty minutes. No. You're going to find your fucking insurance now."

The blond man pulled a handgun out of his Audi.

The first thought that jumped into my head was that someone should call the police. The second thought?

That I was an idiot.

I jumped into the intersection, moving between the two men.

I got shot.

The bullet bounced harmlessly off the armor, but it was still a surprise. I pushed his arm toward the ground with my right hand while pulling the gun away with my left.

Once I had the gun in my hand, I stuck my fingers through the guard and pushed the trigger sideways till I broke it.

Then I dropped the gun and the trigger in the street.

He looked down at the gun and then back up at me. Then he started shouting. "You broke my gun. I'll kill you!"

He went on in that vein for a while.

I had no idea what to do. I had options. The most obvious was threatening him or punching him, but I didn't want to. When I was in costume, I could punch through walls—and people. I knew I had to do something though. In the moment, however, it was hard to think just what that should be.

As some bullies at school had found, I was not all that great with witty repartee under pressure either.

I decided to ignore him. I turned to check on the guy with the truck. He'd shut his car door and stood next to the vehicle, having found what he was looking for or just given up.

From behind me I heard, "Hey, you're not listening to me. Listen to me, damn you! I'm going to sue you. You and this guy, too. He trashed my car. You trashed my gun. That's private property. Did you hear me?

Private property."

I turned around, increasing the volume on the built-in PA as high as it could go. As in, up to eleven.

Now before I go on, I should mention that I've always had mixed feelings about the suit's sonic systems. First of all, because they could have permanent side effects—like deafness. Second, because I had always seen them as the result of forty years worth of feature creep. Back in World War II, Grandpa decided the suit needed a PA. Then he decided it might be useful if the PA could modify a person's voice. Then he noticed that he could break glass with the PA and wondered how far he could take that.

Since the early 70's, in addition to the PA, each arm of the suit has been given 'weaponized' speakers that could focus concentrated sound on an object, sometimes shattering it (even if it wasn't glass).

Not that I was using anything more than the PA, but the PA was bad enough.

"Will. You. SHUT. UP," I said.

I assumed he heard me from the way he put his hands to his ears and how his face whitened.

Not only did he hear me, but so did the crowd (which went dead silent), people several blocks away, and, for all I knew, people inside the International Space Station.

He whimpered.

Lowering the volume to something bearable, I turned back to the guy with the truck. "You may as well find your registration, because I think I hear the police."

He didn't say anything. He just nodded.

"Well anyway," I said to the crowd, "have a nice

night everybody."

I started the rockets and blasted into the night sky just as the police cars arrived.

*   *   *

Lunch tray in my hands, I walked toward the table where Cassie sat. It was on the other side of the cafeteria from where I usually sat and just a few tables away from Kayla and the girls Cassie generally ate with. Kayla glanced in our direction as I sat down.

"You got my note," Cassie said brightly.

I had. It had come in the form of a paper airplane to the back of my head during our only shared class—government.

"You've got good aim," I said.

"Looks like you made national news last night." She put a printout on the table. Headlined "The Rocket Returns?" an Associated Press article gave a brief description of the incident and went on to speculate about whether it was the 1940's era Rocket or a new one, including a quote from a superhero historian who said: "But if he is the same person, he has to be in his eighties or nineties."

"Where'd you find that?"

"Yahoo's got a section for superhero news, and besides, it's been on the local news all morning. Don't you listen to the radio?"

"Not this morning."

I eyed my lunch. In honor of the year's first football game, the hamburger had been renamed The Central High Burger, dyed blue, and placed on a yellow bun.

I supposed that I should be thankful our school colors weren't orange and green.

I took a bite. It tasted normal.

"So," I said, "how did things go for you?"

She grinned. "Boring at first, but remember Syndicate L? We found them. They're here in Grand Lake."

"Where and… How do you know?"

"Daniel," she said. "They've got an old warehouse downtown. He happened to pick up something from the mind of a truck driver making a delivery."

"Did you tell his dad?"

She rolled her eyes.

"Of course not. We're going to do this ourselves. And by we," she said, "I'd like to include you."

I nearly spat out my burger. It's not that I was surprised; I could hardly be surprised since she'd be going on about this for a while now, but at our level of skill, I thought we shouldn't be taking on organized crime, we should be taking down muggers and working our way up.

She didn't wait for me to reply. "I know you've got mixed feelings about this and I know we're not experienced, but we're not going in without a plan. Daniel found out that something big is coming in tonight and it's not legal. Fortunately they're not guarding it with much. Ten people, maybe. Normal people. We can take them. Then we call the police."

"And if you can't handle them…" I said.

"Then we call Daniel's dad or maybe even Larry."

Larry was better known as "The Rhino." He was a nationally recognized hero—though less because of his powers and more because of his nationally branded beer. It wasn't that he wasn't tough. He was just better known for his portrait on the bottle and an over the top Super Bowl ad than he was for any villain he'd ever fought.

"I don't know," I said.

"You don't know?" She put her hands on the table as if she were about to stand up and leave, but didn't.

"I wasn't going do this," she said, "but Daniel tells me that whatever's going on with you is because you feel like I'm making you do this. I'm not making you. You started training with Lee five years ago. You were working with your grandfather longer than that. Whether or not you intended to, you've been preparing longer than anyone but Daniel, and he's had powers since birth."

I opened my mouth to interrupt. It wasn't her—not really. If anyone had pushed me, it was my grandfather.

"No," she said, "Don't say anything. Just think about it. You could have done anything last night after we left, but instead," she lowered her voice, "you went out for a run *in costume*. What does that tell you?

"You want to do it too, that's what. You—" She looked up at the clock in the middle of the lunchroom wall. "I've got five minutes to eat all this stuff." She gestured to the tray in front of her. It held at least three trays worth of food.

"I've got a fast metabolism," she said.

* * *

Flying toward the warehouse that night, I was still thinking about the conversation. I knew that there was more to it.

I sighted the warehouse before I got anywhere. In the twilight, I couldn't see much other than that it was old, brown and brick—which meant it didn't stand out at all in this section of the city.

Daniel and Cassie were on the roof of the warehouse's twin across the street. I landed on the far side of the roof, trying not to be too obvious about it and started walking toward them.

Suddenly, I heard Daniel's voice in my head.

Crawl. They've got cameras and someone to monitor them. I think he missed you, but he's on the edge of my effective range, so I'm not sure.

Right, I thought, crawling the rest of the way across the roof.

The delivery already came. It's over there.

A picture of the loading dock on the other side of the building appeared in my head. A semi had backed its trailer in.

So why are we on this side of the building?

Cassie's idea was that I could clairvoyantly scry from over here since they don't watch this side much.

So do we have a plan?

It's not much of a plan, but it's good enough. We fly over there, take them out, and call the police.

Are you sure that's enough?

They're normal people, Nick. All they've got are guns. And besides they're all in the room next to the loading dock. I'd bet it'll take less than a minute.

Cassie said, "Let's go."

I stood up.

And got shot.

Twice.

"Where'd that guy come from?" I muttered.

He must have moved when we were talking. Sorry. He's behind the top floor window, the third from the end.

I dived off the building with rockets engaged,

hurtled across the gap and broke through the window, flying over the shooter and landing behind him. Landing is actually a charitable word since I stumbled and landed on my chest.

I stood and turned around to find a man in a black uniform pointing a rifle at me. I grabbed the rifle's body with my right hand, bent the barrel ninety degrees with my left and stepped forward to punch the guy in the face.

He fell to the floor.

As I looked down, wondering briefly if I'd killed him despite my training, I heard Daniel in my head again.

He's alive. We're off to the loading docks. Meet you there.

I flew out the window and above the building just in time to see Daniel and Cassie disappearing over the far end of the roof. Not long ago he'd had a hard time moving a basketball with his telekinesis. Now he could move people. It made me wonder what he'd be able to do in five years.

I landed on the loading dock only slightly after them.

Cassie had jumped into a group of three, downing one of them with a punch that knocked him off the loading dock. Two more were firing submachine guns at Daniel, but he seemed unharmed.

The other three are behind the door! Get them before they call reinforcements.

A human sized metal door stood to the left of the larger door meant for unloading the truck. I ran for it, hitting it at as close to full speed as possible and knocking it out of the door frame.

It slammed onto the wooden floor inside and then slid for a few feet, knocking over a cot. The loading bay appeared to be some kind of combination control center and camp, containing cots, sleeping bags, a laptop, guns and boxes of gear.

The laptop on the desk showed eight different views of the building's exterior.

The people inside the room pulled out guns and started firing. I didn't make any effort to disarm them; I just punched them until they stopped.

Cassie walked in after me, stepping over the door. "What did I say? It was easy. Good job, Rocket."

That was probably one of the stranger moments of the evening. In my mind, it was still my grandfather's name. If he'd been there, he'd have known exactly what he was doing. Me? I was still worried I might have accidentally killed one of them, and, disturbed that one of them was a woman. Mind you, she had been firing an AK-47 at me, but it still felt wrong.

Is it sexist that I didn't feel as bad about the men?

"Good job… uh… Captain Commando?"

She laughed. "You know, it's funny that you didn't know. You're right, but I…" She lapsed into silence, eyes sliding to the unconscious bodies for a moment before flicking back toward the door—behind which lay five *more* bodies if she and Daniel had done their jobs.

"It's funny," she said again, not sounding amused at all, "it's his name and his costume and it was all so easy. I should be happier about this, but…"

She trailed off again.

"I think I know what you mean," I said. "It feels off somehow."

Daniel (or I suppose "the Mystic" in this context) poked his head through the door. "My dad says fighting normal people is a lot like fighting ten year olds. You're just so much better that it's not much of a challenge.

"Anyway," he said, "anyone want to find out what's in the semi?"

"You don't know?" I said. "I thought you could sense what's on the other side of walls and stuff."

"Not if they block me."

We walked out to the loading dock and stared at the back door of the truck.

Cassie put her hand on the latch. "How would they block you?"

"Well," he said, "some people use electronics. Sometimes telepaths can do it. That kind of thing."

She pulled the doors open.

It looked more like an expensive hotel suite than I'd expected—wall to wall carpeting (dark red), hot tub, big screen TV, large bed, and a walled off area at the far end that I assumed had to be the bathroom.

A big man sat on the couch in front of the TV.

He picked up the remote, turned off the TV, and pulled himself up to his full height. I'd guess he was around six and half feet tall, but he wasn't especially frightening. He was balding, unshaven, had a bit of a potbelly, and stifled a yawn while he walked toward us.

He wore a bathrobe.

Cassie turned to me and said, "This can't all be for him, can it?"

I didn't answer. I'd just recognized him.

Double V is the fanboy nickname for *Villains and Vigilantes*, a magazine that covers supers. I didn't get the magazine, but my grandpa had. I followed their website's RSS feed and had read his profile a couple years before.

His name was Jason Swan, AKA the Grey Giant, AKA the Rock Goliath, AKA the West Coast ATM Thief. From what I remembered, he was practically invulnerable and incredibly strong. He also had one other power, but I couldn't think of it.

That bugged me.

On his own he wasn't much of a threat. He didn't have much ambition. This wasn't a guy who would be taking Chicago for ransom in exchange for ten billion dollars. Left to himself, he emptied bank vaults and stole ATM machines, but he didn't terrorize people.

When working for other people though... He killed two supers in Seattle three years ago—Lightweaver and the Shield. From what the article said, it wasn't malice. He just hit them too hard. That didn't even count all the normals who died when he knocked out a load bearing wall on a five story building.

In the end, they'd needed half the North Pacific Defenders to take him down.

Basically if you needed a distraction, needed to guard something, or needed somebody beaten up, he'd do it for a price. The article described him as "a small time thug with the powers of a world-beater."

And here he was.

Before our eyes, he transformed from a paunchy, balding, middle-aged guy to a nine-foot tall, freakishly muscular humanoid with grey rock for skin.

"Happy, kids? You fucked up a good payday for me. Should have gone outside the second I heard gunfire." He started walking toward us, clenching his right hand into a fist.

"I don't make a habit of hurting children, but you know, I've got to make an example."

He grew larger, too big to fit comfortably inside the semi-trailer, but it didn't faze him. He just ripped out the roof. I'd say he was fifteen feet tall at that point.

I was about to ask Daniel to send everything I knew about him from my mind to Cassie's, but I was too slow.

Cassie had already jumped into action. She'd closed the distance in one jump, kicking him in the stomach, but not actually hurting him. Hitting him stopped her dead in the air. She managed to fall hands first, back outstretched with feet above, hitting the floor with her hands, using the momentum to flip herself to her feet.

He leaned forward to punch her, but never had a chance. She jumped up, landing on his shoulders, using his own arm for an assist. Then she started pounding him in the head, the ears, and the face... all while dodging his attempts to grab her.

Well, at least for a little while.

Just at the moment I'd revved up the rockets and decided to shoot myself into his solar plexus, he grabbed her leg and threw her out of the trailer and into the building. I heard a thump as she hit the wall and began to fall toward the loading dock behind us.

I received an image of Cassie falling and felt that Daniel was trying to catch her telekinetically. Realizing that I was the only thing stopping The Grey Giant from attacking Daniel, I launched myself toward the giant's midsection.

And immediately experienced pain as a fist the size of my head connected with my chest.

Tumbling through the air, I flew across the street,

struggling to gain control of where I was going but only succeeding in hitting the brick wall of another warehouse.

That also hurt.

Hitting the ground felt pleasant by comparison.

Lying half-conscious next to the factory, it occurred to me that this was what life as a baseball must be like.

When my head cleared, I found myself sprawled on the thin line of grass between the sidewalk and the road. I groaned. My ribs hurt from the punch.

In the twilight, I could make out the Grey Giant next to the ruin of the semi's trailer. He seemed to be studying the roof. I guessed that Daniel might have moved Cassie up there after I'd been taken out.

Right in one, Daniel said.

Was Cassie okay?

Well, she lost a tooth, but it looks like it's already beginning to come back a little.

"Is there any way to make this a three way call?" I thought at him.

Daniel: *Yeah. Why didn't I think of that?*

Cassie: *Oh, great. Now I can't ignore you at all.*

I felt pain in the background as she thought.

Me: *I'm calling 911. This guy is out of our league. I'm pretty sure they can get a hold of Daniel's dad.*

Daniel: *They can.*

Cassie: *Let him take care of it then.*

Me: *Cassie, are you okay?*

Cassie: *I'm fucking fine.*

Her pain pulsed.

Cassie: *You know what they don't tell you? They don't tell you that regenerating hurts almost as much as the original wound… and lasts longer.*

The Grey Giant pulled a large black object out of the trailer, leaned back and threw it into the air.

It flew over the side of the factory.

Daniel didn't close the link so I experienced two simultaneous views of a large screen TV tumbling through the air, bouncing once and shattering. Daniel concentrated, and the pieces shifted to the left, landing just two feet to the side.

For a moment I sensed a double share of relief and then the vision faded, leaving me solely in mental contact.

Me: *Wow.*

Cassie: *Tell me about it.*

Daniel: *I know we can't take him down, but we can't just sit here and see if he comes up with something better.*

Me: *I'll call the cops.*

The suit had a radio transmitter that contacted HQ, which in turn had a device that plugged into the phone network. I thought of it as futuristic 1960's technology. One of these days I needed to put in a cell phone.

It had its uses though. For one thing, the number was a known quantity. When the person on the other end of the line picked up, I could feel sure that their screen showed "Grand Lake Hero League." In theory, this should have gotten me instant respect.

"Hello?" I said.

The woman on the other end said nothing for a moment, but then managed, "Um…."

I supposed that was an understandable response to being called by a defunct super organization.

"This is the Rocket," I said, "and I need some backup here. Call the Rhino and Mindstryke if you can get them. If you can't, get one of the teams in Chicago.

We're facing the Grey Giant at 130 Elm. It's an old factory. Syndicate L is involved somehow. Do you need anything else?"

The pause from the other end was lengthy. Then, "Aren't you retired? I mean, are you real?"

"How real do I have to be? The key point is that the Grey Giant is out of my league. Seriously. I'm not the original Rocket," I said. Then I hung up.

Me: *Well, that was useless.*

Cassie: *Kinda.*

Daniel: *I can call my dad on my cell phone, but there's no guarantee that he'll be able to get Larry.*

Me: *Well, then what do we do?*

Daniel: *I don't know. I'm having a hard time getting into the Grey Giant's head—so mental attacks don't do much. All I've got at this point is flinging blasts of telekinetic force at him.*

I looked over at the Grey Giant. He'd doubled in size, bringing himself just ten feet short of the roof of the factory.

Me: *I'd get off the roof if I were you.*

Daniel: *Meet us on the roof of the factory you're in front of?*

Me: *You got it.*

I got up and ran around the corner, waiting until I got to the opposite side to open up and shoot myself to the roof. When I got there, I found Cassie and Daniel landing on the far end.

Simultaneously, I could hear loud booming and crashing noises. Being on the opposite end of the roof blocked my view of most of the warehouse, but I could see the middle of its wall collapse.

We met in the middle of the factory's roof.

"Dad's not answering his cell phone," Daniel said, with maybe just a hint of nervousness.

"So it's totally up to us," Cassie said, glancing across the street as the left corner of the warehouse shattered and fell in. Was I right in thinking I heard her mood lift as she said it?

"And what are we supposed to do to him?" I asked. "Worse, what do we do with him if we actually catch him?"

"I think," Daniel said, "that there are victory conditions that don't necessarily mean taking him down. If we manage to get him out of town without having him hurt much of anything, I'd count that as a win."

I said, "I'd count it as a win too if I had the slightest idea of how to do it."

"Cut the crap," Cassie said, sounding more confident as she went on. "We've got something he wants. He wants to hurt us to make an example, but—"

"We're faster than he is," Daniel said, having undoubtedly pulled it straight out of her head.

"Right," Cassie said, sounding annoyed. "Here's what we do: we lead him to the lake and then down the coast. Then we ditch him when we get far enough from town."

"I can't think of anything better," I said, wondering where he was now. It had been a little while since the most recent section of wall had fallen in.

"Then let's go get him," Cassie said. She took a step in the direction of the warehouse they'd left.

"If we can find him," I muttered.

The building creaked as a large gray hand appear on the side of roof that faced the now demolished warehouse.

Daniel said, "I hope this building's insurance covers rampaging giants."

Rockets engaged, I shot off the roof toward the ruins of the warehouse, landing next to an enormous pile of bricks that had spilled into the street.

The Grey Giant, illuminated by the streetlights, stood nearly forty feet tall and reached over the side of the building toward Daniel and Cassie.

I picked up a cluster of bricks and threw it at the Giant, hitting him solidly in the back.

It shattered. He turned toward me while Daniel and Cassie lifted off from the roof—or so I assumed. It was dark enough that I couldn't see them until they landed next to me.

"I'm thinking that he might get pissed enough to keep after us if we throw enough bricks at him," I said. "The highway's not too busy at night so we can lead him to it and then just follow the coast when it turns east."

"Right," Daniel said.

A stream of bricks started to fly toward the Giant. It was as if someone had turned on a hose. About the time the bricks hit him in the face, the Grey Giant's expression turned sour.

Growling, he ran toward us. Cassie and I ran west down Boyce Street, knowing we were only four blocks from the highway. Not having any special physical abilities, Daniel flew next to us while the Giant lumbered behind.

Some things seem like a better idea when you're thinking about them than when you're actually trying them.

Leading a forty foot tall super villain down a highway at night was one of those things.

Lakeside Road ran north to Grand Lake and then east around Grand Lake before continuing north. Most of the factories were on the north side of Grand Lake City. It turned into a six lane highway in the middle of town, but before and after, it was four lanes wide.

While it changed from city to countryside fairly quickly, the "countryside" was mostly forest, houses with large lots, million dollar lakeside "cottages," and a few farms.

In other words, we would have to run for miles to lead him some place where he could be left alone.

By the time we reached the highway, we were all in the air again. Daniel telekinetically carried Cassie and himself. I flew under my own power.

The Grey Giant ran behind us. It turns out that when you're nearly forty feet tall, you have a ridiculously long stride. Cassie and I had no chance of staying ahead of him on the ground.

The chase caused as much chaos as you might expect. People stopped their cars and ran into the darkness off the side of the road. The Grey Giant knocked over a couple streetlights, downed at least one power line, and cursed a blue streak.

When we were about a mile out from downtown, he threw a SUV at me. It was a blue Chevy Tahoe. I dodged and watched it disappear into the darkness past the streetlights, grateful that it was unoccupied.

Overall though, I was surprised that I hadn't seen more cars (or crowds) once the fight had started. More often than not, from what I understood, people gathered round to watch supers go at it.

To give credit where credit's due, the government had run a big PSA campaign over the last five years—you know the one—where some old cop tells you what to do when you see supers fighting. "Don't stay and watch. Drive away. If you can't drive away, get out and run away. Don't stay and become a hostage, a missile or a distraction."

However effective the commercials, it was only a matter of time before we ran into someone with a death wish.

We didn't notice it immediately because the minivan sat on the far side of the northbound lane. We were in the southbound.

We noticed when the Grey Giant lurched to cross the median. It was at that point when I realized a middle-aged man and his teenage son were filming everything.

Daniel: *They're planning to upload the video to YouTube.*

Knowing that I was faster than anyone else while flying, I accelerated toward the Grey Giant at full speed and didn't bother to reply.

One of the settings for the weaponized speakers allows me to narrowcast sound at a target. I set it for a decibel level well past the threshold of pain, intending it to be more of a distraction than a serious attempt to harm.

Either too slow to react or too distracted by his goal to notice me, he let me get close. I held out my right arm toward his ear and shot a blast of sound from ten feet away.

He stopped reaching toward the van, missing me as I moved up and away from him, but managing to ding me with his other hand when I slowed down.

I'd thought I was out of his reach.

He followed it up with an open hand smack that sent me back across the median and down into the southbound lane, scraping the road until I rolled onto the gravel and then the grass.

I lay there, winded, wondering what Daniel and Cassie were doing now.

Then I heard a crashing noise, much like that of the warehouse falling down, followed quickly by squealing tires and an accelerating engine.

I pulled myself up.

I saw the minivan, the teenager pointing the camera out the window while his father drove. They stopped fifty feet away.

The Grey Giant lay on the road behind them.

The idiots in the mini-van weren't the only ones taking pictures. A helicopter from the local NBC affiliate, News 10 hovered above the streetlights. Evidently reporters paid no attention to PSA's either.

Of course, I had no right to complain about how stupid a person must be to get anywhere near this fight.

The Grey Giant pulled himself up from the road, leaving deep impressions where he'd landed.

Cassie stood in front of him with the sword out. Behind her, the boy was now pointing the camera out the rear window of the minivan.

Well, at least they hadn't stepped outside for a better angle.

Daniel: *I tripped him.*

Me: *I'd wondered.*

Daniel hung in the air behind Cassie.

Daniel: *I'm going to pull Cassie into the air when he*

attacks and—

But he didn't. The Grey Giant attacked too quickly for either of us to do anything.

First, a word about the sword: it could cut through pretty much anything.

Captain Commando never used it on people, but I could understand why Cassie intended to make a special exception at this moment.

He leaned forward and swiped at her with his right hand. She jumped backward, slashing it.

He looked bewildered, then stood fully and examined the back of his hand. It dripped grayish goo.

Cassie jumped forward, slashing his right shin, then jumped away to the right, into the median and out of easy reach.

He turned and ran. Ignoring the men in the van and the three of us, he sprinted away from Grand Lake, southbound down the highway.

I started the rockets and began to fly after him while Daniel pulled Cassie into the air.

But neither of us needed to chase him.

I'd been hearing police sirens for the last few minutes, but just as I started chasing the Grey Giant I heard a clattering noise from the north.

I knew that noise.

It was Larry, AKA my Crazy Uncle Larry, AKA the Rhino. Like my grandfather, he also used powered armor, but while my grandfather's was elegant, Larry's looked a lot like the Michelin man and sounded like a jackhammer.

He hit the Grey Giant from behind at a couple hundred miles per hour, knocking the Giant's legs out from under him. While Larry skidded to a stop, a tear in reality opened above the road.

Out of it flew too many costumed heroes for me to recognize individually, but it didn't matter. They were on the Giant before I had a chance to do anything.

By the time Daniel and I got close enough to participate (if the fight had still been going on), the Grey Giant lay on the ground. Hands now manacled in glowing blue energy, he had transformed back into his human form. Cassie's cuts to his skin had shrunk to just a couple bloody lines.

One of the heroes, a muscular man in a silver costume, looked from the unconscious body to size us up, commenting to no one in particular, "Damn, the kids get younger every year."

I recognized him. He called himself Guardian and led a team called the Midwest Defenders. He was a pretty big deal. Follow Double V and you'd get the impression that he stopped supervillains from burning down Chicago one week and went into space to fight invading aliens the next.

He stepped away from the Grey Giant's unconscious form and waved us to follow him off to the side of the highway.

As we stepped off the blacktop, Cassie said, "What do you suppose he wants?"

I had no idea.

"You," he was looking at me. "You're not the real Rocket, right? Because seriously, you fucked up. This guy's way out of your league. You should have withdrawn and called us—or hell, even Rhino over there."

Larry was talking with the police a couple hundred feet behind him.

"I called 911," I said. "It took ages before you got here."

"You don't call 911. We've got a number for stuff like this. You call it before you go in and we'll have someone available."

He sounded tired, as if he told me this already a couple times and I'd somehow forgotten.

"What number? Seriously," I said, "is it in the phone book? Do you put it on billboards? I've never seen this number. We had no idea that he was here. We just thought we were dealing with Syndicate L—you know, normal people with guns. This was just our bad luck."

"Besides," Cassie said, "if this is a mess, it's not the Rocket's fault, it's mine. I called him in at the last minute."

"Mine too," Daniel said. "I thought we'd done enough recon." Daniel took a deep breath. He looked tired.

Guardian scowled, suddenly reminding me more of a pissed off coach than a superhero.

"I look at you," he said, "and it's pretty obvious you've been into the Hero League's stuff. Hell, you're probably related to them. But you know what? You're not them."

He glared at each of us in turn.

"They," he continued, "were an experienced combat team. You are a bunch of kids taking a break from your homework to 'fight crime.' If you don't want to remember that your mistakes can kill people, then do us all a favor and go home."

He emphasized the last two words quite loudly. Behind him, the growing crowd of police, costumed heroes, civilians, and reporters all began to look in our direction.

"Tonight you had this guy next to a bunch of abandoned factories and you drove him toward a commonly used highway, knocking out power for I don't know how many city blocks as you went. If you'd done any research at all, you'd have had back up. Our number is *on our website*."

He looked at me directly. What could I say to that?

"If you want to do this," he said, "get serious. This isn't about glory. It's definitely not about money. It's about keeping thugs like that guy off the streets."

Then he turned, glancing toward where the Grey Giant's human body was being loaded into a Box—a small trucks specially modified for holding supers.

"Because if you don't get serious," he said, "you'll probably die young."

* * *

Everything else after that was a blur of police and press questions. I answered the police, ignored the press and we all flew back to headquarters. Daniel and Cassie left for their homes after cleaning up and changing into street clothes.

I stayed in the lab and checked the suit over for damage. Then I went and sat at the table in the main room, turning on the TV.

The massive room filled with a massive screen seemed like a waste for just one person. The trophies hanging on the walls or covered in glass cases told the story of a team twenty years gone.

I flipped through channels on the big screen, finding more coverage of tonight's activities than I really wanted to see. I got to watch myself get smacked across the highway and Cassie slash the Grey Giant via the Channel 10 Choppercam. Meanwhile the reporter talked about a collaboration between "what may be a revival of the Heroes' League and Chicago's Midwest Defenders."

It sounded better than the real story, which would have been "Clueless local heroes saved by jerks from Chicago."

When they shifted to the main news desk to discuss how long the power would be off in the downtown area, I shut off the TV. I didn't need to hear more.

While I walked around HQ, shutting off the lights, I heard the door to the sewer exit slide open and then a familiar clanking. I found Larry removing the head to the Rhino suit in the main room, dumping the helmet on the table in front of the TV next to a pizza.

Then the rest of the armor snapped open. I wasn't sure how. He stepped out of it, wearing a grey coverall similar to a flight suit. With shoulder length hair and a bit of a gut, Larry didn't look like your average pilot. On the other hand, Larry's costume didn't allow him to fly.

"Hey Nick. Free pizza. I'd have brought beer, but then I'd have to arrest myself or something."

"Where'd you get the pizza?" I asked, but that's not what I was really wondering. I was wondering how he could get at the money to pay for a pizza. So far as I could tell, his armor had no pockets.

He grabbed some pizza out of the box. "Antonio's. You know, just around the corner? They usually give me a freebie when I get on TV. Mind if I turn it on?"

Despite the fact that I did mind, I said, "Go ahead."

It didn't take that long to find a channel showing Larry (as the Rhino) knocking the Grey Giant on his back. Actually, we found several—including footage from the idiots in the mini-van.

I got to watch the Grey Giant slap me straight into the pavement on CNN.

"Oh *geez*," I muttered.

"Yeah," Larry said, "bad break there. You're still walking though. That's a plus."

"It doesn't change the fact that I suck," I said. "I mean, what did I do this whole time? I got knocked out of the fight twice and didn't really hurt the guy at all. Daniel at least tripped the guy once and Cassie probably could have killed him by herself."

"Ah, don't beat yourself up," Larry said. "Trust me kid, there are people willing to do that for you."

Larry pulled another piece of pizza onto his plate. "Besides, you stopped the Grey Giant from going after the van. If he'd thrown it at somebody, those guys inside would be pushing daisies."

"That's something," I said, "but in the meantime we managed to knock out power for half the downtown and chased him down a highway. Guardian was right. We didn't plan at all."

"Is that what this is all about?" The expression on Larry's face was hard to read, but it tilted toward annoyance.

"Look Nick," he said, "Guardian's an ass. I missed what he said back there, but you guys did all right for the first time out as team. Did I ever tell you about the first time I ever faced an actual supervillain?"

He hadn't.

"Well okay," he said, "Mind if I take the last piece?"

I was okay with that.

"So here I am," he said. "Nineteen years old. I've taken out a couple muggers, busted a counterfeiter, and I'm ready to take on the world. I've upgraded the Rhino suit and I can throw trucks if I want to. Hell, I'm just looking for the chance.

"I hear on the radio that some supervillain—I think his name was Electroman—is downtown blasting away at the police with lightning bolts. So I run down there. I'm going to take him on. I show up running eighty miles an hour and ready to punch him into next week. The moment I get out in front of the cops, the guy sends I don't know how many volts of electricity straight into the suit and burns out everything in it."

"What did you do?"

"Nothing. I was frozen in place. I had to stand there while the wiseass laughed and told me I should rename myself 'the Coat Rack.'"

"Did he get away?"

"Nah," Larry grinned. "About that time your Grandpa showed up and clobbered him. He got blasted a couple times too, but his armor had better protection. He took the guy out."

Larry didn't stay much longer. After he left, I finished shutting everything down, got into the elevator, and traveled to the surface.

The sky was clear and I could see stars through the trees that lined the street. The air felt warm. It was one of those fall nights when you wonder whether or not summer had ended. I walked away from Grandpa's above ground lab, a bungalow next to Veterans' Memorial Park.

I'd received the bungalow in Grandpa's will. It had

passed without remark in a will reading that included giving away several million dollars that no one had realized Grandpa had.

A few cars passed me. A dog barked. I saw the glow of the David Letterman Show through somebody's window.

I knew that Larry had told me that story to make me feel better, but for the moment it had worked.

The night hadn't been a complete disaster. In the end, the Grey Giant had been caught. Cassie had gotten her chance to take on Syndicate L and we had won that part of the evening hands down.

I walked up to the side door of my parents' house, pulled out my key and unlocked it.

Inside, it was like any other night. My dad sat in a chair in the living room, books on the floor and his laptop on his lap. My mom was already in bed.

"Back a little late," he said. "What were you doing?"

"Nothing much," I said. "Just hanging out with Cassie and Daniel at Grandpa's lab."

"Try to be in before eleven next time."

Next time, I decided, the Rocket would have to do a better job at making his curfew.

CHAPTER TWO

On Saturday morning, Jaclyn and I stepped out of the elevator and into the main room of the Grand Lake Heroes League headquarters. It smelled just as musty as you might expect the HQ of a super organization that had been defunct for twenty years to smell.

"If I'd known what 'Movie Night' was really all about, I'd have been there last week," Jaclyn said.

If I had to choose a word to describe Jaclyn, it would be *precise*. Only a couple inches shorter than I was, Jaclyn wore a blue, button-down shirt and black slacks. She looked good, but her clothes seemed a little formal for Saturday morning.

Granddaughter of the League's only black member, her curly hair had been cut short.

She needed to be precise, first of all because she

wanted to be a doctor. Second, because if her powers were anything like her grandfather's, she was stronger than a locomotive and faster than a speeding bullet.

You wanted someone like that to be careful.

I was about to reply, "Keeping it a secret and then springing it on people was Cassie's idea, so you probably ought to take that up with her," but then the door opened.

Cassie sat directly in front of us. Two empty mailbags lay on the floor and two piles of mail covered half of the table.

"Will you look at this?" Cassie waved her hand toward the piles. "This is just since the fight." She sounded pleased.

I said. "What's in them?"

"Fan mail, mostly. Did you know that the Heroes League even had a fan club? It looks like they're still going and most of them are ecstatic that we're back. And when I say ecstatic, I mean pages and pages worth of gushing praise from old people—you know, baby boomers."

I looked over the piles. There were a lot of letters. "So that's all fan mail?"

"Well, no. There are a few people who complain about the new Captain Commando being a 'little girl.' There's some perv out there who wants naked pictures of me. And back on the fannish end of things, there are a bunch of girls who think Daniel is super cute and want his autograph."

"Anything for me?"

"Do you like bills?"

Jaclyn laughed. I groaned, thinking of all the things we might be charged for. Still, last week's power outage wasn't entirely our fault.

"I'm joking," Cassie said. "Sure. There are a bunch of people who wrote to say how the first Rocket inspired them to go into engineering or something like that. And then there's another bunch of people who want hints on how they can make a suit of powered armor of their very own."

"Oh great."

"Well anyway," Cassie said, "would you mind helping me look through this stuff?"

So that's how we spent most of the next two hours. Daniel was attending his cousin's Bar Mitzvah, but we ended up discussing what Cassie called 'team business' anyway. What sort of team business, given that we didn't officially have a team? You'd just have to ask Cassie—which I did.

"How about a team name? The press will want to call us something and if we don't give them a name, they'll just call us 'the New Heroes League' or something worse."

"Or how about this," she continued. "How do we decide who can join up? I've been talking to Vaughn and he's interested, but it's not like he's got any powers or anything. But, you know, I bet he could get powers."

I paused in the middle of opening a letter and glanced at Jaclyn, whose jaw had dropped a little. "That could work out well," she said, "if he turns out to be a little less completely insane than his grandfather."

"He's not like that *at all*," Cassie said. "You remember him from the picnics? When we were little kids? Nick, you know him a little. Tell her."

Well, I did know him. We were on the Cross Country team together, but he wasn't one of the people

I hung out with on the team. He didn't attend very many picnics either. I didn't know the reason, but I suspected that it was because Vaughn's grandmother might have felt a little uncomfortable hanging out with the people who had probably been responsible for killing her husband.

I didn't say that, though. All I said was, "Do you suppose he ever wants revenge for his grandfather's death?"

"He doesn't," Cassie said, maybe with just a touch too much emphasis. "Just the opposite, the family's had to live with this for years and Vaughn told me he'd like a chance to make things right."

I considered making a sarcastic comment about how the Hardwicks had suffered, but didn't. Still, it was hard to make a good case for shame damaging a family that owned half the city. Well okay, maybe not half the city, but they had a lot of money.

Back in the 19th century, they were lumber barons. In the 20th they'd invested their money in manufacturing cars and office furniture. In the 21st they were funding research in biotechnology from pharmaceuticals and genetic engineering to nanotechnology. Already in the 1930's and 40's, the Hardwicks were considered an "old money" family for the area.

Red Lightning (Giles Hardwick) had done the "rich citizen protects the city" thing starting just before World War II and then somehow ended up in the same "super soldier" unit as Captain Commando, Hotfoot (Jaclyn's grandfather), and my grandfather.

"Alright," I said, "let's say that he does want to make things right. How's he going to do it? Red Lightning's powers only worked when he was juiced up with that stuff he made… What was it?"

"Spinach?" Jaclyn suggested, softly singing a bit of Popeye's theme song.

I laughed.

"Not funny," Cassie said, but she'd laughed too.

"It was called the 'Power Elixir'," Cassie continued, talking over Jaclyn's and my laughter. "I know it sounds stupid, but Vaughn's not planning on using that. Vaughn's planning on using the machine that made Red Lightning's powers permanent. The… 'Power Impregnator'."

She stopped and looked at us warily.

We weren't laughing.

The moment Red Lightning had managed to make his powers permanent was the moment a lot of things began to go wrong for the Heroes League. I wasn't around for it. It'd been twenty years before I was born, but I had heard a few things from my grandfather.

When I asked him directly, he would only say, "I don't like to talk about it."

From comments he'd made while I was growing up though, I'd gotten a general picture of the events leading to Red Lightning's death. When my grandfather and Red Lightning finished the Power Impregnator, it had freed Giles (Red Lightning) from carrying vials of liquid that always seemed to break at the worst moment. Giles had been growing distant from the team for a couple of years before that, but afterward (at least for a little while), it was like it had been during the war—a bunch of guys standing up to whatever the world could throw at them.

I wasn't sure of the details, but within a few years other superpowered gangs began to appear—well organized gangs that were unnervingly capable of not only avoiding, but also predicting the Heroes League's every move. It had to be an inside job. Suspicion fell on everyone in turn, but the Mentalist, Daniel's grandfather, discovered that the gangs had gained their abilities by ingesting an addictive drug similar to the Power Elixir.

After that, it turned into an all out war between Red Lightning and the League—a war the League won, but not easily.

"So," I asked Cassie, "where is the Power Impregnator these days?"

"I don't know. I guess it must be in storage, or maybe… Red Lightning's lab?" She stopped, the sentence hanging, looking up from the mail and at me as if expecting confirmation.

I shrugged, adding, "I've got no idea where that would be."

Strictly speaking, that answer wasn't even a lie—I really didn't know where Red Lightning's lab had been. The comically-named Power Impregnator, however? That was in a cardboard box about 30 feet away, sitting in the corner of the main room next to twenty other boxes of memorabilia.

I'd never been so grateful not to have Daniel around.

"Nick," Cassie said, "would you just talk to Vaughn tomorrow?"

"Sure," I said, trying to think of what I'd been doing before I got distracted.

Noticing the letter in my hand, I finished opening the envelope and scanned the letter's contents. "Hey," I said, "get this: someone wants to sell us life insurance."

*   *   *

I didn't talk to Vaughn.

The next day was Sunday so I went to church with my parents, spent most of the afternoon reading Larry Niven's *Ringworld*, and worked on homework until eleven at night.

After I finished my homework, I read until one in the morning.

I missed him on Monday, too. Honestly, I completely forgot about it until nine-thirty at night when the phone rang. I'd been playing Tony Hawk's Downhill Jam (and to be honest, not doing all that well) when my mom called out, "Nick, it's Daniel on the phone."

I dropped the controller and watched my skateboarder crash. Well, no great loss.

"Hey," I said as I picked up the phone.

"Hi," Daniel said. "Talked to Vaughn yet?"

"Uh… no. Who told you about that?"

"I ran into Jaclyn after school."

Grand Lake had enough of a Jewish community to have a Jewish day school, but not enough of one to have sports facilities. It used Grand Lake South High School's fields and gym—that was where Jaclyn went.

"Is she on the volleyball team?"

"And just about everything else you can sign up for. But you're right. Volleyball too. Our practices ended about the same time," he said.

I walked up the stairs to my room, trying to avoid Grunion (our cat) who had inexplicably decided that the first step of the stairway was his territory. He slashed at my sock as I stepped over him.

With the direction this conversation seemed to be going, I didn't want my mom to overhear and I was willing to risk a bloody sock.

"Any particular reason you haven't talked to him yet?" Daniel asked.

"No," I said, "just busy. Well, that and I forgot. Not that it really matters though. I don't think he's got any powers or anything so it's a moot point."

"But if he had powers," Daniel said, "it wouldn't be particularly fair to him."

"True," I said, "but if he had powers, I'd want you to talk to him. You're the guy who knows what evil lurks in the hearts of men."

"I've already talked to him," Daniel said, "he's okay. He was at Movie Night a couple times during the summer. Remember?"

"Well, no," I said. "I forgot. I must have missed him."

By that time I was in my room. I sat down at my desk and looked out into the dark. It was a quiet suburban street. A few porch lights glimmered. A streetlight illuminated the corner.

It occurred to me that if we were a real team, we'd probably have someone out on patrol right now. I mentioned it to Daniel and he said, "Maybe we ought to think about it. The hard part is choosing the right route…"

We talked about possible patrol routes for ten minutes until Daniel said, "Let's just go. In fact, let's not even plan a route. I've got something I want to try."

If he'd been there, I'd have raised an eyebrow. As it was, I just said, "What?"

"Prescient meditation," he said.

"Ooohkay," I said.

"You know that I can sense the future when I'm fighting," he said. "I can sense just enough to know where not to be. Well here's what I can do. I can turn it around—so instead of sensing danger to me, I sense danger to the city, and instead of going away from the danger, we fly toward it."

"Oh," I said, my mind suddenly awash in possibilities. "So if you had used it last week, we would have found the Grey Giant's truck earlier and—"

"No," he said. "Last week I used it and that's how we found the truck driver and the warehouse and everything."

"I don't want to get into something that big any time soon."

"No," Daniel said. "It's not like that. I try to sense a threat to the city and when I get there it could be anything. I mean *really* anything. Once I went to an apartment building and found that some guy had managed to lock himself out of his apartment. I got him in again and suddenly everything was fine. No threats."

"What does your dad think? Can he do it too?"

"No. He's nervous about it. It's an intuitive thing, so who knows what I'm really preventing? He says it's one thing to change the future when you know why you're trying, but to do it on less than a guess? He doesn't think it's worth the risk."

"The risk of what?"

"Future time travelers coming back to stop me? I have no idea."

"You know," I said, "that might actually be kind of cool."

We laughed.

"So anyway," he said, "you want to go out and see if anyone's getting mugged?"

"Only if we're not out too late."

* * *

Back in the Heroes League's old headquarters, the lights were on. I called out a few times, but no one answered.

I checked the main room, grandpa's lab, a few storage rooms and the entrance to the sewers, but didn't see anyone there either. I even checked in the hanger—which was a waste. You could see the dust. It had been a couple presidential administrations since anything in there worked.

Deciding that someone had just forgotten to turn out the lights, I went back to the lab and suited up. Between Larry, Cassie, Jaclyn and her brothers, the chances that someone had forgotten to turn things off were pretty good.

Once I had the suit on and checked the systems, I exited the complex through the sewer line by the lake again. Then I flew toward Daniel's house.

He joined me in the air.

I hovered for a moment and he floated. I could see downtown's buildings in the distance and the lights of the suburbs spreading around us. It's a strange thing to be able to get the view you'd get from a ten story building while flying under your own power.

Well, strange to me anyway. And awe inspiring, too.

People who'd been at this a while probably got used to it, but I wasn't there yet.

Daniel flew toward me and I heard his voice in my head.

Daniel: *Ready go out and save the world?*

Me: *No. Got anything smaller to save? Like a pebble, maybe? That I could handle.*

Daniel: *Ha. Ha.*

After deciding to fly downtown, we lapsed into companionable silence.

It was a quiet night. Apparently criminals don't do much between nine-thirty and eleven on a Monday—not in Grand Lake anyway.

From the comics, movies, and television, you'd expect something to happen on patrol. In real life, muggers sometimes stayed home—that or Daniel's range wasn't good enough to detect anything interesting.

I suppose we could have tuned the suit's radio to police band, but the whole point was to stop crimes the police weren't aware of.

After twenty minutes of flight, I felt an excitement that I knew wasn't mine.

Daniel: *Let's make this a little more interesting.*

Me: *I don't want to get into anything really big right now. I mean, we're only thirty minutes from my curfew.*

Daniel: *How big can it be?*

I could feel it as he rearranged his mind. Amid the murmuring of the city and its suburbs' nearly one million people, I could feel shadowy presences and indistinct connections. It was overwhelming.

Daniel: *Fly toward the thing that makes you the most nervous.*

Me: *Just guide me. I'll be completely happy to remain in my own head.*

I didn't notice anything interesting at first, but as we flew south, passing over downtown, it occurred to me that we were flying in the general direction of home. Moments later, we were within a few blocks of my house.

Instants later we were over Veterans Memorial Park and Heroes League HQ.

I could see the lights of my grandfather's bungalow and immediately thought, "Lights."

Earlier in the summer, before I'd realized what Movie Night was really all about, I'd given a lot of people the ability to walk into HQ if they wanted. With the exception of Larry, they were all League kids.

This was less stupid and naive than it sounded when you brought another thing into the conversation—"the Block."

As my grandfather told me the story, the team had been talking late one night about their children when Captain Commando, the only team member without kids had said, "So, have they figured it out yet? You know they're going to."

That night they set some very strict policies about secret identities and the Mentalist (Daniel's grandfather) took the duty of being the last resort should their children find out. From what I understood, none of them ever did—with the exception of those (like Daniel's father) who had powers themselves.

I imagined those who did figure it out had that memory quietly erased.

The grandchildren got off easy. The Mentalist created a mental block that prevented any of us from speaking about the picnics outside the group.

It wasn't especially heroic, but how far could you

trust children with something like that?

I wasn't trying to justify it, but I understood the logic.

By the time we got into HQ, it became obvious to me that if the Block had ever included not touching League property, Vaughn's had been removed.

Just as they'd been when I entered the complex before, the lights in the main room were bright. Unlike before, the boxes in one corner were open and a device had been assembled in front of them.

It resembled a futuristic electric chair as imagined in the 1950's. All curves and chrome except for the black seat cushion and leather straps, the device purred quietly, occasionally sending sparks down the length of the body slumped on the seat.

All I could think was that if Vaughn were still alive, I now had no excuse for not talking to him about the League.

I pulled out the plug—a big, industrial plug. Heroes League HQ had been designed with the assumption that you never knew where you might need a high voltage connector.

Well, okay... I tried to pull the plug and it didn't come out. It was a twist-lock plug so I had to twist the thing first. After that, it really did come out.

The hum stopped.

"Is he still alive?" I began to walk toward the Power Impregnator, intending to undo the straps, but Daniel waved me away.

"He's alive," he said. The straps undid themselves and Vaughn's body floated out of the chair, landing on the dusty, olive green carpet.

Vaughn moaned and one of his eyes flickered open

for a moment. A bluish-white spark ran across it.

Vaughn was shorter and heavier than I was, and cultivated what I'd describe as the "sensitive bad boy look." Think black leather jacket, shoulder length hair and one earring. I was told by reliable sources (well, Cassie) that he was "kind of cute," but I didn't see it myself.

Anyway, she'd also said Daniel was definitely better looking—not that it mattered now.

Vaughn definitely looked worse. No one was at their best lying on a dusty floor, face awash in sweat and tears.

"Okay," I said, "what do you think we ought to do with him?"

Daniel looked down at Vaughn's body. "I don't know."

I knew why he didn't know. Red Lightning had originally just been an inventor type whose cringe-worthy way with words had led him to fighting crime while saying things like, "I will stop you in the name of TRUTH and JUSTICE," and crap like that. Beyond his "Power Elixir" and the abilities it had given him (flinging lightning short distances, some strength, and being a little tougher than the average guy), he hadn't had powers.

After being zapped by the Power Impregnator, his lightning power went from being little more than a human taser to being capable of destroying small buildings. Physically, he became considerably stronger and tougher than a normal person. Plus, he could fly.

Between his insanity and his drug-addicted, superpowered goons, he had given the League a hellish five year run as a supervillain.

After Red Lightning had died, opinions were split as to whether it was the Power Impregnator, years of home-brewed drug use in the form of the Power Elixir, or simply native craziness that had ultimately caused him to go bad.

Paranoid vigilante types in the superhero community would argue that we should kill Vaughn immediately and save everyone trouble later.

"We should take him home," I said.

Daniel didn't say anything. His face showed no expression.

"Daniel," I said. "Hey? You there?"

"What? Sorry. I was trying to run through a few possibilities. I don't sense any possibility that he'll die from this. There is some kind of danger connected with him, but it's not big… and not immediate. So yeah, we should take him home."

"As superheroes or as ourselves? Personally, I favor being heroes. That way his mom won't ask us as many ques—oh no…"

My suit had a line of readouts at the top of my vision inside the helmet. When I was flying I could find out air pressure, altitude, speed and few other things— including the time. Just then the clock began blinking red. It was 10:55pm—five minutes before curfew.

Or to put it another way, five minutes before I got grounded for neither making curfew nor informing my parents why.

My suit had a phone, but since I didn't want to show up on the caller ID as "Grand Lakes Heroes League," I took off my helmet and ran to the lab for my cell phone.

I began to call home, but remembered that I was in a concrete bunker a couple hundred feet below the ground. This would not do wonders for cell phone reception.

I ran to the elevator, shot up to Grandpa's old workroom in the bungalow, and phoned home.

My dad answered. "Hello, Nick."

In the background, I could hear an announcer and cheering crowds, leaving me to wonder which version of ESPN he was watching.

"Dad," I said, "Something kind of bad just happened. Daniel and I were at Grandpa's house… um… studying and we were just about to leave when we found Vaughn… Do you remember Vaughn? He was sleeping on the front doorstep. Would you mind driving him home?"

*   *   *

Within ten minutes, Dad had parked his SUV in front of the house. He stepped out of the car still dressed for work—no tie or jacket, but wearing a button down shirt and slacks.

Dad was all business, immediately walking up the steps to the front porch and checking Vaughn over where he sat on the front step. Dad was a psychologist who'd written a few books on marriage and family issues—including addictions. It didn't surprise me then when he sniffed Vaughn's breath for alcohol, discreetly rolled down his sleeves to look for needle marks, and felt Vaughn's wrist for his pulse.

He touched Vaughn's shoulder and said, "Can you hear me?"

Vaughn mumbled something.

I didn't know how Dad felt, but I was relieved. Daniel had said that Vaughn was probably okay but I knew that I wouldn't feel secure until I saw him walking away under his own power.

Dad said, "I didn't understand that. Could you repeat yourself?"

Vaughn said, "Dr K?"

So in case you were wondering, that meant that Vaughn was either a current or former client. Not that it was particularly surprising. I didn't know whether Dad was the best psychologist in the city, but he definitely had the most publicity, especially with evangelical Christians.

Vaughn's family went to Grand Lake Community Church—a church, I suddenly remembered, where the pastor had once interviewed Dad as part of a sermon.

All of which went to show that the best advertising was the kind you didn't have to pay for.

Dad put his hand on Vaughn's shoulder, ready to help him stand. "Can you walk?"

"Walk? Sure I can walk. I just…" and here Vaughn looked at Daniel for a moment, "fell asleep."

He pushed himself up, stumbling where an old oak tree's roots made the sidewalk buckle. My Dad frowned, but didn't say anything.

Moments later everybody else followed him into the car and we started the twenty minute drive to Vaughn's house. After Vaughn gave Dad his address, we didn't talk much. Normally Dad got my friends to talk about what they were doing in school, hobbies, and whatever, but tonight he just said, "Everybody buckled in?" and drove off.

Bearing in mind that it was after eleven by that time, I was guessing he wanted to go to bed. Also, with Vaughn being a client and all, asking him about his life probably felt a lot like work.

This meant that theoretically Daniel and I had twenty minutes to talk telepathically if he wanted to—but didn't. He was looking pretty drained. In addition to flying around with me, he'd flown home to grab clothes before my dad had gotten to Grandpa's house. I don't know how much probing the future took out of him, but it probably wasn't free.

Both he and Vaughn fell asleep in the back seat, leaving Dad and me as the only people still awake. I took advantage of the moment to watch the streetlights as Dad's Saturn Vue chewed up the pavement. The local NPR station played Jazz after ten, so we found ourselves listening to Miles Davis' "Kind of Blue" as we drove deeper into the suburbs.

Vaughn's family lived near Lake Michigan on a street where the houses grew ever larger and the grass greener—at least from what I could see on this side of the fence.

Vaughn's family's house, for example, included both a tennis court and a helicopter pad. I'd heard that there was a swimming pool back there too, but you couldn't see it from the street. Mind you, a swimming pool seemed redundant when you had one of the largest freshwater lakes in the world in your backyard, but what did I know?

Vaughn woke up as we stopped in the driveway and passed my dad his keycard. The gate slid aside, and Dad drove the Vue about a quarter of a mile to the end of the driveway.

A light turned on, illuminating our car as well as the front of the six-stall garage. The middle garage door opened and a woman stepped out. She looked a lot like

Vaughn—if Vaughn were forty-ish, short haired, and female.

Vaughn got out of the Vue, talked to his mom for a minute and then went inside. Dad rolled down his window as she walked toward us.

"Thanks for bringing Vaughn home," she said. "Could I speak to your son for a moment?"

"It's not a problem, Suzanne." To me he said, "Nick, why don't you step out and talk to her?"

I did. She walked around to my side of the car as I shut the door.

"Hi," I said.

"Thanks for bringing Vaughn home," she said. Then, out of nowhere she said, "Did I see you on the news last week?"

"Not that I know of."

"My mistake," she said, keeping her tone light. "I thought I might have seen you on television with a couple of your friends."

"No," I said.

"Well," she said, voice a little harder now, "I don't want to see him involved in anything like that. Do you understand?"

"Uh… Yeah."

She waved goodbye and left, managing to smile until she disappeared into the garage. The garage door shut behind her.

The ride to Daniel's house was a blur of suburban lawns, passing cars, and blinking red lights. The major difference from the ride to Vaughn's was that Daniel was awake.

Daniel: *She knows.*

Me: *Yeah. How?*

Daniel: *Well, you know about my Grandpa's Alzheimer's or whatever it is. So, if she discovered any of her dad's stuff after Grandpa stopped caring... My dad hated the whole idea, so it's not like he's going to erase stuff from people's heads.*

Me: *This is bad. If Vaughn's mom knows, who else does?*

*   *   *

We stepped into the house. The lights were all off and Mom was in bed. With my older sister Rachel at college, the house felt empty. When she was home, you could count on someone being awake after midnight.

Dad pushed the button that closed the garage door, shut the back door behind us and locked it.

"Nick," he said, "is there anything I should know about what just happened?"

"No," I said. "You know about as much as there is. We found Vaughn asleep on the porch when we were about to leave, and so I called you. That's all."

He stopped by the kitchen table and looked at me, passing his keys from his right hand to his left and then back again.

"I'm trying to figure out how to say this without breaking confidentiality," he said. He stood there for a moment. Then he seemed to come to a decision.

"Vaughn's parents came to me for other reasons last year, but as we did therapy, I learned that Vaughn was involved in things he shouldn't be. I can't go into any details, but if it looks like he's having problems, tell someone."

"Like what problems?"

Dad put his keys into his pocket. "I can't talk about

it," he said in the voice that he used with clients: calm and professional.

"Drugs?" I said.

"I can't tell you," he said, then paused and asked, "What did his mom talk to you about?"

"Nothing," I said. "She thanked me and then she asked me if she'd seen me on TV."

"Had she?"

"Not that I know of. It's not like the cross country team gets a whole lot of press."

He laughed, and that was it. We both went to our rooms.

I was off scot-free.

I was also off scot-free on the whole Vaughn thing, at least in my mind. Probably not in Cassie's, but seriously—his mom knew and she'd told me to stay away. It wasn't like she'd miss it if our team (assuming we had one) now included a guy who flung lightning bolts.

It was only the next day, while I was doing my calculus homework during study hall, that I realized I was ignoring an obvious problem. Whatever I thought, Vaughn would be the one deciding whether he should be involved with us, not his mom.

After a few minutes, I disappeared completely into the world of limits, derivatives, and integrals. I lost track of time, the cafeteria, and the silent students around me.

The bell rang as I began the last problem. I considered finishing it, but the cascade of noise from books and feet made it hard to think. By the time most of the other students had left, I had given up on the idea and started hauling my books back to my locker.

As I began turning my combination lock, my cell rang. Picking up the phone, I heard Vaughn's voice.

"Nick. Let's talk."

"Yeah, okay. Give me a second." I held the phone to my ear with my shoulder and finished opening the lock.

We agreed to meet outside the front door and talk for a little while before heading off to cross country practice. It didn't start till 3:30 anyway.

Central High was three blocks from downtown in a century-old, brown brick building. The parking lot was across the street and surrounded by a six-foot high fence. Only fifteen minutes past the end of the school day, the parking lot already seemed to be ninety percent empty.

I looked around the front steps and noticed Vaughn sitting on the lowest one, black leather jacket unzipped, hair spilling across his back, leaning back and looking to the sky.

I walked down and sat next to him on the cold, concrete steps.

"So what's up?" I said.

He sat up, pulled a strand of hair out of his face. Then he looked up toward the entrance. We were alone.

"I just thought I'd thank you and your dad for bringing me home last night, and apologize… for breaking in and making a mess and all that."

"I'll pass that on to my dad," I said, thinking that even though he'd apologized, I would still be revoking his ability to get into HQ without me.

"Yeah," he said, sounding frustrated, "about that. See if you can do it and leave the impression that I'm not on drugs or something."

"I can try."

We sat in silence for a moment.

"Do you know anything about my grandfather's powers?" He looked down at his right hand and flexed it.

"Not much more than anybody else."

"I'm sure he could do more than this," he said, curling his fingers into a fist and then opening his hand, spreading his fingers as far apart as he could. Electricity crackled and bluish-white sparks flew from finger to finger, making the hand hard to look at for a moment.

"Wow."

"It is cool," he said, "but I read that Grandpa could blow up buildings. I'm not much more than a taser."

"It's only been a day," I said.

"I suppose the powers could grow," he said. "That would be cool."

The front door opened behind us.

Sean Drucker walked out. Sean was tall, blonde and curly haired. Last year he'd gotten kicked off the basketball team for drinking.

"Got what you owe me?" His upper lip curled as he looked at Vaughn. He barely glanced at me.

Vaughn said, "No." His tone suggested he was tired of the question.

Sean didn't seem to have expected a yes. He didn't even stop walking.

"What do you owe him?" I asked.

"About a thousand bucks," Vaughn said. "And a new car."

"How do you owe somebody a thousand dollars?" I didn't need to ask about the car. Everybody in school had heard about Vaughn crashing Sean's car.

I'd heard three different versions of that story and I was mostly unaware of the school rumor mill.

"Last year was a wild year," Vaughn said.

On the sidewalk in front of us, Sean got into the passenger seat of a red jeep. He gave Vaughn the finger as the jeep drove off.

"For you," I said.

"Yeah," he said, nodding, "for me. My parents gave me a pretty big allowance and weren't paying much attention to what I did with it. So I spent a lot of it on parties and sometimes when I was out of cash, I borrowed."

"You borrowed a thousand dollars?"

"Not all at once. Just when Sean added it all up, you know? And he's not the only guy I owe money to. I could have paid it back, but then my parents cut off my allowance and sent me to rehab."

I knew enough about Dad's style to know that he recommended that parents create clear and immediate consequences.

"Who else do you owe?"

He threw up his hands. "Look, I didn't come here to tell you everything I ever did wrong. I came here to apologize. I'm sorry I broke in. I'm sorry you had to take me home. That's it."

He stood up and started walking back up the stairs and into the school. I hurried to keep up with him, passing under Central High's arched doorway. I didn't want to risk a fight (what with him being a walking electrical outlet and me being out of costume), but some things still bothered me.

We walked past the glassed in trophy display case

on one side and the windows into the computer lab on the other.

"Vaughn," I said, still a couple steps behind him in the hall. "Why now? If you wanted power, you had all summer. What were you waiting for?"

So yeah, brilliant move. Instead of leaving a guy who may have the ability to electrocute me alone, I went ahead and pointed out to him that logically he should have broken into Grandpa's house earlier.

He stopped and turned to face me. It may have just been my imagination, but I thought I saw something arc up his forearm from his right hand.

"They told me I had a week to get more of Grandpa's stuff or else, you know, they'd—they never said, but it sounded like they were going to go after my parents next."

"Wait a second, you were breaking in to steal something?"

"I wasn't stealing anything. I was breaking in to get the power to *protect* myself."

"Why didn't you call the police?"

"It's not that simple," he said and opened the door that led to the school locker rooms. Central had special locker rooms for people on the sports teams. Both the athletes' lockers and the regular lockers were part of a 70's era addition and included a lot of cinder block painted blue and yellow, but the athletes' locker rooms had bigger lockers.

The athletes' locker room smelled of BenGay and sweat-soaked uniforms. It was empty—except for Coach Michaelson.

Coach Michaelson was also known as Mr Michaelson, one of the math teachers. I'd always liked him, but being cross country coach struck me as a bit of a blow off job. As far as I could tell, ninety percent of it was saying, "Today we're going to run six miles. Go out and have a great time."

Granted, it wasn't always six miles, but it was basically the same line.

"You're late," he said, "but it's okay. Everyone else is already gone, so you guys can buddy up and do a four mile run. Have fun."

He wrote something on his clipboard and left.

Vaughn and I put on our sweats and walked out of the locker room into the gym. From there we stepped outside, exiting through big metal doors to the track behind the school.

We didn't talk while running warm up laps. Then we left the school grounds to do the run. Central High was in the middle of the city so we did a lot of our training on the road.

It was a decent day for running. The sky was blue and the temperature wasn't too hot or cold. Goldilocks would have been pleased.

A couple of blocks into the run I asked Vaughn, "Who are 'they?' I mean seriously, you make it sound like the Men in Black or the Mafia."

We were leaving downtown, passing into old neighborhoods of Victorian houses, wooden homes with towers and turrets.

"A couple guys who were hanging out at the parties I went to. After my parents cut off my allowance, they gave me a few loans."

"And all they wanted was your grandfather's stuff? That's crazy."

Vaughn stopped running. When he replied, he was

almost shouting at me. "You don't know what it was *like*. Sean and everyone else wanted their money back and I was panicking and they had money. They gave it to me no strings attached."

I began to open my mouth and point out that handing over his grandfather's equipment was more like a rope than a string, and it probably had a noose on the end to boot.

He interrupted me before I even got a word out, saving the metaphor from abuse.

"I know it was stupid. Don't tell me."

"What did you give them?"

"Some gadget from his costume and book full of formulas. After that they left me alone—or at least they did until you guys turned cape."

"What did that have to do with it?"

Vaughn said, "I don't know. After I gave them a little bit of my grandfather's stuff, they left me alone for months until you guys fought the Grey Giant. That night they dropped by and let me know that they wanted more."

"What did you tell them?"

"I told them to go away." He glanced toward the house next to us. It was a big red Victorian house with a huge lawn. "Let's start running before these people begin wondering why we're in front of their house."

We started running again, but this time it was different. Vaughn started a little fast, but I sped up to match him. Then I passed him. When I got a little tired, he passed me.

Within a few blocks we were running almost all out. Not sprinting, but as close to it as we could knowing we still had three miles to run. I didn't exactly know why we did it. It just seemed like the thing to do.

We may have been pissed off at each other. I wasn't happy with the idea of bringing him into the League, and I was beginning to guess that he was sensitive about discussing last year. So rather than talk about it, we attempted to run each other into the ground.

I wouldn't claim that it was one of the most mature things I'd ever done.

We were running through some of the less desirable older neighborhoods, places where the roads had big potholes from last winter. Paint flaked off the wooden siding of most houses and too many windows had cracks.

Vaughn shot away from me, running around a car at a four way stop and passing in front of a black Cadillac Escalade. It had been rolling forward, but stopped as he crossed the street.

Lungs and legs burning, I followed him, glancing at the Escalade as I did. Wondering where I had seen it before, I realized that I'd seen it parked in front of the school while we were talking.

I put on a burst of speed and tried to catch Vaughn, managing to get close halfway down the block.

"Vaughn," I said, barely able to talk, "behind."

We both turned around in time to see the Escalade disappear behind a house. It had followed the cross street without turning in our direction.

"What?" He tried to breathe in the middle of it, turning the word into three syllables.

"Car," I said, "saw it at school."

We slowed to a walk, both of us breathing hard. We were next to each other in the street, cars parked along both sides almost all the way down the block, leaving only a lane and three-quarters for traffic to pass through.

"Sidewalk?" I suggested, and we walked up the nearest driveway.

I turned my head to look behind us again and didn't see the Escalade. I looked ahead in case it might be coming around the corner. It wasn't. The only moving vehicle on the road was a yellow sports car. Well, I decided, I could just be paranoid.

The yellow sports car pulled up in the driveway directly in front of us.

Two men stepped out. I pegged them as mid-twenties. One was blond and stocky. The other, the driver, was dark haired and average build. Both wore suit jackets and looked... I don't know. Well-manicured? They looked clean cut. Like they were the kind of people who paid attention to haircuts, fingernails and color-coordinated clothes.

I guessed that everyone was supposed to do that, but personally, I'd always figured everything matched blue jeans.

The blond one said, "Vaughn, how're you doing?" Meanwhile, the dark haired one stepped around the front of the car. He leaned against it and gave Vaughn a little wave.

Wiser people would have turned around and run away by now.

"Hey Stevie," Vaughn nodded to the blond guy. "And Dom, great to see you too."

As far I could tell, that was Vaughn's default face to the world. Even if you were hiding a semi-automatic under your sports jacket, you still got treated as if you were an old friend coming over to hang out.

Dom gave him a small, quickly disappearing smile.

Stevie said, "I'd like both you guys to step into the car. A friend of ours wants to speak to you."

Vaughn said, "Sorry. We're both in the middle of cross country practice. We've got to get back, but maybe later, right?"

Dom's right hand moved toward the inside of his jacket.

Vaughn held out his right hand and the air between them crackled.

I didn't bother to find out what exactly Vaughn was doing. I stepped forward, punching "Stevie" in the nose. It was a great punch, delivered exactly as my martial arts instructor had taught me. Unfortunately, Stevie didn't go down. He only stood there looking stunned.

My second punch hit him instants later in exactly the same spot, propelled forward by another step to give it just a little added oomph.

He went down, falling backwards, his head hitting the car and then the driveway. He didn't move.

To my right, Vaughn stood over Dom's unconscious body, his hands still glowing with bluish sparks.

It reminded me ever so slightly of the ending to Return of the Jedi; the bit where the Emperor stands over Luke's body. Except where the Emperor looked happy, Vaughn looked scared.

Well, we had that in common.

I looked down at Stevie again. He moaned, but didn't open his eyes. Now that he was lying on the ground, his jacket gaped, exposing his gun and shoulder holster. I pulled out the gun, yanked out the clip, and dumped the bullets into the storm drain next to the driveway.

Then I opened up his cell phone case, popped out the battery and stole the SIM card. I assumed that Dom's SIM card had been annihilated when Vaughn shocked him, but I took his too. You never know.

As I was dismantling Dom's phone, Vaughn managed to pull out of his funk long enough to ask me, "What are you doing?"

"Stealing their SIM cards. Without them they can't call anybody, and I can check out their contact list."

"Is that legal?"

"Probably not, but it's the best way I can think of to find out a little bit about them."

"What about looking through their wallets?"

He had a point there.

I pulled out Dom's wallet and flipped through his identification. He had plenty of driver's licenses, none of which identified him as Dom. He also had ID's that identified him as FBI, CIA, a US Marshal, a Secret Service agent and an employee of the NSA for good measure.

Stevie's wallet had just as much variety.

"This can't be real," I said.

"No kidding," Vaughn said, looking over my shoulder.

"Well," I said, "we should probably get out of here. Would you open the car and nuke the inside? That way they can't drive around and look for us."

"I'll try." He opened the passenger side door and stopped, picking some photographs off the front seat.

He flipped through them and handed them to me, saying, "Nick, look at this."

They were glossy, blown up to 8½ by 11 inches

and showed the faces of everyone who had attended a Movie Night: Daniel, Cassie, Jaclyn, Vaughn and myself, plus her brothers and a few other people who had only attended once.

All of them seemed to show Grandpa's house, lawn, or a neighbor's house as background. How had we failed to notice? Had they used more than one car? Or had they placed cameras nearby?

More importantly, why were they bothering?

My thoughts were interrupted by the sound of Vaughn's lightning and the smell of burnt plastic.

As the lightning's afterimage faded from my eyes, I said, "Maybe we ought to go. If the guys in the Escalade are working with them, they could get here at any time."

"Never mind the Escalade," Vaughn said, "Look at that… A few shots and I might be able to destroy the whole car."

Blackened and smoking, the steering wheel lay in the front seat. The clear plastic over the speedometer had shattered and in some spots the dashboard had melted.

If it was a rental, they definitely weren't getting their deposit back.

"I get a little stronger each time," he said.

"I still don't want to find out if they've got backup," I said.

We ran back toward the school.

We cut through backyards, climbed over fences and hid in the bushes as we decided where to cross the street. When we crossed, we sprinted.

We saw the Escalade three times. First we saw it as we left Dom and Stevie on the ground, turning the corner slowly. We ran around a dark house with grimy windows into the backyard and followed the alley almost to the end of the street, cutting through another backyard to escape.

The second time we were hiding behind a yellow, plastic slide/swing set. Vaughn peered around the slide as the Escalade stopped at the corner. It turned right, traveling away from the school and us.

"They're giving up," Vaughn said.

"Maybe," I said, stretching out the word as I panted.

The third time, we were almost at the school. We were running down the sidewalk in a nice neighborhood just north of Central's athletic fields. The houses were obviously beginning their second century, but were kept up and the lawns mowed.

A boy that couldn't be older than five raced past us on his bike shouting, "I winned you!"

Vaughn turned to me, grinning. "Race you to the gate," he said.

He sprinted and I took chase. We'd decided to make for the back entrance to the school fields, betting that if the Escalade did show up, they wouldn't have the nerve to go after us in public.

We were wrong about that.

The moment that Vaughn and I began to sprint, I heard a deep roar behind us. I didn't even look behind to check what it was.

"Backyard," I shouted. He didn't reply. He'd already left the sidewalk and begun scrambling up the front yard of the nearest house. All houses on the school side sat at least five feet above the street.

I followed Vaughn up the hill, past a brown house, around the plastic chairs on their back porch and into the backyard.

The gate through the school fence was three houses down. Between us and it stood a seven foot tall wooden fence, extending from the house back to the twelve foot tall school fence.

The Escalade drove straight up the driveway and stopped in front of the small, single car garage. The doors opened and four men in black suits stepped out, pistols in hand.

Technically, they probably weren't the Men in Black of conspiracy theory fame, but I didn't have an opportunity to ask about that.

"Halt!" that nearest one shouted.

I was frozen, not because I was listening, but because I couldn't think of what to do next. The fences seemed too tall to climb and I didn't see a way to get past the men and around the side of the house.

Vaughn didn't stop.

Out of the corner of my eye, I saw him run toward the school fence, jumping to give himself a head start on the twelve foot climb.

He flew into the air, hands outstretched, ready to grab the chain link fence.

But he never grabbed it. He flew past and turned around in the air, facing us and suddenly giving a laugh.

The nearest Man in Black raised his gun toward Vaughn, but he never had a chance. Vaughn's hands seemed to explode with bolt after bolt of lightning.

I couldn't see in the brightness and closed my eyes. I opened them to find Vaughn standing next to me and all the men unconscious on the ground.

"Did you see that? It was incredible." He looked over the yard—the unconscious men, the Escalade (now with four flat tires), and a hole in the lawn that I assumed came from a miss.

"Some of it," I said.

"I had no idea I could do that stuff. I've only ever seen it on TV," he said, mumbling the last sentence.

"You okay?"

"No, fine," he said. "Maybe a little tired."

"Well," I said, "let's get out of here."

* * *

Vaughn seemed tired and a little punchy on the way back. He stumbled as we walked up the hill to the gate and then again on the way down the hill to the school's tennis courts. Tennis being a spring sport, the courts were empty.

As we walked toward the soccer fields and the entrance to the gym, he seemed unable to stop talking.

"I'm in a position to do some good in the world now," he said, "and change things. I know who sold me drugs. I bet I could find out where they live. I'd collect evidence and bring them, you know—KER-POW—zapped unconscious to the police. I'd just have to get a costume. Leather would be cool, but I wear leather a lot of the time anyway so that wouldn't be much of a disguise... And a name, I'll need a name."

Daniel got that way when he overused his abilities too. Well, not precisely that way. Daniel got quiet and fell asleep a lot.

I felt tired myself. We had covered around four miles, most of it running. That wasn't a massive distance, but it counted.

We stepped into the gym to find the volleyball team just finishing practice. A couple girls were still practicing their serves, but most of them were standing and talking.

Cassie stood in one of the bigger groups, laughing loudly with girls I recognized but couldn't name. As I shut the door, she waved and half-ran over to us. "Hey Nick, Vaughn. Have a good run?"

Unlike anyone else in the room, she didn't look tired at all.

She smiled at me, living temporarily in a happy world where Vaughn and I walking in together meant that we'd had a long talk and were now best friends forever.

Vaughn barely seemed to notice her. He leaned against the wall. "White Lightning," he said. "That's a cool name. I could go with that."

"I'm pretty sure 'White Lightning' is synonym for moonshine," I said.

"No way? That'd piss off my mom. Not that that's hard."

Cassie said, "Is he drunk?"

Vaughn laughed. "I am not drunk. Just tired. And I mean bone tired."

He sat down on the floor.

"He really isn't drunk," I said, "but a few things happened during the run that we probably shouldn't talk about here."

She glanced toward the rest of the volleyball team. Most of them were leaving for the locker room. A few still stood talking next to the bleachers.

"Tell you what, I've got my mom's car. I'll drive you home."

"That would take care of everything," I said. "Um… You want to help me get him over to the guy's lockers?"

Vaughn's head lay on his chest. He had fallen asleep.

"Only if I don't have to go in. The boys' locker room reeks. Do any of you guys ever wash your uniforms or do you just keep them there for the season?"

I decided to take that as a rhetorical question and started to pull Vaughn up by his right arm. Cassie took the other arm, and to be honest, did most of the work. Not that that should surprise anyone.

Vaughn woke up enough to get himself into the locker room. We showered and changed into regular clothes. While I rearranged my locker, it occurred to me that Cassie was right about the smell. The reason wasn't hard to explain.

I left my sweats there all week and took them home to be washed on Friday. I was also sure I wasn't the only one. In fact I was pretty sure some people left their stuff even longer.

Don't judge me.

I pulled my backpack out of my locker and put the SIM cards and pictures in the front pocket.

Vaughn already had his jacket on, one strap of his backpack now over his shoulder.

"So," he said, "rumor says you and Cassie are going out."

"Where did anyone get that idea?"

"I heard it from Kayla first, but she's not the only one who says it. I'd wondered myself. I've never seen you together before this year and now you're talking in the hall. You're having lunch. You're riding home from school together... Everything but PDA."

"No."

Which went to show that the school rumor mill was pretty much full of it. Last time I'd heard anything about Cassie it was that she was a lesbian. Bearing in mind that *that* rumor circulated about all female athletes who were any good, and every female phys ed teacher, I didn't pay any attention to it.

It made me wonder if anyone bothered trying to reconcile contradictory rumors, or if these things just washed ashore like waves on the beach and then disappeared.

"I'll bet you can think of one other reason we might be hanging out," I told him.

Vaughn looked puzzled for a second, but then said, "Oh, duh. I'm a moron."

I grabbed my backpack and we walked out of the locker room. Cassie was waiting for us in the hall. We walked quietly out of the school and through the parking lot.

Cassie's mom had a late model blue sedan. It looked distinctly like a mom-mobile—as in clean, had a tissue box, a trash receptacle, and didn't have bags of fast food garbage on the floor or the seats.

Once we shut the doors she said, "Okay, what have you got for me?"

I pulled out the photos and the SIM cards.

I told her everything.

CHAPTER THREE

So it was Friday night, the night (if popular culture was to be believed) when everybody who was anybody was out doing something fun.

I was in my grandfather's lab in Heroes' League HQ setting rules for the security system. During the summer, when I'd decided to use HQ as a massive home theater/video game room, I'd set it to let in anybody connected to the original League.

Recent events had made it obvious that this was not a good idea.

I set the security program to let in Daniel, Jaclyn, Cassie and myself without question, other people if they were with one of us, and for everyone else, the program would email me a request.

I walked up to one of the computers at the main

table, setting the screen to display a publicity picture of the Heroes League circa 1965. It showed the team posing next to the computer in costume. Ghostwoman sat next to the console—just transparent enough to see the outline of the chair she sat in. Grandpa stood behind her as the Rocket. Next to her crouched Night Wolf, all in dark gray and looking feral. Behind him stood Hotfoot, recently renamed as 'C', and probably just back from marching for civil rights somewhere in the South.

Captain Commando (wearing an enormous utility belt) stood next to C, and Red Lightning stood in front of Captain Commando, electrical sparks covering his arms. The Mentalist stood next to Captain Commando and partially behind Red Lightning. He appeared deep in thought.

I backed away from the table to admire the photo, briefly wishing that they were dealing with all of this instead of me.

Jaclyn arrived first. She could run at the speed of sound so that wasn't much of a surprise. She walked into the main room through one of the tunnel entrances.

She wore a purple costume with a mask that covered all of her face except for her mouth. It didn't have any markings or symbols.

She turned to a blur between the tunnel and the table. By the time I could make out her features, she'd taken the mask off and sat down.

"I didn't know you had a costume," I said. "Do you have a name?"

"My grandpa gave me the costume last year but no, no name." It didn't sound like she cared about coming up with one either.

Jaclyn looked a lot like her grandfather. I couldn't put my finger on why. Both of them were thin, but with toned muscles that somehow conveyed power. On the other hand, maybe that was all in my head because I knew what they could do.

"I never really intended to wear it," she said. "My brothers didn't bother to use their powers until after they'd graduated college and moved to Atlanta. Besides, I don't want to run around the city looking for muggers when I've got schoolwork."

Schoolwork that she's probably doing at Mach 1, I thought. Between sports, school council at South High, playing cello in the orchestra, and being a member of South's yearbook team, she was probably using her speed just to get through daily life.

"I barely have time to be here," she said.

"What," I said, "you have something else going tonight?"

"No, it's just that I could be working on my homework or researching colleges for my applications or practicing or… I'm sorry. I don't really want to stay for the meeting. Could we just talk about it now?"

"Well, we're really going to need everyone. After we talk about what's going on, we're going to have to figure out what to do about it."

"What exactly," she said, "is going on?"

"Um… It looks like someone's watching us and I don't know for sure, but they might be trying to kill us."

* * *

"I don't like this," Jaclyn said.

I'd just told her about Vaughn and I discovering the pictures in the car. The fact that all of them seemed to have been taken next to Grandpa's house hadn't escaped her. She put the pictures on the table and turned into a purplish blur, moving from one side of the room to the other, the dust on the carpet practically exploding around her feet.

Pacing, I guessed.

After a few times across the room, she stopped by me again.

"What I really hate about this is that I can't ignore it. They know who we are. They probably know where we live."

She paused, frowning. "Do you know anything about them?"

"I'm working on it."

"Work faster," she said.

Easy for her to say.

I occupied myself with the computer, making sure I could get at the results of my research on the contact list. Not that the results were all that impressive since I was only half done.

Jaclyn had sat down again and was surfing the internet on one of the other consoles.

"What do you think about Vaughn? Do you think he's working with them?"

"I doubt it," I said. "He seemed as confused as I was."

She sighed.

"This sounded like a lot more fun last week," she said.

It was funny; aside from Daniel, with whom I'd been best friends since I was four, Jaclyn had been the only one I'd kept up with after Captain Commando died, the Mentalist developed dementia, and the picnics stopped.

I still had no idea what to say to her.

I could have told her that fighting the Grey Giant wasn't really fun at all. I'd felt terrified half the time and utterly out of my depth for the other half.

It didn't seem like the right thing to say, but not saying anything felt wrong too.

The console beeped, saving me from replying.

The security cameras showed three different groups coming through three different tunnels. After clicking the mouse pointer on each window, I was relieved to find that I recognized everybody.

Daniel and Cassie exited first—from the tunnel on the far wall, both of them in costume. Three mailbags floated behind them.

"More?" I asked. "Didn't we just do this?"

"Did you see Time magazine this week?" Cassie said.

The confusion must have shown on my face, because she followed with, "You don't pay any attention to the news at all, do you?"

"I read Reddit," I said.

Judging by her expression, Reddit didn't qualify as a news source.

"We're on the cover," she said. "They did an article called 'The New Old Heroes.' I don't have one here, but I'll bet there's one in the sacks."

"It's not just about us," Daniel said. "There are a bunch of second or third versions of heroes showing up. Mostly no one you've heard of."

"Why did you pick up the mail now?"

"I thought it'd make us seem more real. Also," Daniel continued, "we can't just let them stack up in the storefront downtown."

Unlike a lot of superhero groups now, the Heroes League never built a big shiny building in the middle of a city. They built a bunker under Grandpa's house and bought an old shoe store and former speakeasy. During the 50's and 60's, they staffed it with a secretary, but in the 70's they turned it into a futuristic, automated office.

I'd thought about making things work again, but it would probably take weeks.

Daniel floated the mailbags in between the table and the screen—where it would be impossible to miss them.

"You're worried about seeming real?" Jaclyn said.

"You know," Daniel said, "like we're more than a bunch of teenagers."

"Maybe you should give everyone issues of Time magazine," she said. She didn't sound sarcastic exactly, but her tone had an edge.

"*Funny*," he said. "I'm not obsessing about this. This is a big deal. We're getting together a bunch of people who haven't seen each other since they were five and asking them to trust each other. We're going to make decisions that might put our lives at risk. So the details matter. A lot."

"Hey," Jaclyn said, "I'm not arguing. I know what's at stake. That's the only reason I'm still here."

Daniel breathed in, paused and then spoke, "Sorry. I'm just trying to make this work. I've been thinking about it maybe a little too mu—"

"Yo, Danny-boy," said a voice from the other wall. "Are we late?"

Two of Night Wolf's grandchildren came in

through one of the tunnel entrances.

Daniel turned around and checked his cell phone. "You're on time. Hi Travis."

Travis held the metal door open, waiting for a moment as his sister Haley stepped through. He closed it as casually as I did when I was wearing the suit. Travis stood about six foot eight and had the musculature of a body builder.

Haley was a foot and a half shorter.

Both of them wore dark gray costumes modeled after their grandfather's and had the same black hair— except Travis's was short, and Haley's hung a little past her shoulders.

It amused me. Night Wolf's whole shtick was being a nocturnal predator. He would step out of the darkness and lay them on the ground before anyone knew he was there.

I found it hard to imagine darkness big enough for Travis to hide in. By contrast, Haley could definitely hide, but being barely over five feet tall, how hard could she hit?

As Travis started talking to Daniel and Cassie stepped over to Haley, I remarked to Jaclyn, "We've only got Marcus and Vaughn to go. And Marcus is in the tunnels."

"Where's Vaughn?" Jaclyn said.

"I've no idea. He hasn't been in school since Tuesday so that's two… no, three days. He was looking really tired after the uh… incident. So he's probably at home."

I'd called his house (his parents still hadn't given him back his cell phone), but only got his mom. She'd told me he was sleeping, and she may have been telling the truth. Cassie had said she'd try to talk to him in person, but she'd never told me if she had.

"Well," Jaclyn said, "I'm not running this, but if I were, I'd say let's start the second Marcus gets here. Like how about now?"

"Is Marcus here already?" I checked the monitor. The tunnels were empty.

"Behind you," Marcus said.

Marcus was the son of one of Jaclyn's aunts and one of Travis and Haley's uncles—which made him the grandson of both C/Hotfoot and Night Wolf.

I turned around.

Marcus was about my height, had curly hair, light brown skin and wore black sweats.

"I know Daniel said we should come in costume, but I don't have a costume. So I came in this…" He gestured to his clothes.

"Fine with me," I said.

Daniel was the one who'd thought costumes were a good idea. "People need to see things," he'd said. "If we get them into costume, putting together a team will be easier to imagine."

All I cared about was that people came through the secret entrances so they wouldn't be seen. We'd discussed it Tuesday night in a seemingly endless three way instant messaging session. Getting together tonight was step one of the plan.

While Marcus and Jaclyn talked, I leaned over and tapped Cassie on the shoulder. "Did you ever talk to Vaughn?"

"A little," Cassie said, stepping away from Haley, Travis and Daniel. "It went wrong. *All* wrong."

"What happened?"

"You know how Vaughn's parents have decided to protect him from ever doing anything wrong again and took away his cell phone *and* his bank account *and* his car?"

Cassie sounded more irritated on Vaughn's behalf than I would have been.

"Yeah?"

Cassie sat down at the computer next to mine.

"I called Vaughn's house on Tuesday night and got his mom —you know, just to see if he was available tonight. I left a message for him to call me, but he didn't. So I called back on Thursday and his mom answered again. Only this time she told me I was a bad influence and not to call back. Then she hung up on me. Seriously, what the hell is going on with that?"

Cassie rolled her eyes and then grinned at me. Everyone else had stopped talking.

"I'm standing there with my phone in my hand and I'm pissed. I *did* drop him off after a party once last year, but it's not like I made him get drunk. I took away his keys that night. And anyway, all I wanted was for him to answer one very simple question. So screw it, I decided, I'm breaking into Fortress Mom."

"Uh... wow," I said.

Travis snorted.

"I grabbed one of Dad's old utility belts and drove over. I jumped the fence and then went to the side of the house where Vaughn's room is—except his room is on the second story. So I threw up the grappling hook. After that it was easy. I just crawled up the side of the house."

I glanced over at Daniel. He had an extremely blank facial expression.

Cassie continued, "I knocked on Vaughn's window and you should have seen the look on his face. He opened it and I'm hanging there on a rope. I started to tell him about the meeting while I was stepping inside, but we didn't get very far. His mom opened the bedroom door and started shouting at me. I jumped out the window, yanked the grappling hook until I dislodged it and ran back to the car."

"I may have missed it," I said, "but is Vaughn coming or not?"

She stopped and looked uncomfortable for a moment. But when she spoke she sounded just as amused as ever.

"I told him about the meeting," Cassie said, "but your guess is as good as mine."

"So," I said, "we might as well get started. I think we've got chairs for everyone."

I sat down at the table and pulled up a few things on the monitor—the photos and the contact list I'd retrieved from the SIM card.

By the time I looked up, everyone had taken a seat around the table. Daniel sat on the closest end and Cassie was to the left of me. Travis and Haley were across the table. Marcus sat at the far end and Jaclyn to my right. We still had room for Vaughn if by some miracle he actually showed.

For a moment I felt a little thrilled to see the seats filled and wondered what it had been like for the original League. Less cluttered by piles of cardboard boxes, trophies, and mementos of course, but it was still a group of people around a table. It felt good to imagine that we might be like them.

I stood up and began to describe how Vaughn and

I had almost been kidnapped by the guys in the sports car and then attacked by the men in the Escalade. I started a slideshow of the scanned copies of the photos Vaughn had found. They cycled through the big screen on the wall, giving each picture a long enough appearance so that each person could be recognized.

Then I showed everyone the contact list.

"I'm still going through this," I said. "Right now all I know is that there are a few more numbers here with Chicago area codes than anywhere else. I'm sure I could have found out more, but I also had homework to finish. I'm hoping to learn a little more this weekend. And if you want to help, I'm open."

Travis raised his hand. "Didn't the League used to have connections with the FBI's Superhuman Affairs Department? That list sounds like the kind of thing they'd handle."

"It does," I agreed, "but I've got no idea how to contact them or anything."

"I'd try the phone book," Travis said. Haley and Marcus laughed a little.

"Good point," I said, "though Daniel and I were talking about passing it to his father if I couldn't find anything useful."

Travis nodded. "That's right. He's a lawyer."

"Better yet, he's got connections in the police and FBI." Daniel said matter-of-factly.

"Anyway," I said, "that's longer term. Shorter term, I'm more worried about us. They've got our pictures and they might know our names."

I pulled a box out from under the table. It contained rings, necklaces and watches.

"Take any one you like," I said, passing the box to

Jaclyn. "They're homing signals my grandfather made. They probably belong in a museum, but they work."

Jaclyn sorted through the box. "I'm sure your grandfather was a great inventor, but his taste in jewelry—oh God. Look at this..." She pulled out a big silver medallion shaped like a peace symbol. "What were they doing? Infiltrating a group of hippies?"

Eventually she picked a gold ring and passed the box to Marcus.

When everyone had pulled out something, I closed the box and put it back under the table.

Cassie took over from there, talking about how important it was to practice fighting together just in case we had to operate as a group.

I pretended I was listening, but had other things on my mind. I didn't know if Travis had thought it all the way through, but if he had, he was right. We shouldn't be handling this ourselves. We should have been storming Daniel's dad's office and asking for advice.

Or honestly, just finding someone who actually knew what they were doing and handing it all over to them. Like Guardian over in Chicago if we had to... Or Larry. He wasn't much of a detective, but he had at least been living this life for twenty years.

What got me was how few options we had. Telling the police would mean revealing our grandparents' secret identities, and Daniel's dad's too. Not to mention it would open up our families to revenge by who knew how many people.

Handing it over to a group of experienced heroes wouldn't take us out of danger either—even if I could persuade Daniel and Cassie that it was a good idea.

They had some kind of drive to revive the League,

a drive that I somehow didn't receive as part of my inheritance.

However much Daniel wanted this to feel real, I still felt like I was just pretending.

* * *

After every party comes the cleanup.

I stood alone in the League HQ holding six empty pizza boxes in my hands. I'd already put the pop and leftovers in the refrigerator.

David Letterman kept me company. Twenty feet tall on the Leagues' TV, he joked about the president, the current presidential candidates, and how the next big super team would be eight year olds from Indiana.

It didn't get much of a laugh, but I stared at the screen, dumbstruck. Was that a reference to us? Hadn't our fifteen minutes of fame run out yet?

I dumped the pizza boxes into the trash compactor, shut the door, and heard a satisfying *crunch*. The next time I opened that door, it would be empty. One of these days I would have to find out where it all went. Given the world's level of environmental awareness when Grandpa had designed this place, I wouldn't be surprised to discover it all shot into Lake Michigan.

While I pushed the chairs underneath the main table, I heard a low-pitched beeping. Looking up at the screen, I noticed a blue bar running across the bottom of the screen. The words "incoming call" floated from the right side of the screen to the left.

Crap.

I knew what that meant. It meant official. As in federal. As in a representative from our actual government wanted to talk to someone here.

I ran into the lab and put on the Rocket suit. I'd taken it off after everyone had left.

With any luck, they'd give up before I finished. I had to pull on the arms, gloves, legs, chest piece, and helmet separately, each one with its own special connections.

The beeping didn't stop.

I ran back out to the main console, clicked the "receive" button and watched as the FBI's seal appeared on the TV. Underneath the symbol were the words "Superhuman Affairs Branch."

In a moment, the seal dissolved into a dark haired man standing in front of a wide desk in a cramped office. Piles of papers threatened to crowd out his computer, the biggest pile on the left just about ready to fall over.

He was in his mid-forties, had Asian features, and wore a blue suit. Just as he became visible, he had been putting a gold colored action figure on his desk. I couldn't see exactly what sort of action figure it was, but the idea of an FBI agent playing with C3PO in his spare time amused me.

I wondered how he would take it if I asked about it.

The fact that he was smiling also didn't quite fit with my mental image of the FBI. Of course, my image of the FBI came mostly from X-Files reruns.

"Hi," I said, "I'm the Rocket."

"Good to meet you Rocket," he said. "I'm Isaac Lim, Super Team Liaison for the northern Midwest."

His accent sounded like it was from one of the northeastern states. I couldn't place which one.

"I'm calling," he said, "to let you know that your team is part of our agency's National Hero program."

"I knew that the Heroes League was," I said, "but what we've got here right now only barely qualifies as a team. Besides, aren't there some requirements for that? I think I remember something about five years of supervision and needing... I don't know... a security clearance?"

"Don't worry about it. You've been grandfathered in."

"Well that's good, I guess. What do we get out of it?"

He looked a little surprised at the question, but said, "The usual. Federal resources for your cases and sometimes equipment if you need it. You get paid when you're on call. You also get guidance from an experienced field agent—me, in this case."

"Okay," I said. "What do you get out of it?"

"We get heroes and in your case, we get legendary heroes back from beyond the grave," he replied, laughing a little as he said the last part.

"More like replacement heroes," I said.

"No," he said, "I'm serious about that. The League was legendary. I idolized the original Rocket as a kid. Most supers are born with powers, but here was a normal person who could go toe to toe with them. You don't know how much I wanted my own suit or how many hours I wasted daydreaming about it..."

He stopped, a little embarrassed. "Don't mind me," he said. "It's been a late night and I ought to go home."

"So should I," I said, "but if we really do have access to FBI records, I've got a list of names and numbers I'd like you to check out."

"Absolutely." He told me how to send him the file. Apparently our network had a secure connection to the Feds.

Then he signed off.

After I sent him the contact list, I wondered whether I should have trusted him with so quickly. But it was too late to take it back. Besides, I told myself as I took the suit off, he seemed to really like Grandpa.

Funny to imagine an FBI agent having a Rocket action figure in his office. It was a strange world.

Chapter Four

"The hot lunch menu says that it's called Mystery Pizza," I said. The pizza appeared to be crust covered with baked beans, red onion and cheddar cheese.

The only thing I found mysterious was that someone could actually believe high school students might recognize it as food.

Cassie said, "I'll eat it if you don't."

She'd come with her usual three trays worth of food and had already finished half.

"Don't worry about it," I said, "I'll deal." I picked it up and ate it. What other option did I have? I didn't particularly feel like listening to my stomach growl for the afternoon.

"Hey there 'Bad Influences,'" Vaughn said, putting his tray down between the two of us. "Ready to save the world?"

Cassie and I both replied simultaneously, Cassie saying, "Not that loud," while I said, "Not here."

Granted, we were sitting at the back table in a corner with basically no one around. Still, you didn't talk about superhero stuff in a high school cafeteria— at least not loudly.

"When did I become a bad influence?" I added.

"Ah, don't worry about it," Vaughn said, "you're not. I just didn't want you to feel left out."

"Thanks."

Cassie scowled. "What I don't understand is why I'm a bad influence at all. It's not as if I brought you to parties. I brought you home because you were too drunk to drive."

Vaughn poked at the pizza with his fork.

"Look, I don't know. I think she's decided everyone she saw me with right before going into rehab is a bad influence." He laughed. "Of course, now she thinks you're a crazy stalker too…"

He turned to me. "She told you about climbing through the window, right?"

"Yeah. Friday night," I said.

"Wish I could have made it. I swear, it's like Mom never stops watching me." He picked up the pizza and took a bite. "You know, this stuff is okay. Better than the 'Mystery Casserole.' I never did figure out what was in that." He chewed the pizza thoughtfully. "Did she tell you about the shingles?"

Cassie looked away.

"She jumps out the window and starts yanking on the grappling hook, only it doesn't come out. It's stuck. She yanks again and there's a ripping noise and geez... ten shingles came down with the grapple. It was hilarious—the shingles were raining down and my mom was finally too shocked to shout at anybody."

"About Friday," Cassie said, her face now slightly red, "Daniel and I worked out a patrol schedule and a response procedure if one of us gets attacked. I'll get it to you after school."

"And I'll get to use it when they finally let me out of my cage," Vaughn muttered.

For a few minutes after that, we just ate.

Cassie finished first. "Did either of you see the news over the weekend? There were a bunch of fights in Chicago on Friday night and a few more on Saturday and Sunday."

"Oh yeah," Vaughn said, "All the Chicago supers were in on it, plus Defenders groups from both coasts."

"Fighting gangs, right?" I had actually paid some attention to the news this weekend.

"Not just any gangs," Cassie said. "Powered gangs. Not hugely powerful individually, but there were a lot of them."

"And CNN said that even the normals had military grade weapons," Vaughn said.

I zoned out while they discussed the highlights.

"Guardian opening a gate like he did when we fought the Grey Giant..."

"—that fire guy—"

"Supernova dusting the building..."

"All that water just pouring through downtown—"

I could see how the Superhuman Affairs Branch guy would have been in the office on a Friday night. From what I'd read, the major action would have been finished by the time he'd called me.

"Vaughn," I said, "weren't low powered gang members your grandfather's MO? Addicted to that 'power elixir' stuff and rampaging through the city?"

"Shit, yeah," Vaughn said. "You don't think he's alive, do you? That'd be way too much like a comic book."

"No. I was thinking more of the stuff you passed on to Stevie and company back when you were on drugs."

The expression on Vaughn's face moved from shock to despair faster than I'd thought possible.

Before he could reply, Cassie's friend Kayla walked up to the table, a tray of food in her hands. Kayla was a little taller than Cassie and always seemed tanned.

Previous to this year, I'd almost never seen her apart from Cassie.

"Mind if I sit down?"

Still halfway into the conversation we'd been having, we were silent.

"I can go if you don't want me," she said, looking at Cassie.

"No, no," Cassie said, "sit down."

"We were just talking about Chicago," I said.

"Oh," Kayla said, "all those poor people who lost their homes."

Funny how that aspect of the weekend had never entered into our discussion.

* * *

Haley hung her legs over the edge of the roof while I stood a couple of feet away from the ledge. Despite being able to fly when I wore the Rocket suit, I still hadn't gotten over the fact that eight stories was a long way to fall.

We were looking over downtown.

Downtown was a mixture of modern glass buildings like you'd see in any big city and 19th century architecture. The 19th century stuff included buildings intended to be beautiful—marble pillars in front and ornate sculptured cherubs holding up the roof—and brick factories that existed only to pump out as much furniture as possible.

Back then, Grand Lake had been known nationally for furniture production.

The building we were on had been a movie theater in the era of silent films. Now the bottom story was "The Black Crow Tavern." The other stories held offices.

According to Daniel and Cassie's list, Haley and I were on patrol tonight.

The evening so far had all the awkwardness of a first date and none of the excitement. Just like the time I'd gone on patrol with Daniel, we hadn't found any crimes that I felt comfortable interrupting. I'd been listening to police and fire departments over the suit's radio, but they seemed to have everything well in hand. After half an hour of running across rooftops Matrix-style, Haley had suggested we find someplace to sit down.

"Not what you expected?" I stepped a little closer to the ledge where she sat. The street still looked a long way down.

"Oh," she said. "I'm not expecting anything. I'm just along for the ride."

"Along for the ride?"

"Travis loves the idea of bringing back the Heroes League," she said. "He was so excited, he called me at one in the morning from his dorm to tell me about the meeting. And I thought it sounded fun, so I came."

"I think we've got different definitions of fun," I said.

"I didn't mean the meeting. I meant Travis. Seeing him excited about something is fun. Don't tell him I told you," she said, "but I don't think he's been this into anything since before the Air Force Academy rejected him." She paused, then said, "What about you? What got you into it?"

"Me?" I asked. "I don't know. I think Cassie and Daniel nagged me into it."

We talked for a few minutes about classes and then just watched the city. It was around nine at night and very few cars moved down the streets. Once the tourist season ended, Grand Lake didn't have much nightlife.

Just below us someone crossed an intersection diagonally, ignoring the stoplight.

"Hey," I said, "we could go down there and tell off that jaywalker. I think that's the only illegal action we're going to see tonight."

She laughed. "That's okay," she said. "It sounds like we're both just out here for the exercise anyway."

Just as I was about to ask her if she wanted to go home, I saw a beam of bright red light strike something and then realized that the pole in front of Channel 10's studios was burning.

"Did someone shoot Willy?" Haley asked.

Willy the Weather Worm is a metal earthworm covered with lights. It glowed in different colors for different forecasts. The local NBC affiliate, News 10, came up with it in the 1960's, took it down in the late 70's and pulled it out of a junkyard in the late 90's—though it briefly had to compete with the Weather Worm remnant that Channel 6 had pulled out of a different junkyard for being the real Weather Worm.

I wish I was joking about that.

"Are you up for checking it out?" I said, running through a systems check on my suit. Glowing readouts appeared on the inside of my helmet.

Over the radio, I could hear the police and the fire department being dispatched. "We've got a 10-80 downtown…"

A 10-80 is an explosion.

*   *   *

Channel 10's studios were in an old former factory. A big brick box on the edge of downtown, it had a strip of lawn in front and a large parking lot on the opposite side.

That was what I could see in the streetlights, anyhow.

I had landed in the front, not wanting to land in the middle of any trouble without having a chance to look it over first. I'd carried Haley to save time.

"Your armor's *cold*," she said.

"Sorry," I said. "It's warm on the inside."

"Then I get to be inside next time," she said, rubbing her arms.

Lights ablaze in the night, police cars passed us without stopping, either not noticing or not caring that we were there. Over the radio, I heard the dispatcher give the request code for the SWAT team.

"I'm going to take a look around the corner and find out what we're up against," I said.

"Not without me."

I made it to the corner in a few long strides. She kept up.

I peered around the edge of the building. Now decapitated, Willy the Weather Worm burned, his pole listing toward the parking lot. Willy's head partially smashed in the roof of an SUV.

Five police cars were parked on the street, police behind them, guns out and pointed toward someone standing in the middle of the parking lot.

Man-machine. Until now, I'd assumed he was dead.

Almost every superhero seemed to have a stable of regular villains, the people who showed up again and again, apparently more interested in making the hero's life hell than committing crimes. Man-machine was one of Grandpa's.

Just like Grandpa, he was into powered armor. Unlike Grandpa, the armor he'd created couldn't fly. Man-machine concentrated on strength. Where Grandpa's armor looked slim and elegant, Man-machine's looked blocky and angular. Though only slightly taller than a normal man, the armor was twice as wide.

The laser cannon mounted on his left shoulder explained the red beam of light I'd seen earlier.

Above me, I heard Haley say, "I didn't know he was still alive."

She hung on the wall between the first and second story, her fingers and toenails digging into the brick. They were longer and more claw-like than I remembered, and dull grey in color.

"Looks like it."

"Do you have a plan?"

"Does calling for backup count?" Yesterday I'd set things up so that my suit would transmit my address along with a message calling for help to League members' phones. I activated it.

"I suppose," she said. Her tone of voice suggested that it only barely counted. Her brother, I imagined, would have probably already been dismembering Man-machine by now.

In fairness, I should mention that neither Grandpa nor anyone else had ever succeeded in catching Man-machine. He'd been defeated, but had always managed to get away. Stepping out from behind the building and challenging him seemed like several kinds of stupid.

From the parking lot, a police officer addressed him over a megaphone. "Man-machine," she said. "It's been a long time. What brings you out tonight?"

A dry, wheezing laugh filled the area. Grandpa wasn't the only one who'd put amplifiers into his armor.

"Officer Van Kley? It's been years. Still working on the front lines? I'd have thought you would be further along in your career by now."

"I'm a lieutenant," she said, "but they still let me out on special occasions."

"It will be just," he gasped for breath, "like old times."

Lieutenant Van Kley lowered her megaphone for a moment, then asked, "Are you alright? We have medical personnel on the way. If you need to be looked at—"

"I'm not sick." He took another breath. "Just old. Call the Rocket if you haven't already."

"Man-machine," she said, "the old Rocket is gone. The new one's just a kid."

The laser cannon swiveled toward the side of the parking lot opposite the police cars and fired. A car exploded.

"The Rocket. In five minutes."

When faced with people whose skin repelled bullets or who shot lasers out of their eyes, cops didn't have a lot of options. From what I understood, standard policy was to stall them until someone with half a chance of taking them down arrived.

Officer Van Kley was doing her best. I could hear her talking again. I wondered whether anyone would arrive before Man-machine got bored.

"I'm going in," I said.

Haley said, "With me."

"Right," I said. "Can you fight?"

From what I remembered, her grandfather, Night Wolf, had the ability to hide, could climb walls and had inhumanly good senses, but an enhanced sense of smell (no matter how good) seemed pretty useless at the moment.

"Yes, I *can*," she said.

I looked up the wall to find her glaring down at me. Her eyes were slit like a cat's and glowed slightly.

"Sorry," I said.

From the parking lot, Man-machine said, "Time's up."

A red beam hit the nearest police car, melting the right side window and setting the front seat on fire. The two policemen that had been crouching behind it ran to the next car.

"We better get in there," I said and engaged the rockets, shooting across the parking lot toward him at full throttle.

I crossed the parking lot in seconds, readied myself to punch him, and missed. I'd misjudged how close I'd had to be and passed him about two feet to the left. I didn't even try to blast him with the sonic weapons on my arms. I was too busy climbing to avoid the former factory on the other side of the parking lot.

That factory used to make bikes. Now it was a store called Lavender West. They sold clothes and hippie paraphernalia. It had a skate park on the fourth floor.

I'd been told (though I'd never had any reason to check) that they also sold bongs.

If I'd turned a little slower, I could have smashed into the building and found out. Instead I missed the wall by inches, flying directly in front of a third and then a fourth floor window. I could have reached out and shaken hands with all of the people crowding to see the fight.

Of course, moving at 286 mph, I would have ripped their hands right off.

Once above the building, I gave myself a little spin, rotating so that I was facing the parking lot. Then I dove. I had a plan this time.

Grandpa used to tell a lot of stories about fighting Man-machine. Nearly half of them ended with Grandpa finding a way to smash the transparent faceplate. Sometimes he'd punch Man-machine unconscious. Sometimes he'd smash the glass without breaking it, leaving it in one piece but impossible to see through.

I was going to fire the sonic weapons directly at the faceplate. All I had to do was get close enough.

Three-quarters of the way down, I realized that Man-machine had turned to face me. Then I saw a flash of red and felt heat on my chest.

Systems reported the damage as medium—suit integrity intact but heavy damage to that spot. I'd better not get hit there again.

The blast distracted me from my intended approach. I leveled off fifteen feet above the ground and some twenty feet away from Man-machine, beginning a tight circle that I hoped would put me on a near collision course with him.

It did.

He barely had chance to turn and had no chance to turn the cannon. I fired a sonic blast directly into the faceplate and then I was past him.

I managed to turn more quickly this time, without even leaving the parking lot. I didn't know what I was going to do next, but I did want to see what damage I'd done.

Tactically that wasn't such a great move and I probably would have gotten shot a second time if Haley hadn't chosen that moment to enter the fight.

By "enter the fight", I meant that she threw a Prius at him.

At least I assumed it was Haley. I never saw her do it, but cars don't generally launch themselves into the air.

It knocked him over, but not out. He pushed the car off with one hand and stood up, shouting into the darkness.

Disappointingly, the sonics didn't appear to have hurt his faceplate at all.

"Why of all the cowardly things…" he began, but couldn't seem to finish the thought.

Beginning again, he said, "It'll take more than that—"

I didn't allow him the time to finish. I gave the rockets fuel and flew toward him, arms outstretched. Once over his head, I dipped, pulling my forearms up in front of my helmet and using them to smash into the side of the laser cannon.

It broke off from the mount point on his shoulder with a satisfying crack.

The momentum took us both and I scraped across the parking lot, stopping several cars away from him.

I pulled myself up. He lay there, unmoving.

The Man-machine of my grandfather's stories would have been up by now, trying to crush the life out of me. His armor had always been stronger than Grandpa's and in straight hand-to-hand combat, that was what counted.

"Are you okay?" I edged a step closer to him. It *could* be a trick.

I could hear labored breathing over his speakers.

"Damn..." he said. "Damn you."

Haley stood next to me. I hadn't seen her appear.

Man-machine said, "You're one of Night Wolf's grandkids, right?"

Haley looked at me for a second. When it was obvious I didn't have any advice, she said, "Could be."

"He didn't fight fair either."

"Fair?" Haley said, sounding irritated, "You were blowing up innocent people's cars with a laser cannon. When is that fair?"

"Forget about it," Man-machine said. "You win. Just get me an ambulance. My chest hurts."

We stepped away as the police surrounded him. Officer Van Kley read him his rights while Man-machine told the paramedics how to remove his armor.

I kept watching him the whole time. By reputation, Man-machine would have slipped away by now, having hidden a mini-rocket pack or smoke grenades inside his armor.

Instead he just looked old as they pulled the armor apart and lifted him onto a stretcher—just a gray-haired man wearing a t-shirt and jeans.

The armor lay open on the ground. I wondered how long it would be before the FBI picked it up.

It got crowded after that. Now that the violence was over, the people in Lavender West came out to gawk. The journalists in News 10 rushed out the front door of the studio, cameramen in tow.

As Haley and I were being interviewed, I saw a blur appear at the edge of the crowd. It turned into Jaclyn.

"Sorry," I said, "I've got to talk to someone over here."

The crowd opened to let her through.

"I am so sorry," she said. "My dad caught me on the way out and wanted to know where I was going. It took a long time to get away. Where's everyone else?"

"You're the first one here," I said.

"You're kidding."

Vaughn and Daniel flew in after that. Vaughn was in a black leather outfit that I could only describe as superhero bondage gear. Marcus flew in, having taken the form of a faceless, bat-winged man. Travis and Cassie arrived last—probably because they'd taken cars and parked two blocks away to avoid being identified.

I decided it was safe to conclude that this test of our alert system was completely unsuccessful.

* * *

By the next morning, it was all over the news. Man-machine turned out to be the secret identity of Gerald Cannon, owner of a small garage chain called G's Auto

Parts. Apparently he'd been having a heart attack the entire time we'd been fighting.

It was his second. The first had happened in 1981, the year Man-machine had disappeared.

Gerald had survived the night, but was now in Grand Lake University Hospital under guard and not allowed any visitors.

I'd had time to read about it on Tuesday morning because school had been closed for the day. Central High had received a bomb threat. The FBI was investigating it, but I had good reason to believe they weren't investigating very hard.

I'd gotten a call on my cell phone at 6:30am, practically at the moment my alarm went off.

"Good morning, Nick. It's Isaac Lim," said the voice on the other end of the line.

His voice oozed cheerfulness.

I managed to get out a "Hi."

He gave me an address. "Be there at 10:30, fully dressed and ready for action. You'll want to see this."

"I have school," I said.

"We've taken care of that."

Four hours later I landed on a lawn in a subdivision just south of Grand Lake. The house I was in front of stood out for a number of reasons. First, it was a one hundred year old, white painted wooden farmhouse in a neighborhood of nearly identical aluminum-sided McMansions with three car garages.

Second, it had ten cars and a semi-truck in front of it. Four of the cars were police cars. The rest had government plates.

Third, the house was squared off with a yellow "Police Line Do Not Cross", which held back more than twenty members of the media with their cameras, trucks, and satellite uplinks.

Isaac stood in the middle of the lawn and shook my hand almost immediately after I touched down. "Good to see you, Rocket. Follow me in."

He turned and started toward the house's front porch. "Don't mind the civilians," he said. "They're having a bad day."

The inside felt comfortable, a place where needlepoint versions of Norman Rockwell paintings hung on the wall, complete with pictures of grandchildren.

A grey haired older woman sat in the living room in front of the TV. It was shut off. A red haired woman in a flannel shirt sat on the couch next to her, holding a cup of coffee. "Two teaspoons of sugar, Mom?"

We walked through without a word and stepped into the kitchen. A teenaged boy stood behind the counter eating a ham sandwich. He was watching a small TV that hung from the bottom of a cupboard. From its tinny speaker, I heard a voice say, "The Rocket just entered Cannon's house."

I knew him. His name was Chris Cannon, and he was a sophomore. We'd both been on the school's Science Olympiad team together last year.

I'd never felt more grateful for the helmet.

He watched us, saying nothing, as we opened the door to the basement and walked downstairs.

The basement was little more than concrete walls, a furnace, tools and a workbench. Cans of paint, two by fours, pipes, and plumbing fixtures lay next to the workbench. Evidently Man-machine was a bit of a do-it-yourselfer.

At the far end of the basement, a piece of the concrete wall swung outward. Had it been shut, I'd never have looked at it twice.

It opened up into a room three times the size of the basement, and one that seemed oddly familiar to me. Man-machine used some of the same tools and machines as my grandfather. At least eight recognizable versions of Man-machine's armor filled the space.

The older ones all had broken faceplates.

FBI personnel were everywhere in the room, documenting, photographing, investigating…

Isaac turned to me. "I think this may be the best moment of my career."

One of the nearer agents, a short, dark-skinned man said, "Nah, just of your childhood, Isaac."

Isaac laughed with them.

After a little while, he said, "You'll want to take a look at this for sure. We'll have to classify most of it, of course."

He led me to the far end of the room, our footsteps echoing on the concrete floor. Newspaper clippings and photographs covered the wall. A few showed Man-machine with other villains, the products of short-lived teams set up to oppose the Heroes' League.

Photographs of the Rocket covered the rest of the wall and overflowed around the corner to the next. The pictures went as far back as World War II up to this year.

Up to me.

Maps of the city hung on another wall, Grandpa's patrol routes drawn and dated on them. Photographs of Grandpa's armor had been enlarged to nearly full height. Each redesign's picture was covered with scribbled speculations about weak points and improvements.

The speculations written about the redesign that I wore were unnervingly accurate.

Not as unnerving as some of the pictures, though. Starting in the late 1960's, the photographs included pictures of my grandfather even when he was out of costume and they continued past 1983 when the League disbanded and he retired.

I recognized pictures of my mom and her older brothers playing in the front yard of my grandparents' house. I found a picture of myself as a toddler on the porch swing with my grandfather.

I didn't remember hearing of him ever attacking Grandpa out of costume or kidnapping any of the kids. I could only guess that he would have thought that unfair.

I told Isaac to let me know if he found anything important, flew back to HQ, took off the armor and left it in the lab.

Then I sat on the porch swing for a while.

CHAPTER FIVE

HQ had become busy.

Okay, that might have been an overstatement, but it no longer felt deserted. Travis sat at one of the computers at the main table, leaning forward, too big and too muscular to be truly comfortable using normal furniture.

A pile of books sat next to him. His Spanish book was open and he was making flash cards with a Spanish word written on one side and the English equivalent on the other.

"It got too noisy in the dorm," he'd said, his voice a deep bass. "I didn't want to go to the library, so I came here. Hope you don't mind."

"No problem," I'd said.

So now he sat there, flashcards in one huge hand,

pen in the other.

Meanwhile, I sat in front of one of the other computers going through the messages in the voicemail system. There were a lot of messages because I'd never gotten around to listening to any of them.

And by "never gotten around to listening to them," I meant it in the most literal sense possible. My grandfather's voice still welcomed people to the Heroes' League even though he had been dead for five months, and he was the last person who had checked for messages.

There were hundreds. Scrolling down the screen, I highlighted everything except the last week's and deleted them, hoping that I wasn't losing anything important. Then I listened to the hundred or so that were left.

I instantly deleted reporters asking for interviews, leaving the ones that were more problematic. A few were from established teams, like the various regional Defenders units congratulating us on reestablishing the group. Did we have to make a response? I decided to put it to the rest of the group later.

Then there were the calls from people who probably should have called the police or the fire department instead. We had a "my cat's stuck in a tree" call from a couple days ago. Hopefully it was down by now, but we really needed to set some sort of policy on things like that.

We also had a call from an angry sounding man who ranted about the state of the world and finished by shouting about how kids our age ought to be in school instead of beating people up. I deleted it.

Finally, the mayor's office had left a voicemail

asking us all to come down and meet him. I kept that one.

Then I headed off to the bathroom—though "bathroom" was a bit of a misnomer. It was actually more of a locker room. It had six stalls, four urinals and ten showers. Plus lockers.

The original League only had one woman—Ghostwoman—and she wasn't all that active after the 50's, making the old League something of a sausage fest. The New Heroes League (or so the press had named us, much to Cassie's annoyance) was closer to equal and had three girls and five guys and it looked like we were already beginning to compete for control of the facilities.

At any rate, that was how I'd interpreted the existence of three boxes of tampons and pads beneath the sink.

When I finished my business in one of the stalls, I discovered that someone had once again flipped the toilet paper—which made it twice in the past two weeks. Instead of going over the top, it now fell behind. I switched it back.

I checked the other stalls. They'd been changed too. I switched them back for good measure.

When I returned to the table, Travis put down the cards. "We missed all the action a couple nights ago."

He managed to put more certainty into that statement than I'd ever felt about anything.

"It worked out," I said.

"We can't count on these guys having heart attacks. We need a better system. Instead of having everyone do backup, we should have a couple people we assign to do backup. That way they've already made their excuses and they're ready to go.

"I was in the library talking with a girl, and then my phone went off and I had to run across campus to get my costume and my car. If I'd been prepared, I'd have been there faster."

We talked about it for a while longer and then he said, "What we really need is faster transportation. The League had all that shit. Any idea what happened to it?"

"It's probably all in the hangar," I said. "You want to take a look? My grandfather mothballed all of it so I'm sure it can work, but I doubt it does right now."

I went back to the main menu on the computer, clicked to open the hanger doors and turn on the lights.

The big metal doors rattled open, revealing the hanger. Travis and I both sneezed.

In the far left corner, a light shattered and the place went dark.

That still didn't detract from the awesomeness of the scene. I mean, I had this huge room that could just as easily have been on an aircraft carrier (or the Death Star), and in the middle of it sat the Heroes' League jet, covered with some kind of form fitting white plastic sheet. It was surrounded by a few other things under tarps.

Travis and I started pulling the tarps off. We'd uncovered Night Wolf's corvette (still black and shiny) and Captain Commando's motorcycle (red, white and blue) by the time we heard the hum of the elevator.

"Cassie's back," I said. I was pulling the tarp off a rack on the wall. The rack held ten small, silver rocket packs.

"Here's what they did," I said. "All the people who

couldn't fly got rocket packs so they could get to HQ and grab their stuff. They don't have much of a range, but they fit in a briefcase."

"Think it could hold me?" Travis picked one up. It wasn't much longer than his hand.

"No idea."

Cassie stepped into the hangar, still in costume from patrol. "What are you guys doing?" Then she noticed the motorcycle. She didn't even wait for an answer before hopping on the seat. "Oh my god, Dad's motorcycle. Does it work?"

"He's going to get it to work," Travis said.

I didn't even have a chance to object. By the time I was able to think of a response, Travis had already started on how to solve our response time problem.

"The only problem I see with using this stuff," Cassie said when he was finished, "is that I don't know how to drive a motorcycle and none of us can fly a jet. Nick can teach us how to use the backpacks, but the rest of it…"

"I can fly a plane," Travis said.

"Jets are different," Cassie argued.

"I think I know someone who might be able to get us lessons," I said. Then I told them about the FBI and Isaac Lim.

"You were just sitting on that for days?" Cassie sounded a little annoyed.

I shrugged. "I was going to tell you on Monday at lunch, but then Kayla showed up."

"She's my friend," Cassie said.

"I know," I said, "but she still blew my only chance of bringing it up."

"Never mind that," Travis interrupted. "Do you

have any idea how hard it is to qualify to work with the FBI?"

"We don't qualify," I said. "I think they're just allowing us in for the publicity."

"Who cares?" Travis said. "All that matters we get their stuff, or hey, *our* stuff. It's our tax dollars paying for it."

"Whatever," Cassie muttered. "I'm changing back into clothes and taking a shower. Don't come in."

As she walked away, Travis asked me, "You think you can get this stuff working again?"

"I think so. Grandpa was pretty good about leaving instructions."

"Cool." He walked back to the table and started looking at his Spanish flash cards.

I picked up one of the rocket packs. They wouldn't be hard to fix at all. The jet? That would be a challenge, but oh, *so* cool. I tried to remember where I'd seen the jet's plans and documentation.

I found it in one of the file cabinets in the main room, along with the car's manual, the motorcycle's and most of the others. The jet's documentation was hundreds of pages long.

As I flipped through the three ring binder, I heard Cassie shout something from the bathroom.

I walked to the door and said, "What was that?"

"I said," Cassie shouted again, "who keeps on messing with the toilet paper?"

*   *   *

Mayor Bouman's office was less impressive than I'd expected, but was big enough to fit all of us, which helped. Located in City Hall, a Victorian era building, it had intricately carved woodwork, old paintings and a view of downtown. The mayor's desk appeared to be the size of a small boat—though it had a richer finish and probably included more gold than most boats (or at least those boats not crewed by pirates).

Despite all of that, it was still just an office.

Maybe I'd been expecting too much.

Mayor Bouman shook our hands. He was in his forties, brown haired and blandly handsome.

A photographer snapped another picture as the mayor struck up a conversation with Vaughn. If nothing else, they were a study in contrast. The mayor wore a blue suit while Vaughn wore black leather pants, a mask covering the top of his face, and a matching jacket. The pieces of his clothing had more straps and loops than what seemed functionally necessary.

"So, if it's not a secret, how did you get into this?" Mayor Bouman smiled at him.

"Oh," Vaughn said, "I just woke up one day and found I had powers beyond the reach of mortal man, you know. Some shit like that."

The mayor laughed and asked, "What sort of powers?"

Vaughn paused a little too long, but then said, "Weather powers mostly… Look out the window for a second."

Mist gathered outside, forming gradually into a small cloud. Vaughn breathed out. "Okay, I'm letting it go now."

It drifted away, floating downtown toward the suburbs, shrinking as it went.

Vaughn said, "Some things come easier to me than others."

"What comes easily?"

"Wind," Vaughn said, "and a couple other things."

"That's impressive. I'll call you in if it rains during Cityfest next summer." He then held out his hand to Haley. "And what can you do?"

He went down the line. He asked us our powers, our names, acted impressed by any demonstrations we gave, handed each of us his card, and generally pressed the flesh.

When he was done, he said, "Feel free to sit down if you want. I'm afraid I've got to give you a little bit of a speech."

I sat down, still holding his card. The suit wasn't designed for social occasions and so there weren't any pockets. Leaning back, I realized that the chair hadn't been built to accommodate rocket packs. I stood up.

"Sorry," I said, "I don't fit in the chair."

"Don't worry about it," the mayor said. "I'll try to make this short."

I spent more time pretending to listen than actually listening. Helmets are good for that. Mind you, it's not that he was actually boring, but all he'd really called us in to do was let us know how much (or how little) the city supported us.

Here's the gist of it: the city was honored to see the Heroes' League active again, but they'd prefer that we concentrate our efforts on things the police can't handle (like supervillains) and leave normal crimes alone. The city wasn't going to specifically give us missions because that might leave them open to charges of child endangerment, but we were welcome to warn the police if we were working on something. Finally, while it was true that technically vigilante justice wasn't legal, he wanted to let us know that we had his support.

"Keep the streets safe," he said as we walked out of his office.

I slowed next to Vaughn. "Hey, I didn't know about the weather stuff."

"I just figured it out recently," Vaughn said. "And it's great. If I can do some other things, maybe people won't pay so much attention to the lightning, you know?"

"That'd be cool," I said.

People inside the offices stood from their seats to stare at us through the windows as we moved down the hall. I was grateful when we made it to the stairs.

I was not grateful, however, to experience the head rush of an eight-way mental contact, and I wasn't alone. I could feel Cassie grabbing the railing while Travis tried to avoid falling into her. Marcus grew an extra leg to balance himself.

Daniel: *Sorry, I couldn't—*

Cassie: *... while we're walking down a stairway? Daniel, what the fu—*

Haley: *Does anyone else feel like they're floating?*

Jaclyn's thoughts were too fast to make any sense, but I could feel the irritation.

Daniel: *He's corrupt. I couldn't read everything but he was trying to get something out of us. Maybe out of Vaughn.*

Travis: *What?*

Vaughn: *Yeah, what?*

Daniel: *I don't know. He's hard to probe.*

Travis: *Let's table this for now.*

Daniel: *No. I should go back up there and try and—*

I found myself in the middle of what Daniel must

experience in minds: whirling eddies of thought, fluid rivers of emotion, and unmoving structures. He intended to thread his way in and do something, but I never got time to figure out exactly what.

Travis: *Dammit Daniel. You can't just go up there and rummage through the mayor's head on suspicion.*

Daniel cut the connection. We walked out silently.

*   *   *

Fall. Leaves lay in piles next to the street. The air felt just a little cooler on the skin as I walked down the sidewalk. It was dark, slightly past ten o'clock at night, and I'd already finished my homework.

I wanted to be alone. Just call me Greta Garbo. … Or was it Bridget Bardot? I could never get those old movie stars straight.

In the not-so-distant past, I might have gone to League HQ and spent an hour fiddling with Grandpa's tools or going through League memorabilia. League HQ had changed utterly in the past two weeks. Instead of being the nearly deserted place where Grandpa had shown me how the Rocket suit worked and sometimes told me stories, it had become a place where, at any given moment, any of us might show up.

I wasn't sure I liked that.

Tonight, for example, Daniel and Vaughn were going on patrol and Travis was still using the main room as a study hall.

Were I to walk in, people would want to know about my progress with getting the vehicles ready and whether Isaac had gotten back to me on the contact list.

And since there wasn't any progress on either front,

I'd decided not to show my face.

So I walked around instead, kicking a few leaf piles while imagining ways of improving the rocket pack's fuel efficiency. My parents' house stood in a section of town developed in the mid-sixties on what had once been the edge of town. It was still a nice area, but not that far from older and slightly rougher neighborhoods. Their reputations might have just been the product of racism due to there being more black than white residents, but there was no denying that people were poorer and their houses cheaper. Whatever the case, I'd never had any trouble there.

I saw a few other people out, including Terrence and Darius, a couple kids I recognized. Passing each other on the sidewalk, we all said, "hi," which was something we never bothered to do in school. Then we all continued on our separate ways.

That was fine. I really wasn't in the mood to talk. Of course, the fact that I wasn't in the mood to talk didn't mean that people weren't in the mood to talk to me.

My cell phone rang. I didn't recognize the number, but took the call.

"Hi Nick." It was Haley, Travis' younger sister.

"Are you in trouble?" I couldn't think of any other reason she might call.

"What? No. I just thought I'd call and see how you were doing after, you know… everything."

"Which everything?" I asked. "Do you mean 'talked with the mayor' everything or 'fought Man-machine' everything?"

"*Everything*, everything," she said. "But mostly Man-machine."

"I'm feeling kind of guilty," I said, though I hadn't

realized it until then. I'd won a fight with an old man who was having a heart attack. Then I'd seen Chris Cannon, Man-machine's grandson, at school. He still looked lost.

In a slightly doubtful tone, she said, "Really? Why?"

So I told her about going to the Cannons' house, seeing Chris, and the wall of photos in the basement. "I know I didn't make him do it, but going in there… It felt like I'd killed him."

"But you didn't. He tried to kill you. He blew up people's cars just to get your attention. And filling a wall with pictures of your grandfather and his family? That's just creepy. *He* should be feeling guilty."

I lingered under a corner streetlight, checked for cars and then crossed, deciding that I should probably go home.

"True, I guess," I said, deciding to change the subject a bit. "How are you doing after... um, everything?"

"I had fun," she said. "I've spent most of my life trying to avoid having people notice what I can do, but in a costume I don't have to pretend at all. I can climb walls—"

"And throw cars," I added.

"I felt a little guilty about the car," she said. "I liked the Prius. I should have thrown an SUV, but I wasn't sure I'd be able to toss it far enough."

I laughed.

"What's so funny?"

"It just occurred to me that I'm having a conversation about which cars are best for throwing."

"That's what I mean," she said. "We really could have a conversation about throwing cars and it wouldn't be weird at all."

"I think it'd still be a little weird," I said.

We talked more while I walked home. The walk wasn't bad—just step after step down the sidewalk in the dark.

I got a voicemail during our conversation. I hadn't recognized the number so I'd ignored the call.

"So, does gymnastics start soon?"

"I... wouldn't know," she said. "I'm not doing it this year."

It sounded like I'd struck a nerve, but that didn't stop me from asking more questions.

"Why?" I asked. "You were really good last year. Didn't South High almost win State?"

"We did, but... Do you remember Jackie Thomas?"

I did. Jackie Thomas was the state wrestling champion two years ago, or at least he had been until he saved some kid from being hit by a truck. He saw it bearing down on a four year old boy who had wandered into the road. Instead of grabbing the child, he'd picked up the four-ton truck, dug his feet into the road, and held the front end in the air until the child managed to get out of the way.

He was hailed as a hero at first, but within a week things changed. The association that regulates high school sports stripped him of his title. The media argued about whether he was a cheater. Thomas' protests that he hadn't known he was so strong fell on deaf ears.

I didn't know what had happened to him in the end. I thought I'd read that his family left Detroit, but I didn't know where they'd moved.

"I can see your point," I said.

We hung up a couple of blocks away from my house,

about twenty minutes before eleven. I had enough time to make my curfew and listen to that voicemail.

The message was from Isaac Lim. "I checked out your contact list and sent back some notes. You'll find them interesting."

I shut the phone and put it back in my pocket. "Interesting" wasn't a promising word.

Well, at least talking with Haley had gone better than I'd expected. Of course, the fact that she'd called me at all was pretty odd.

*   *   *

I could thank the fact that everyone else apparently had more of a social life than I did for HQ being empty Friday night. Other nights Daniel and I might have done something, but he was Jewish and Friday night was a family night.

I logged into the computer and found the files Isaac had sent me. They contained pictures and reports pulled from government databases that Isaac assured me we would soon be free to peruse ourselves. It included several hundred pages, including death certificates and photos.

I wasn't going to finish all this tonight.

I walked to the kitchen and found more food than I'd expected—three-fourths of a large pepperoni pizza and a couple two liter bottles of Coke (one of which was diet). Ordinarily I wouldn't have taken someone else's food, but someone had written "eat me" on the pizza box and "drink me" on the Coke in black marker. I poured some pop and warmed up a couple pieces of pizza in the microwave, hoping that taking the food would work out better for me than it had for Alice.

Then I walked back to the table and began to read.

For each number, they included basic personal information about the number's owner, a criminal record if the person had one, and any relevant files that the government kept on them.

The one thing that most of the contacts had in common was being dead. Almost all of the dead people had died last weekend in Chicago during the massive dust-up between a few teams of supers and super powered gangs. From what the reports said, the people who had died weren't gang members. They'd just died because they happened to be downtown during the fighting or because their apartment building happened to burn down that weekend.

I didn't buy it and apparently neither did the FBI. The report pointed out that each person who died had worked directly or indirectly for Martin Magnus. I'd never heard of Magnus before, but according to the reports he invested in a lot of businesses and had a personal fortune of one hundred million dollars.

The FBI had investigated the connection between Magnus and the violence as far as they could. Magnus' people didn't have any obvious link to the violence outside of dying from it. They'd interviewed Magnus himself, but didn't get anything worth including in their report.

I moved on, clicking through page after page of photos. Only one caught my interest. It showed an office in downtown Chicago. It was an insurance office owned by a person named Ron Hirschfield, who had once been part of Martin Magnus' personal staff.

The office had been ransacked. Files lay on the floor next to a dead man. His arms were outstretched in front of him. A gold ring inscribed with symbols glittered on his right hand. The FBI's photographer must have thought it interesting too because the next photo showed a close up of the ring. The symbols were Egyptian hieroglyphics.

I'd seen those symbols before.

I got up and walked over to the cardboard boxes full of memorabilia. Sifting through the labels, I found the boxes from the destruction of Red Lightning's lab. I opened the boxes and dug through journals full of ranting and experimental chemistry, stoppered vials still containing colored liquids, and old tools that I didn't recognize.

I sorted through the boxes until I found Red Lightning's uniforms. He had a lot—a necessity when you led fanatic, drug addicted hordes.

The uniforms smelled like HQ—musty, but with a hint of cardboard. They were made from the damage resistant material my grandfather had designed. The colors weren't faded.

Gold, black and red, Red Lightning's costume had been designed in a pseudo-Egyptian style. A jagged bolt of red lightning ran through the middle of the chest under a gold arch decorated with Egyptian hieroglyphics. It was the same collection of symbols that I'd seen on the ring.

Packed with the costume, of course, were Red Lightning's crook and flail. I tried to remember what they could do, but it slipped my mind. Ultimately, it didn't matter. Grandpa had undoubtedly left schematics and design notes somewhere.

I wondered if the FBI had made the connection with Red Lightning, but doubted it. The hieroglyphics on his chest were too small to be anything but blurry outlines in photos.

So now, what was I supposed to do about it? It always seemed so much more obvious in stories.

*   *   *

Daniel and I sat in my room. He sat in the chair by the desk while I sat on my bed.

Even though he sat quietly, I could tell he was excited about something.

While hanging out with Daniel had never been completely normal, it felt as normal as a Saturday night used to be. Now some things felt a little different. For example, the poster over my bed displaying the original Heroes' League made me feel a little nervous.

Glancing at it reminded me that I should already be further along with the vehicle restoration than I actually was. Meanwhile, the dots on Red Lightning's chest made me wonder what exactly the hieroglyphics meant. It was probably in the report—which meant I had one more thing to add to my "to-do" list the next time I stepped into HQ.

"We'll have to bring in everyone," Daniel said, "but what I think we should do is bug Magnus' house."

Even though he was suggesting illegal wiretapping, his voice was completely calm. . He was like that most of the time.

"That would tell us some things," I admitted.

It wasn't clear yet whether Magnus was the villain or the victim of last weekend's brawl. On one hand, he had lost a bunch of current and former employees, and friends. On the other, he could have used the fighting as a cover to off people he couldn't trust. Either way, the deaths had to be connected somehow.

"Do you know how cool it would be if we solved this thing? We wouldn't be a bunch of kids who inherited everything. We'd have our own reputation," Daniel said.

"It'd suck though," I said, "if it'd be a reputation for butting into other people's business. It's not like Chicago doesn't have the Defenders plus a few independents."

"Screw 'em," Daniel said. "They missed their chance."

That wasn't how it really worked. From what I understood, it was polite to let people know if you were working on their turf—at least if you could find them. The Defenders' headquarters was a big building in downtown Chicago so we didn't have much of an excuse.

"I know," Daniel said, "we'll tell them, but we don't have to have them looking over our shoulders the whole time."

"Which begs the question of what exactly we're going to do about it," I said. "We could figure out a way to electronically bug Magnus or just, I don't know, station you on the roof for a few hours?"

"Sounds like fun times," Daniel said. "But count me out for now."

I barely had time to notice my own surprise when he continued.

"Don't count me out forever. Just for the bugging part. I assume that's your thing, not mine. I'll be in whenever you need me, but I've got another project going on too."

"Another project?"

Daniel smiled. "I'm going to expose the mayor."

"For what?"

"I don't know. My dad's been saying the mayor's corrupt for ages, but he's never been corrupt enough for my dad to make a special project out of it."

"Is this about the meeting?" I asked.

Daniel leaned forward in the chair. "He was trying to find out something about Vaughn back there in his office, but it wasn't for himself. It was for someone else. I want to find out who's got enough power to enlist the mayor."

I sat up on the bed. "Can you do that?"

"I don't see why not," Daniel said.

"What I meant was, are we really allowed to just overthrow the government or something?"

"Right," Daniel said. "As I said, I don't see why not. Besides, it's not as if I'm going to try to lead the city in revolt. I'm going to expose the mayor's connection with illegal activities. After that, it all goes to the courts."

"Are you talking to your dad about it? I don't want you to end up in trouble."

"Do you talk to him before doing anything? I don't either. We're vigilantes. Technically almost everything we do is illegal."

Daniel sounded irritated. I'd noticed that he got that way when we'd talked about asking his dad for advice before. I also knew that he wasn't as strong a telepath as either his father or grandfather and I'd sometimes wondered if the two facts were somehow connected.

"I *don't* feel inferior to my father," Daniel said. He hadn't said that calmly.

We sat silently for a moment. I tried to think of nothing in particular.

"You want to go downstairs and play video games?"

I pushed myself off the bed.

Daniel said, "Why not?"

*   *   *

A week later, I stood in the HQ hangar surrounded in tools. My hand released the hood of Night Wolf's Corvette and I heard it click shut.

"Done," I muttered.

I'd spent most of Saturday testing the car. Grandpa had a long and detailed list of what needed to be done and I didn't want to miss anything.

Night Wolf drove a black, 1964 Stingray—sort of. By "sort of" I meant that I doubted that any of the parts were original. Even forgetting that the car was forty years old, I seriously doubted that an armored body, windows made of transparent metal, or hidden wings that could extend out below the doors were standard on any model of Corvette.

I had worked on Night Wolf's car and Captain Commando's motorcycle as a way of passing the time while waiting for the parts I needed for my redesign of my grandfather's eavesdropping system.

My back felt sore after standing for six hours—standing under the car while it was on the lift and standing under the open hood while reaching into the engine.

I opened the door and sat inside. The seat felt good. I touched a button and the window disappeared into the door. My eyes swept across the dashboard, its complexity rivaling the control panel of the still-mothballed jet. I now knew what all the controls did. Travis would have a good time with it.

I put my hands on the steering wheel and thought

about taking it out for a drive. Then I closed my eyes. My grip loosened and I fell asleep.

I woke to find Cassie's hand on my shoulder. She gave me a gentle nudge. "Nick? Are you awake?"

"I was just thinking about taking this car for a test drive."

"Did you say thinking or dreaming?"

She wore street clothes—jeans and a dark blue hoodie. A motorcycle leaned against the wall behind her. I guessed it might have been from the 1970's.

"What's that?" I asked.

"Dad's other motorcycle. Mom had it in the back of the garage. Would you mind looking it over?"

"I guess," I said. "I already finished the other one."

"I know," she said. "And I'd prefer to take lessons as myself instead of in costume."

Covered with dust and spider webs, the bike looked like it had sat in the back of the garage for ten years. I got out of the car and started wiping the bike off with a rag. It was a Honda CB400F.

"Did you ride it over here?"

"What? No, I pushed it. I should have had Daniel float it over."

So now I had another vehicle to fix. On the other hand, it didn't have to break the sound barrier or hide a machinegun—which meant it would be much simpler. I considered ways I might improve it. I could just toss the engine and replace it—maybe with a turbocharged diesel. But why stop there? Why not put in something interesting like a rocket assisted speed boost?

Cassie said, "Earth to Nick. What the hell are you doing?"

I realized that I was holding a screwdriver and had

already begun to take the bike apart.

"Nothing that can't wait," I said. "You want to come along while I test drive Night Wolf's car?"

*   *   *

We exited the tunnel of the Heroes League's mostly defunct downtown office. There was too much to fix there for me to even bother trying, but I'd made sure one thing worked: the mechanism that opened the garage door.

We moved through the garage and out onto the small exit ramp. By small, I meant it was only a car length from the road.

Sunlight hit my eyes for the first time in eight hours. I blinked and then watched for a break in traffic. You couldn't expect a lot of traffic at four o'clock on a Saturday, but enough cars passed that I couldn't instantly enter the right lane.

It made sense. This part of downtown was a mile-long strip of hospitals and other medical and genetic research facilities. Hospitals never closed down.

Further down State Street, the company that ran most of the city's hospitals had a data mining operation. I intended to get in there someday.

"Nick," Cassie said, "go. The lane's open."

"Right," I said.

"Honestly," she said, "you're so distractible."

I pulled out and merged into traffic. The car responded beautifully. It had a smooth acceleration, matching the speed of the other cars almost before I noticed. I wondered if I could get away with testing how it handled high speeds on the freeway.

"Hey Nick," Cassie said, "how's the research on the

contact list going?"

"Well," I said, "that depends on your point of view. Almost everyone on it is dead, but they work or worked for someone named Martin Magnus who might not be dead. I plan to bug his house as soon as the parts I need come in the mail."

Cassie sighed. "We should have just called the Midwest Defenders and had them look into it. It's been more than three weeks since we got that list."

"With everything that happened in Chicago, Magnus is probably dead too. Whatever was going on might have died with him."

"If we're lucky," she said.

I was paying too much attention to cars on the road to know for sure, but it seemed like she frowned.

"I didn't know it was going to be this hard," she said, sounding frustrated. "Do you know how many people skipped out on their patrols this week? Jaclyn and Haley had tests and wanted to study and Vaughn's mom kept him home again. Daniel went, but he barely put any time into it."

"Everyone is pretty busy," I said. "Maybe patrols aren't the best thing we can do. Or maybe just less often would be better?"

"I don't know," Cassie said. "I just thought it would be *good* to bring the League back."

"It is. We're all just feeling our way into it," I said. "Pretty soon we'll know what works for us."

It was the nicest thing I could say. Personally, I'd enjoyed the quiet.

We had gone far enough down State Street that we'd passed Grand Lake University Hospital, the Hardwick Institute for Biomedical Research, the non-descript brown, brick building that housed the data mining facilities, and the street had turned from four lanes into two.

The traffic was sparse. The nearest car in front of us had to be a couple hundred feet ahead. A police car was close behind, but not much of anything was behind it.

"Cassie," I said, "I think we're about to have a problem."

"Why? We aren't breaking any laws."

"We don't have a license plate," I said.

Before Cassie could reply, the lights started flashing and the siren began to wail. I started to slow down, but Cassie shouted, "Don't stop. Go!"

She had a point. Neither of us were wearing costumes and I had no way of explaining who exactly this car belonged to.

I gunned it.

I'd watched a lot of car chases on TV in my life, but it was interesting to learn that at least one thing about them was true. The police really will chase you if you drive away from them at high speed.

If anyone else had been behind the wheel, we would have lost them without a problem. Beyond being able to corner well, the car could easily pass two hundred miles per hour. It had all the standard accessories for a hero's or villain's car—caltrops for popping tires, the ability to release a blinding wall of black smoke…

I could have used them, but I wasn't willing to risk killing people who were, after all, just doing their job.

When you're watching TV, the drivers in these chases never slow down. They don't stop for signs or they'd never pass them. They had the sense to move the chase to the highway instead of residential streets.

Me? I slowed for stop signs and barely ever exceeded forty miles per hour. I drove down the twisting streets of nice neighborhoods, doing everything I could to avoid dead ends, worried that I might slam into a kid on a bike.

It was exactly that kind of neighborhood too—cut lawns, trimmed bushes, houses that always got painted when they needed it. Children rode bikes down the streets and played soccer on their perfect green lawns.

Cassie seemed to know more about the layout of the streets than I did. "Don't go that way. Go *that* way!"

I swerved and went the opposite direction to the one I'd been intending, skidded a little, and stayed away from the police a moment longer.

"That way," Cassie pointed. "Get on the highway and you can really make the speed count."

We were getting close to where one of the development's streets—Northwood—exited onto Belmont (a four lane road) when I realized that the police had blocked the intersection.

Three cars were parked at the end in front of the traffic light. Two more followed behind us. It was almost a relief. I was finally in a situation that could be solved by technology instead of my driving skills.

I pressed the button that extended the wings, guessed how much thrust it would take to clear the cars, and fired the car's rockets. It couldn't fly far, but this was exactly the sort of situation that it was designed to handle.

Taking off felt just like the suit or an airplane—like I'd left my stomach behind.

We easily flew over the cars, crossing all four lanes of the intersection and smashing into the traffic light on the other side of the street.

They were bigger than they'd looked from the ground.

I managed to touch down without destroying the car and we drove off.

"They're not following us," Cassie said, craning her neck to look out the back.

"Do you think they finally recognized Night Wolf's car?" I asked.

"Let's hope not."

*   *   *

You never knew how the press would spin an accidental car chase. Would they portray you as a menace? A fool? Or would they fail to even recognize you?

With that in mind, I was relieved to find the story in the lower right corner on page three of the Grand Lake Sentinel's Sunday edition under the title "Mistaken Identity Causes Low Speed Chase."

A quote from the article…

"An unidentified police officer stated, 'If the officers on patrol had properly identified the car, I'd have told them to leave it alone. I remember Night Wolf. He never bothered to stop either.'"

I left the paper in a pile on the couch. Dad would read it when he and Mom came home from the conference. I spent Sunday afternoon re-reading David Brin's *Kiln People* while sprawled across my bed. Fixing the Legion's old vehicles and attempting to play superhero had cut into the time I normally would have used to play video games and read.

It felt good to be normal for a change.

My parents came through the door around five. The conference had been relatively close to home—just a few hours' drive to Indianapolis.

Although my dad specialized in teen therapy, he was also an author and wrote books with titles like, "What Your Teen Wants from You."

According to Dad, most teens want consistent rules, love and appropriate discipline. Personally, I could have used a copy of *Firefly* on DVD, but that had yet to show up.

Ever since the publication of his first book (when I was five), Dad had gone to conferences, acting as a speaker and panelist, attending either just to network or to get a booth to plug his books. Mom, as his business manager, always went with him.

I opened the door to my room. On the other end of the upstairs hallway, I could see Mom, still in her blue suit, dumping their dirty clothes down the laundry chute.

"Nick, how did your weekend go?"

So here was a bit of irony: in his books Dad claimed that one of the reasons teens began having massive parties in the house or got involved with the wrong crowd was because their parents weren't home enough.

Dad and Mom ended up going out of town on speaking engagements at least once a month. So far I hadn't set up any parties or joined a gang. I didn't even get invited to those sorts of parties. In fact, prior to hanging around with Vaughn and Cassie, I hadn't even known when I'd missed one.

On the other hand, you could argue that a superhero team wasn't that much different from a gang.

"Not a whole lot happened," I said. "I did my

homework. I read a book. I hung around with Cassie a little on Saturday afternoon."

"She's nice," Mom said. "You've been spending a lot of time together lately."

She leaned against the wall, waiting for my reply.

"We're friends, Mom."

She only smiled and walked into the bedroom to help my dad unpack.

I returned to my room, read for another hour and then went downstairs. Dad was on the couch reading the paper. Mom was fixing herself a sandwich.

"So now they're joyriding in Night Wolf's car," Dad said. He sounded amused.

"Who?" Mom said.

"The kids who fought that thug a few weeks ago. The Grey Giant?" Dad flipped open the paper, following the story to page four.

"I don't think the article said they were joyriding," I said.

"What else would kids be doing with a car like that? I had this old rust bucket of a Camaro back in high school and tried things that should have killed me a couple times over."

He scanned the rest of the article. "The city's not going to fine them for destroying the traffic light either."

"Should they?" I walked over to the refrigerator and pulled out the leftover Chinese takeout from Saturday night.

"They should. Kids need accountability."

"I'm sure they feel guilty about it." I poured the rest of General Tso's Chicken over a small mountain of rice and put the plate in the microwave.

"They probably do." He put down the paper.

"But that's not good enough," he continued. "It's the whole package that causes problems. There's the secret identities—which means these kids can't talk to anybody about what's going on in their lives, the constant exposure to violence which could give anybody post-traumatic stress disorder, and then there's the government. Some kid, or even an adult, goes over the line and they just smooth it over.

"It's corrosive," he said. "It takes a child's community away and it gives them what? Adulation for hurting people? And they wonder why some of these people go over to the other side of the law."

I pulled up a stool and ate my dinner at the counter.

"I hadn't thought of it quite that way," I said.

He shrugged. "Neither had I, but I had a client a couple years ago. Basically a good kid, but with a bad case of PTSD. He started skipping school and killed a man outright. It turned out that the man was a villain who had abducted and killed the kid's girlfriend as part of a plan to kill him. The government covered it up and told him to take a break for a while. His parents brought me in because they knew something was wrong, but they didn't know what."

"Is he still active?"

"I don't know. I haven't seen him lately. He's not from around here."

Chapter Six

Sometimes, when you realize something for the first time, there's a certain excitement as your whole world changes. Other times, the realization makes you feel like an idiot.

For example, imagine that after three weeks, you finally decide to check out a lead that you should have followed up on earlier, but hadn't because you'd assumed traveling to Chicago was a huge hassle. Then you actually calculate how long it would take to get to Chicago--if you were using your grandfather's powered armor that just happens to include a rocket pack.

A direct flight from Grand Lake to Chicago was only about twenty minutes.

I realized it on Thursday while sitting in Grandpa's lab at League HQ. I'd just scooped the bugs I planned to plant into a bag, and thought about the practical details involved.

That was when I realized that I could fly to Chicago in about the same time it'd take to drive across town. Theoretically, I could have flown to and from Magnus' house during lunch hour at school.

I was an idiot sometimes.

I told my mom that I'd be at Grandpa's house studying and didn't worry about my dad because Thursday nights he stayed late at his private practice.

Then I suited up and shot out of the tunnel that exited over Lake Michigan, flying across the water.

The sun had already set, leaving the stars and moon to glow in a cloudless sky, dark waves churning below. I saw the blinking lights of a jet above me and checked for planes at my own altitude.

Moving at three hundred miles per hour, it seemed that I'd barely put Grand Lake behind me by the time I caught sight of Chicago's lights. The Sears Tower's top story shone while the two antennas gleamed red in the night.

I had a sudden urge to buzz the building, but didn't. You know that wouldn't generate good press.

I shifted course a little after being informed by my GPS that Magnus' house lay to the north of the city.

Passing over endless suburbs, cars and well-lit streets, I wondered how well Grandpa's suit showed up on radar. I knew he'd done his best to make it hard to see, but that didn't guarantee anything. After having to avoid the police last weekend, it would really stink if the Air Force scrambled fighters to investigate me today.

Worse, I supposed, would be if the Midwest

Defenders decided I was a threat. I had left them a voicemail saying I'd be in town, but how often did they check it?

I landed half a block away from Magnus' house, guessing that I'd probably make too much noise if I landed on the roof, and suspecting that landing on the front lawn might be a little too "in your face" for comfort.

The neighborhood had big lots, large lawns, and enough trees that it felt like a forest. Magnus' house looked like an Italian villa with a square tower, a wide arched doorway and three disjointed sections, each as large as my home.

None of the lights were on. I wasn't sure if this was good or bad. It would make bugging the place a little easier, but on the other hand, it could mean that Magnus had already made a run for it.

I stood on the sidewalk next to the brick wall that divided Magnus' property from the street.

Unhooking the pouch from the powered armor, I pulled it open and fished around inside for the controller. With the controller in hand, I activated the bugs and watched them swarm out.

Long and multi-legged, they could pass for large cockroaches. I adjusted the picture on the controller to include the house and pressed the 'infiltrate' button. Most scuttled down the other side of the wall while a couple flew upward to tap the telephone line, both to listen to Magnus' calls and so that they could broadcast any information back to League HQ.

The thought that I was bugging a house with cockroach shaped robots amused me *much* more than it should have.

Seriously. I actually giggled a couple of times.

I briefly considered moving somewhere less visible while I watched the roachbots (a nickname that also seemed considerably funnier at that moment) do their initial once over of the house. A guy in golden armor doesn't blend into any neighborhood.

Unfortunately, I got distracted.

Flipping between the viewpoints of thirty different bots, I found that one of them had made its way into a very interesting room. Bookshelves lined the walls. Beakers, jars, and test tubes covered the tables along with human skulls and animals preserved in jars of formaldehyde.

I tried to decide whether the room fit better in one of the Harry Potter movies or Frankenstein, but was pulled back to reality by a more pressing issue.

"Don't move," said a voice from behind me. "Turn around and hold your hands where I can see them or I'll blow you away."

I held up my hands and began to turn around, curious. If all he turned out to be was a guy with a gun, he was about to have a very unpleasant surprise.

If I had to choose one word to describe him, it would be 'professional.'

Clean-cut, clean shaven, and wearing black jeans, shirt and jacket, the man pointed a submachine gun at me.

"What's that in your hand?" He gestured to the controller with his gun.

I decided not to bother with replying, putting the controller back into the pouch.

"What do you think you're doing? Pass that thing over here."

Shrugging, I tried to think of my next move. The classic answer would be knock him unconscious, but he hadn't done anything other than point a weapon at me.

That's not much of a threat.

Of course, it was possible that he had armor piercing bullets.

"So," I said conversationally, "do you work for Martin Magnus?"

"Do you have a hearing problem? Give me that thing or I'll shoot you."

He stepped toward me.

I smacked the muzzle of the gun with my left hand, forcing it away from my body and then grabbed the top of the gun with my right hand, yanking it away from him.

Unfortunately, it was on a shoulder strap. So by yanking the gun away from him, I'd pulled him toward me. He took advantage of it, diving into me like a linebacker and catching me in the stomach with his shoulder.

I fell over. He landed on top of me, pulled himself up and punched me in the head.

It didn't hurt. The helmet took the blow but it was still a strong punch, easily in line with what Cassie had thrown at me during practice.

I landed an open-handed strike to his face, knocking him unconscious. Then I rolled him off me and stood up, checking him over.

His trigger finger pointed at an odd angle relative to the rest of his right hand. I must have done that when I'd pulled the gun away. Looking at it made me a little queasy. I turned my attention to his head, hoping

I hadn't cracked his skull when I struck him.

His face seemed to be normally shaped and didn't give when I touched it. Without an X-ray, that was as much as I could tell.

Anyway, he seemed to be breathing normally. With any luck, whatever gave him that strength also gave him some kind of healing ability.

I could only hope.

Originally I'd been planning to let the bots do a quick once over and then let the bugs report after that. Now, I could count on people removing anything interesting as soon as he either reported in or failed to.

Leaving him on the sidewalk, I started the rockets and flew up to a balcony on the wing to my left. I ducked under an arch while floating over the railing and landed in front of a door. It was locked. Punching through the window next to the doorknob, I reached in and unlocked it.

I walked into a guest bedroom that should have been in a motel—a carved wooden bed and dressers, a couple paintings, a big television, a radio, and no clutter or personal items.

From there, I went out the door and down the hall, following the information from my controller. I had to break the door open to get in, deciding that I ought to learn how to pick locks.

It was much weirder than it had looked from the robot's perspective. From where the bug had been, I'd seen the books, the skulls, and the jars of preserved animals, but I hadn't noticed the number of plastic containers filled with different colored dust. The refrigerator turned out to be stocked with animal parts (I closed it quickly).

Another thing I noticed was that though there were glass beakers and test tubes just like I remembered from chemistry lab, the beakers seemed much larger. Whatever Magnus did in this lab, he clearly did in bulk.

The books were another mystery. An entire shelf held three ring binders filled with photocopies and pictures of writings in other languages—Egyptian hieroglyphics, Sumerian cuneiform, and others I didn't recognize. Near them were another shelf of grammars and dictionaries.

The rest of the books seemed to be a mixture of anatomy, biology and chemistry.

I had no idea what to do next. It was obvious that this all connected somehow to Vaughn's grandfather. It also seemed obvious that the ancient writings were somehow useful in creating whatever Magnus worked on in this lab, but I still couldn't piece the overall picture together.

In an ideal world, one of the books on the shelf would be 'The Book That Explains Everything'. Unfortunately, if such a book did exist, it appeared to have been checked out. What's more, I didn't have enough time to go through all this stuff.

Fortunately, I had an idea. I didn't like it much, but it was the only idea I had.

I activated the cell phone I'd recently wired into the suit, placed a call to one of the numbers I had on speed dial.

"Hey Isaac," I said. "I was wondering how good the FBI is at confiscating property for no apparent reason?"

* * *

Shortly after, the FBI arrived in unmarked vans

and cars. I'd explained the connection between Red Lightning, the ring in the picture, and Magnus to Isaac over the phone. When the FBI got there, I showed them where the room was, but they didn't need me after that.

They took the still-unconscious man I'd fought away in an ambulance. I watched the flashing lights disappear down the street from the sidewalk. Then I walked away from the house, barely able to see the stars in the sky thanks to all the trees. The streetlights didn't help either.

Not paying any attention to my surroundings, I thought about the last hour. If I'd taken anything that I'd just done at all seriously, I ought to have turned myself in.

Crimes committed? Breaking into Magnus' house, tapping his phone lines, bugging his house, and knocking some guy unconscious (a guy who had threatened me, but who, to be honest, had no real way to hurt me).

Crimes prevented/criminals caught? None.

Amusingly, Isaac had simply told me "good job" and called in a crew to confiscate the evidence I needed.

Whatever had prompted Dad's rant about the corrosiveness of being a superhero, he had a point. I'd just been given positive reinforcement for breaking into somebody's house on a hunch. It made me wonder how far I could go before they tried to reel me in. On the other hand, the FBI had to have a policy against allowing teenage supers to do whatever they wanted.

I was probably overthinking things again.

An annoyed voice shook me out of my rumination. "So you're just going to leave?"

A man-shaped cloak appeared in front of me,

transparent at first, but slowly becoming more solid. Once the cloak was opaque, I glimpsed the hint of a face in the shadow of the hood.

"Dark Cloak?" I asked.

He fit the description I'd read on Double V's website. Dark Cloak was one of Chicago's independent heroes. From what I could remember, he specialized in gang activity but he hadn't been active for the last two years.

His voice revealed something Double V hadn't, however. He sounded my age, maybe a little older.

Ignoring me, he continued, "No matter what they say, they don't really give a damn about you. If something happens and you stop, they'll move on to the next guy."

"I'm sorry," I said. "I followed less than half of that."

"They're using you. What's to follow?"

I started to say something, but stopped. Being used wasn't a concern, and Isaac hadn't promised me anything besides assistance... I was more worried about becoming dependent on the FBI for things we could do ourselves.

"Don't believe me?" he said. "I worked with them for years and then they told me to quit. I can't say they didn't have their reasons, but I'm back and they still aren't talking to me. Where's the gratitude? I gave them Death Mask when I was just sixteen and I'm better now than I was then."

"I remember Death Mask," I said.

It had been a big deal three years ago. National news. I remembered seeing him on Late Night with David Letterman. Or was it Jay Leno?

"Well," I said, "I probably ought to go. Got to get

back home before my parents miss me, you know."

He seemed to stiffen, then took a small step toward me. "Don't believe me, then."

"It's not about belief," I said. "I just don't think we're in the same situation."

Then I pressed a button on my palm and shot into the night sky.

As I flew home across Lake Michigan, I wondered if he'd been the client Dad had mentioned.

I wished I'd thought of it earlier, then decided it wouldn't have made much of a difference. I couldn't mention my dad without blowing my own secret identity, and Dark Cloak probably wouldn't have taken the more general question, "Have you ever seen a psychologist?" particularly well.

* * *

After supper the next day, I walked over to League HQ, deciding I might as well check for any messages. I arrived to find Vaughn watching Channel 10 News on the big screen in the main room.

A copy of the Grand Lake Sentinel lay next to a computer. I picked it up and glanced at the front page.

The headline was "Mayor Denies Influence" while the article argued that the mayor had received money from a group called Michigan Citizens for Business, and then hired members of the group into his administration.

Much of the evidence came from an "anonymous source"—Daniel, probably. Telepathy was tailor-made for gathering dirt.

The next story's headline was "Storm King Continues War on Local Drug Pushers." The picture showed police leading handcuffed men out of the shattered doorway of a house. As a former client, Vaughn would have had some insight into the local drug scene.

I began to skim the article, but put the paper down as News 10 covered the same story on TV.

Vaughn grinned as a reporter interviewed a round-faced woman in a bathrobe about what had happened.

"The fog came out of nowhere and surrounded the house across the street, and then lightning shattered the front door. I always knew something was wrong over there, but I never did know what."

"Got 'em," Vaughn muttered. Then, "Hey Nick, is that cool or what?"

"It's cool," I said, giving my response just enough enthusiasm so that hopefully Vaughn wouldn't ask me again. Meanwhile, I checked through our voicemail. We had about forty messages, some of them two week old complaints about my joy ride in Night Wolf's car. Why didn't anyone else bother to check for messages? It wasn't hard.

The most recent one had come just ten minutes ago. Mayor Bouman had asked me to drop by his office because he had a few questions. I called him back to let him know that I was coming, put my suit on, and flew downtown.

For someone who could fly without help, I imagined flight would be all about the wind against your face and the roar of it in your ears. For me, it was the warmth of the rockets on my back and the smell of plastic, metal, and my own sweat.

The city of Grand Lake blurred beneath me, all lights and suburban lawns at first, but ending in the mixture of glassy, modernism and turreted Victoriana we called downtown.

Within minutes I stood in the mayor's office.

He shook my hand, thanked me for coming and said, "I made sure you could sit down this time."

The chair in front of his desk had no arms.

He gave me a smile as he took a seat behind his desk. The sight of a high-backed chair in front of large window that looked out onto a dark sky gave me flashbacks of the Emperor in *Return of the Jedi* or *Revenge of the Sith.*

I suppose that ought to have frightened me.

Not that Mayor Bouman looked like the Emperor. Despite being in his forties, he could have passed for thirty: tanned, with no wrinkles to speak of. Maybe he used botox.

Next to the window hung a framed copy of the Grand Lake Sentinel. The headline read, "DynaChem Loses Appeal."

Before he had become mayor, he'd been a lawyer who'd successfully sued DynaChem after people began to die of cancer near one of their storage facilities.

"It was one of my best moments," he said, glancing toward the framed paper. "They'd gotten so big, they couldn't imagine that an ordinary person could do anything to them. They thought they could hide evidence and lie on the stand. It turns out that they couldn't."

Inside the helmet, I rolled my eyes. Even two years after the election, he couldn't stop campaigning.

"But enough about that," he said. "I imagine you're wondering what I wanted to talk to you about."

Yup.

"You've heard about the scandal," he said. "I'd like you to talk to your friends and see if you can find out who's behind it."

"I can talk to them," I said, knowing that I didn't have to look very far to find the culprit. Turning him in was, of course, a completely different thing.

"Great," he said. "That's all I can ask for."

As he spoke, I felt something in my mind. Growing up with Daniel, I'd long ago learned to recognize the feeling. Everyone in his family, from his parents to his younger brother and sister, had been in my head at some point.

And whoever was attempting to hack my brain definitely lacked their skill.

I felt pressure—not a painful pressure, but a solid if slightly clumsy touch.

Mayor Bouman had stopped talking and held the edge of his desk with both hands.

I tried to think of what to do next.

Daniel often found it difficult to read my mind when I was working through a technical problem, so I focused on some lingering issues from the roachbots I'd released in Martin Magnus' house.

They needed to move faster. I ran through some possibilities in my head, making some general calculations. With any luck, all the details in my head would hide the fact that I could feel his intrusion.

The pressure of the mayor's mental touch lessened, but didn't disappear.

"Someone's trying to destroy me," he said. "You work your way into a position where you can do some good and people try to tear you down."

He leaned forward, his hand next to a picture of his

wife and twin sons.

"I have a right to defend myself," he said.

"You do," I said, more as a way of indicating that I was listening than expressing any actual sympathy. Still, I was distracted enough to wonder if he'd seen anything in my head.

That was a mistake.

All of a sudden the pressure on my mind intensified and I could feel a certain exhilaration mixed with fear that wasn't my own. My attempt at defending myself by calculating technical details such as the optimum power of the roachbots' motors dissolved upon contact.

Oh well. Defending oneself from a telepathic assault via the Power of Math sounded like something out of an educational kids show anyway—the sort of TV show where the villains say things like, "Fractions will not save you now, foolish mortal!"

Sadly, I would have totally watched that show as a seven year old.

Touching Daniel's mind felt like a conversation between equals—a little more intimate than I preferred—but the mayor's felt like an invasion. I could feel him searching frantically through my head, not finding what he wanted.

It felt as if sections of my memory were closing down as Mayor Bouman's mind touched them. I knew I was the Rocket. I knew I was being attacked. I could feel and see, but for the moment I had no past.

My mind echoed with his frustration.

I felt empty.

Well, not quite empty.

I had one thing. I had memories of my martial arts training. I remembered my teacher (whose face

I couldn't see and whose name I couldn't think of) and the hours I'd spent running through patterns of moves—both in and out of the suit.

There was something odd about my teacher, but I couldn't think what.

I heard Mayor Bouman think, "Wow, it's amazing how many years you've spent training for someone so young…"

Then I punched him.

My gloved fist hit him squarely in the nose, pushing his head back into the chair. I felt surprise, a brief moment of pain, and then he was out of my head.

I leaned over the desk, pulling my right hand back into ready position at my waist, my left arm raised in a block. He slumped forward in his chair, face hitting the desk.

Standing up, I realized that I was myself again. I then realized that I'd just knocked the mayor unconscious. This struck me as considerably more serious than trashing a stoplight. What kind of trouble had I gotten all of us into now?

But had it been entirely me? I'd been stripped down to little more than my martial arts training and my basic urges. In my opinion, I'd almost been somebody else. The mayor couldn't have done that, but I knew people who could.

For the moment, I could even remember their names.

* * *

An hour later, I stood in Daniel's room in my street clothes. I'd left the suit back at HQ. Putting it away and borrowing my mom's car had given me enough time to calm down.

Mostly.

Daniel's room used to be his dad's home office. Bookshelves were built into one wall, filled with books, CDs/DVDs, and video games. Unlike my room, everything in Daniel's room had been put away—no piles of books on the desk or the floor.

He had a lot of books about the Civil War. I flipped through a couple as I waited for him.

"Dad's just about to fly back from Chicago," he said, shutting his door as he stepped into the room. He seemed as calm as ever, even though he had to be sensing my emotions.

"I'll have to go home before he gets here," I said.

"I know."

I paused, trying to figure out a good way to accuse my best friend of secretly planting something in my brain.

"Look," he said. "I'm sorry. I should have told you."

"I didn't know my own *name*."

"I know. Here's what happened: you remember the block Grandpa put into everybody's heads? So none of us would talk about the League in front of outsiders? Well, a couple years ago I looked at yours and I realized I could improve it. Now, if a telepath tries to invade into your head, the block shuts off access to anything he touches."

"And not just for the telepath," I muttered.

"Not really," he said. "It's all there. You just can't consciously think of it. That's the beauty of it all. Just trust your instincts and you've got unconscious access to everything."

"What about the martial arts training? That didn't

go away."

"I thought you might need conscious access to *that*."

I bit back a reply about how having conscious access to my name and history might have also been useful. Unfortunately, I understood why he'd done it. If he hadn't, I'd still be in the mayor's office, spilling out my guts. Worse, however irritated I might be with Daniel, had the mayor been given the chance to change things around in my head, who knew what *he* would have done?

"If you feel the urge to screw around with my brain in the future, tell me first," I said.

"I get it," he said. "I'm sorry."

We stood there quietly for a moment. I wanted to move on to another topic, but still couldn't quite let this one go.

"So," Daniel said, "how do you suppose the mayor's going to play this? Think that he'll ignore it or call the police?"

"I have no idea." I said. "Haven't you been investigating him or something?"

"Sort of," Daniel said. He sounded a little frustrated. "My dad said he was corrupt, but I haven't found any evidence of it. I mean, there's the thing I fed to the paper, but there's no direct evidence that he was involved at all. The organization gave money to his campaign and he did hire a former staffer of theirs, but that's all. If it weren't for what happened to you and the way he was trying to get information out of Vaughn, I'd be worried I was going after the wrong guy."

I considered asking him why he'd released the information to the media if he wasn't confident about it, but I never got a chance.

"I was trying to push him to do something," Daniel said.

"It worked."

"Not very well," he muttered.

I laughed, and after a moment he did too.

"Well," I said, "if you want to check, I think FOX 50 has news at ten. Punching the mayor would make the news no matter who'd done it."

Daniel had a TV in his room. The remote floated from the dresser to his hand and he turned the it on.

We watched the broadcast. It contained the usual litany of car accidents, the presidential campaign, an exposé on a local contractor who was ripping off the elderly, sports, and finished off with a report about a water skiing squirrel.

Near the end of the program we heard shuffling footsteps in the hall.

Then each door opened one by one, swinging with enough force that the metal doorstops buzzed upon impact.

Daniel got up quickly and stepped into the hall. I could hear the doors beginning to shut—softly this time.

I got up off the floor and followed him. The second story hall in Daniel's house looked down onto the living room, on the right. The bedrooms were all to the left.

A short, white haired man stood a few doors down the hall, leaning on the railing. He was wearing a dark blue bathrobe and had a confused expression.

"Zayde?" Daniel said.

"I can't find my room. Do you know where it is?"

"You're standing next to it," Daniel said. "It's the

only door that's still open."

His grandfather took his hand off the railing, turned toward the door and looked inside. "That's not my room."

I heard Daniel's voice in my head: *I hate this.*

"Zayde," he said. "Come on, I'll show you."

He walked down the hall, reached into the room, and turned on the light. "See?"

"Oh." His grandfather peered in. "It looked different. Thank you. You're both fine young men." He stepped into the room, then turned to face us. "Shouldn't you be in uniform? There's a war going on."

The door shut behind him.

Daniel turned to me. "Sorry."

"That wasn't too bad," I said. "Remember the time he thought I was *my* grandfather?"

Daniel nodded. "Yeah, that was worse."

*   *   *

I stopped by HQ the next day after cross country practice, knowing that I could squeeze in twenty minutes before my parents started wondering where I was.

Daniel's dad had left an email at my official government-supplied account. Don't ask me where he'd gotten it. Between being city prosecutor, ex-military intelligence, a telepath, and Daniel's dad, he had his resources.

The email advised me not to talk about punching the mayor (like I would have) and said that we should meet soon to discuss the public relations end of the situation.

Okay.

The next email was from Isaac Lim, letting me know that I should call him about some things they'd found at Magnus' house—nothing urgent, but I should definitely call.

I wanted to, but I had a bad feeling that it would take a lot longer than twenty minutes.

Which brought me back to the real reason I'd stopped in—the roachbots. Despite calling Isaac in, I'd left a few roachbots around to monitor the house and I wanted to know if they'd been able to send anything back.

They had.

Most of the pictures showed Isaac's people tearing apart the lab. One showed Dark Cloak materializing inside after all of Isaac's agents were gone. The last few showed three people in dark clothing sneaking into the house and removing something from a safe in Magnus' office.

I couldn't see their faces, but the footage had made leaving the bots there completely worth it—well, except for the fact that I knew nothing about them.

I walked home still speculating over who they were.

When I returned to HQ after supper, Vaughn was there.

He was sitting at the main table, hair wet because he'd probably just taken a shower, books lying next to a monitor. A chemistry textbook lay open in front of him. His leather jacket hung on the chair.

"You're here a lot lately," I said. "I thought you were basically grounded forever."

"Me too," Vaughn said, "but I realized something lately. I realized that I can go anywhere I want. I mean, what are my parents going to do about it? They've taken away my bank account and car and shit. So what's left?"

"Aren't there supposed to be conditions where you can earn everything back?"

"Oh yeah," Vaughn said. "Sure. In a year."

"A year?"

"One year clean and they give back my car and my bank account. Just in time to leave for college."

"Shouldn't there be some sort of graduated system," I said, "where you get more back the longer you go?"

"Heh," Vaughn scoffed. "That's what your dad said too. Trouble is, they tried it before, back when I was using. I went right back to everything the second I got my bank account back."

"But you're not using drugs anymore," I said. *...Right?*

"No," he said. "I'm clean. My grades are good. I'm not going to parties. I'm doing everything they want. So I figure screw them, I can fly. I don't have to stick around the house if I don't want to."

This didn't quite seem like the best way to prove that he was responsible and should get his stuff back early, but I suspected that this wasn't about being rational.

"So what are they doing about it?" I asked.

"Nothing," Vaughn said. "It's just like when I was using. I pretend I'm not ignoring them and they pretend I'm not doing anything wrong."

They'd been pretending pretty well given that his mom had recognized Daniel, Cassie and I our first time out. Of us all, Vaughn was now the person most visibly using his powers. If she'd recognized us, his mom had to have recognized him.

"Oh hey, I'm probably going to be on the news again tonight," he said, excited.

"Yeah? Another bust?" I sat down at a computer and got ready to call Isaac.

"Nope. Interview on the evening news. You should do higher profile stuff and get some press attention."

"I don't need more attention." I clicked on Isaac's name.

"What are you up to?" Vaughn leaned over toward my screen. "Top secret FBI stuff?"

"Not top secret," I said. "I'm still following up on the contact list from those phones."

"Cool. I'll listen in."

That wasn't the reply I was hoping for. I was about to say that it was private, but then Isaac answered. His face appeared on the screen and he said, "Hi Nick. And this is?"

"Vaughn," I said, clicking a button to move the picture over to the big screen, which made Isaac's face twenty feet tall. It wasn't private, but at least this way Vaughn wasn't looking over my shoulder.

"Red Lightning's grandson?" Isaac's expression wasn't hostile so much as appraising. "Well, this concerns you as much as anyone else," he said. "We've had people translating the books from Magnus' house and they claim to describe how to create the 'drink of gods.' From our records, it appears similar to what Red Lightning used to brew."

"So what does this 'drink of gods' do?" I asked.

Isaac's gaze flicked toward Vaughn. "It depends on the drink. Each one does something different. It could be anything from throwing lightning to increased strength. Some don't do anything. They just test which recipes will work on a person."

"That's wild," I said. "It sounds a lot like Red

Lightning. He gave stuff like that to his henchmen after he decided to turn on the League."

"Are they exactly like Red Lightning's?" Vaughn pushed his hair out of his face, looking uncomfortable.

"I don't know," Isaac said. "We don't have Red Lightning's recipes to compare them to. All we've got are old samples of his work. Do you have something more?"

Even I could hear the interest in his voice.

"No," Vaughn said. "I used to, but I gave it away. You haven't seen it with the other books? An old brown journal in my grandfather's handwriting?"

"Nothing like that," Isaac said. "Everything we confiscated is in a dead language."

"Huh," Vaughn muttered.

"Well, that's all I've got," Isaac said. "I'll let you know more when I get it. Email me if you've got questions."

His hand moved to cut off the call.

"Wait," I said, "I've got one more thing I should mention. I… punched the mayor in the face yesterday."

He nodded without expression, then said, "Was it in costume?"

I told him the whole story. Isaac took notes. Vaughn just said, "Whoa."

"Nick," Isaac said. "The time to tell me this was yesterday. If he starts pushing this we've got no plan for damage control."

"He hasn't."

"Yet," Isaac said. "But he will. It's just a question of when."

"Daniel's dad has a plan."

"Mindstryke? Okay. What is it?"

"I don't know."

Isaac sighed. "Nick, I'll get back to you later. I've got some calls to make."

He cut off the connection.

Above us, the television screen on the wall went black. It felt like the whole room turned dark. As my eyes adjusted, Vaughn said, "Think he's pissed?"

"I don't know." I stood up. "I think I'm going to go home."

"No problem. Get some sleep or something. I'll shut things down on my way out. Or you know, you could stay and watch my interview—shit, it's on now."

He put Fox 50 on the big screen and I heard the announcer say, "Our lead story tonight is 'The New Heroes League: Too Young?'"

The very tanned and fit reporter continued, "A little more than a month ago, the New Heroes League appeared, seemingly out of nowhere, reviving identities that were household names in the 1950's.

"But the original Heroes League were first of all soldiers who had been tested in the battlefields of World War II. The current members of the League don't appear to be any older than twenty. Do they have the judgment necessary to defend a city? Let's go to City Hall where—"

The picture showed the mayor and a reporter standing in the mayor's office. Wind blew through the broken windows behind the desk. I'd shattered them with the sonics after knocking the mayor unconscious.

Back then, it had seemed like the quickest way to leave. Now it seemed like a really dumb idea.

I started paying attention again midway through Mayor Bouman's reply to the reporter.

"—we were talking about the scandal when he

punched me. I don't know anything after that."

The camera moved in for a close up of the mayor's face as he talked. They definitely hadn't covered his black eye with make-up for the broadcast. It looked bad.

With the segue, "And we all remember this from just a few weeks ago," they went into footage from the car chase—including the moment where we'd hit the stoplight. Had one of the police cars been filming? I couldn't remember seeing cameras at the time.

Following that, they showed a small interview with Vaughn as the Storm King, ending Vaughn's clip with him saying, "I know from personal experience how much drugs can hurt a guy. That's why I go after the dealers so hard."

Next to me, Vaughn said, "Well that's not the worst thing. I was getting worried that they'd show—oh no…"

The screen showed Vaughn in the parking lot at the station answering a question. "You know," he said, "weather powers. Rain, fog, lightning… You want to see? Sure. And what's really cool is I've got a lot more control than I used to. Watch this…"

He pointed his hand at the station's mailbox. Electricity arced across the gap, blasting the metal box off camera and turning the wooden post into blackened shards of splintered wood.

The camera turned toward Vaughn, who winced. "Oh man, I meant to stop just short of the mailbox. Sorry, guys."

Back inside the studio, they showed the interview stage. In one chair sat the reporter. In the other, my dad, wearing the dark blue suit he always wore on television.

"To add some perspective, we've asked noted child psychologist Dr John Klein to comment on what we've seen.

"Dr Klein," the reporter said seriously, "do you think teenagers are ready for this kind of responsibility?"

Dad said, "To be vigilantes? I don't think anybody's ready for that."

"But Dr Klein, what about teenagers in particular?"

"I'd say it can be a corrosive force in your life whether you're a child or an adult," he began.

I overrode Vaughn's control of the screen and shut off the broadcast.

Now the wall TV showed my desktop wallpaper—a picture of a spaceship called Serenity.

"But that was your dad," Vaughn protested.

"I can listen to him at home." I started to walk toward the elevator. Even before the elevator door opened, all four phones began to ring.

Vaughn stared at the phones. "Aren't you going to help?"

"I can't deal with this," I said.

* * *

Walking around at night can be relaxing, but I didn't even get a block from HQ before my cell phone started ringing. Initially, I thought about ignoring it, but then I checked the number on the display. It was Daniel's dad.

In addition to being a prosecutor and a superhero, Daniel's dad was also responsible for managing a number of assets related to the Heroes League, including Grandpa's house, its connection to League

HQ, and a few million dollars Grandpa had intended to be used to stop supervillains.

In short, until I was 18 I'd have to get Mr Cohen's permission every time I bought anything for HQ— ranging from toilet paper to thermite. You never knew when you might need thermite.

I took the call.

"Hi Nick. I'd ask how you were doing, but I'd guess you're feeling lousy right now."

"Good guess," I said.

"I doubt it will comfort you much, but this all goes with public life. Sometimes you're the hero of the day, sometimes you're not. The bad press gives me at least as much motivation as the good—it gives me the chance to show them just how little they really know."

I stepped over a bit of sidewalk that had buckled because of a large tree root. I didn't say anything.

"Here's my plan: Larry and I are going to make sure that the local media knows that we support you. If the mayor still pursues you after that, I'll try to raise issues about the mayor's credibility and piggyback on the scandal. If that doesn't work, well, we've got options."

"You're not going to unmask him as a telepath? Or, I don't know, just stop him?"

"It'd be nice if it were that easy, and sometimes it is. But not this time. If I'm going up against the mayor, I want it to be an open and shut case. If I meet up with him, rip everything that he might be planning out of his head and accuse him of it, it'll be his word against mine.

"So what I want is evidence that no one can argue with. Daniel and I are going to do our best to dig some up. What I want you to do now is lay low."

"I can do that," I said.

At that moment, laying low sounded like a great idea. I was up for it. I was up for lying low till the end of my senior year and maybe college. Because seriously, before putting on the armor I'd had no idea that the city's mayor was psychic, that my grandfather's arch nemesis was alive and knew where I lived, and that the FBI used superpowered teenagers against supervillains.

Ignorance really *was* bliss.

"Glad to hear it, Nick."

A pause.

"Nick," Mr Cohen said, "you know why I'm saying it, right?"

"Uh," I said, "because if I'm out of sight, I'm out of mind?"

"No," he said. "It's because tomorrow this is going to hit Reuters, the Associated Press, all three networks and the cable news channels. It may not be the top story, but it'll be watched. After that we'll have a mini-convention of ambitious, no-name heroes showing up to take out the Rocket's crazy replacement. And then there's Vaughn... People remember Red Lightning. The people who'll come to take him out aren't going to be no-names. They'll be a paranoid sonovabitches like Vengeance, and he'll be armed for war."

I could see my house down the block, living room windows bright with light. I wondered if Dad was home. He could be if the interview had been taped, but it would be easier if he wasn't.

"Even if I'd really punched the mayor for no good reason," I said, "isn't this way out of proportion? And Vaughn hasn't done anything wrong."

"Nick, there are a lot of good people in costume,

but we've also got more than our share of crazies. That's what happens when you have no choice but to hand off law enforcement to anyone who's willing to do it in his spare time."

CHAPTER SEVEN

Call it the geek lunch if you need a name. More accurately, you could call it the male geek lunch, because there weren't any females at our table.

We were sitting just a few tables away from the entrance to the cafeteria, ensuring that a constant stream of people passed by, all carrying lunch trays and talking. Andy, Mike and Kyle were having an in depth discussion about whether the new version of Dungeons and Dragons really was a rip off.

It felt like a throwback to last year even though it shouldn't have. Most days I still ate here—hanging around with Vaughn and Cassie at school was still more the exception than the rule, and today I had more reason than ever not to stand out.

His name was Future Knight and he circulated

around the cafeteria, asking questions, sometimes even cracking jokes. He looked like a thin Cylon (minus the roving red eye)—silver armor reflecting the lunchroom like a mirror. A sword hung on his left side and a pistol on the right. He wore a rifle strapped across his back.

According to an interview in Double V, he claimed to be a normal guy from Detroit who had been pulled into the future, trained to be a cop and then sent back to our time. Normally he worked with a crossbow-wielding partner named Red Bolt.

I guessed that Red Bolt was at a different high school.

I concentrated on my pizza, hoping that Future Knight didn't have the ability to notice my stealth suit.

Grandpa had designed different versions of his armor for different situations. The stealth version was little more than a black bodysuit that fit under clothes. It acted as armor, gave extra strength (though not anywhere near the full suit's strength unless I wanted to run out of power), and included a full power version of the sonic systems. Along with that, there was an underpowered rocket pack that passed as a backpack.

On a practical level, the suit meant that I could go to school and still feel like I wasn't completely defenseless.

Chris Cannon, Man-machine's grandson, sat down next to me.

"Did you see the cape?" His tray hit the table with a clunk, making his milk carton fall over. Fortunately it wasn't open. He picked it up, opened it, his hands shaking, and put in a straw.

Chris knew me from Science Olympiad and ate with me occasionally. It felt a little awkward sometimes, but that might have been entirely in my head.

"Only just now," I said.

"He questioned me. He was all friendly about it, but he wanted to know if I'd ever heard what happened to the old Rocket or his suit. I mean, it was like he thought *I* might have it." Chris sounded like he was on the verge of shouting or maybe tears.

"That would be… bizarre," I said.

"No shit," he said. "Grandpa wasn't always the nicest guy in the world, but I wouldn't have beaten him up. Besides in order to have the old Rocket's armor, I'd have had to meet him first, *and* have him train me *and* tell me all his secrets. After which, I'd do what? Commit myself to making up for my grandfather's crimes? How far-fetched is that?"

"It sounds pretty typical for a superhero."

He snorted, then laughed. "Point," he said. "How hard do you think it would be to make armor like the Rocket's or my grandfather's?"

There weren't many sentences I wanted to hear less than that one—though, "Hey Nick, watch me crush this car," was right up there.

"I'm sure it would be nearly impossible," I said. "First of all, you'd have to get the right materials— by which I mean you'd probably have to create them yourself and—"

Then I stopped talking. It wasn't because I'd realized that I was beginning a technical monologue that risked exposing me (and giving Chris specifics on constructing powered armor). It was because Kayla and Cassie were walking past, and Cassie had punched me in the arm.

It hurt less than usual. I should have worn the

stealth suit every day.

"Nick," she said, "still need a ride home?"

She didn't really need to ask. We'd arranged it the night before. This was actually a bit of theater that would allow us to avoid explaining why we were leaving together after practice.

"If it's okay," I said.

"It's totally okay."

They left for the other side of the room to eat with about half of the volleyball team.

After that, Chris and I got drawn into the Dungeons and Dragons discussion.

* * *

Sixth hour: Kayla and I had the same American Literature class. She sat a couple seats behind me and to the left. It wasn't normally worth mentioning because it wasn't as if we ever talked. We didn't even say "hi" when we passed each other in the hall.

She always hung out with Cassie, both of them a study of how similar different people could be—Kayla always looked tanned, had dark hair, and wore nice clothes. Cassie was a tomboy: blond hair pulled back in a ponytail, pale skin, and generally wearing a mix of t-shirts, jeans and a hoodie.

But physically, their bodies were the same— muscular, but not bodybuilder muscular. Well, except since this summer, as Cassie had bulked up a little after a series of unknown treatments.

When Kayla and Cassie walked together, it was a little like seeing differently colored twins.

So when the bell rang and I walked into the hall only to realize that Kayla was walking next to me? That was a little weird, verging on uncomfortable.

"Hi," she said.

"Uh… hi."

I wasn't sure where to go from there. All I knew about Kayla was that she was a good basketball player, and I watched basketball about as often as I played golf on the moon.

She opened her mouth, closed it, frowned, then blurted, "What's going on between you, Cassie and Vaughn?"

I didn't quite know how to answer. It was obvious that I'd have to lie. If Cassie hadn't told her, I certainly wasn't going to.

The problem was, of course, what I could tell her that fit the facts. Given the way we hid it, it had to be something shameful or illegal. Recreational drug use? Strange sexual practices? Maybe we'd all joined a cult?

I decided to go as close to the truth as I dared.

"We're just friends," I said. "Our grandfathers all served together in World War II and we used to get together as kids. We're just getting together again now."

"Every night?" Kayla stopped walking.

"Well, if Cassie's out every night, I don't know what *she's* doing," I said.

"She's never home anymore. No one is. Her mom has barely been there for years." Kayla raised her hands in what I guessed was a gesture of frustration. If she'd moved her right arm much more, she'd have lost half the papers in her notebook.

"I don't know why," I said. "We've just been getting together every once in a while since school started."

The crowd in the halls had thinned. I still had half the school to cover to make it to the cafeteria for study hall.

"Where's your next class?" I asked. "Because I'm going to have to run."

"The cafeteria," she said, sounding irritated.

Should I have known that?

The warning bell rang. We had less than a minute before we were late.

We looked at each other and began to walk quickly. Running in the halls wasn't allowed.

We made it just barely before the bell rang. Kayla sat at the next table down.

Funny. We were halfway through the semester and I'd had no idea she was there. It made sense, though. They'd assigned seats in alphabetical order. My last name was Klein. Hers was Ketchem. Go figure.

I spent most of study hall working on my math homework. When that was done, I thought about the mayor. Whatever Daniel's dad had said, I didn't think that laying low was a good idea. Obviously I wouldn't start running around in costume, but there had to be another way to contribute.

By the end of study hall, I had a plan.

When the bell rang again, school was over. I picked up my books and began to walk out—except that Kayla caught up with me again.

"Nick, do you have just a second?"

I stopped and leaned against the table near the door while a quarter of the school filed past us.

"I'm not trying to pry into your life," she said, "but I'm worried about Cassie. You know how she was sick this summer? Ever since then, something's been different. She disappears. She's been hanging around Vaughn a lot and you know what people say about him. And have you looked at her lately? She doesn't look like a guy, but look at her muscles... Do you think she's using steroids?"

Everything she'd said seemed to come out in one breath. I tried to take it all in.

"No. Vaughn would be against that more than anyone. He' s been off drugs for a while now—at least since the summer, anyway. His parents sent him to some kind of camp."

She held my gaze, but didn't say anything. I guessed she didn't believe me.

"Well, I know *you're* not like that," she said.

We left for our respective practices after that—her for volleyball, me for cross country—but not before I'd promised to let her know if I noticed anything strange.

* * *

Practice was a relief. Getting out on the road and just running—having the time to daydream and not needing to talk—was almost like sleep. Not *exactly* like sleep, when you considered the aching muscles and the constant need to keep up with everyone else, but it did relax me.

Afterward, Cassie, Vaughn and I met up on the front steps of the school. I was the last to arrive.

"Finally," Cassie said. "What kept you?"

"I don't know," I said. "My shower?"

I looked down the stairs and across the street to the parking lot. Future Knight stood next to the gate of the fenced-in lot, his armor gleaming red under the setting sun.

"Maybe I should just walk home," I said.

"No. That would look weird. Stay with us," Cassie

said.

"Yeah," Vaughn said. "You can handle it. You're Vomitman, right?"

Moments like these made me regret ever mentioning the fact that if I found the right frequency, I could probably use the sonic systems to induce nausea.

We crossed the street.

"Greetings, humans," Future Knight said. His electronically modulated voice and clipped delivery made me wonder if he was a robot.

Then he started laughing. "Ah-hah-hah," he said. "Your faces...."

His laughter still sounded electronic, but stupid jokes like that? That was all human.

"Sorry," he said, "I've got to keep myself awake somehow. If you give me a second, I'd like to ask you some questions. I'm trying to find some kids. Do you know anyone who's been disappearing a lot lately? Or who's changed physically? Maybe changed groups of friends?"

"No," we all said simultaneously.

He looked us over. I hoped he couldn't somehow detect the stealth suit—though if anything he'd probably notice the amps attached under my forearms or maybe the rocket pack. I'd been hanging onto my backpack by the strap. I pulled it up and put it on my back.

"Try it in harmony next time," he said, evidently amused. "Move along."

Cassie's mom's car was on the other side of the parking lot. As Cassie unlocked the doors, I said, "That could have been worse."

Cassie stepped inside. "We're still in the parking

lot," she said.

On the way out of the lot, we saw Kayla and a few other girls from the volleyball team talking to Future Knight. Cassie waved to Kayla. Kayla waved back weakly, eyes wide, her mouth hanging just a little open.

My dad often said that the best part of his job was seeing the moment when a client finally came to a new understanding. I had a feeling I'd just seen that look. I didn't like it much.

* * *

In superhero cartoons, the square-jawed leader described the plan and all the other heroes recognized his wisdom. Then they went out and trashed the baddies.

It didn't work that way in real life. And if it did, it was only with grown-ups.

Cassie had called a "Special Emergency Team Meeting" last night via email/IM/cellphone until she'd reached everybody. Her idea being that there had to be a team response to the mayor's accusations and the growing negative media coverage.

Travis (who seemed to think that *he* was the square-jawed leader) suggested a raid on City Hall, in which we would force the mayor to explain what was really going on, then give it to the media and emerge as heroes. Daniel and I shot that down. First, because a telepathically-forced confession probably wouldn't hold up well in court. Second, because that sort of thing only worked on *24*. Third, if it didn't work, we'd all end up looking like a bunch of power-mad freaks.

Cassie asked, "Does anyone else have an idea?"

"Kind of," I said. "It's a variation of the last

suggestion. Sort of."

I described the idea I'd had in study hall. I wanted to use the roachbots to bug the mayor's house, car, office and anything else I could manage. Everyone looked interested enough at the beginning, but then I got distracted and ended up describing technical problems I'd had while redesigning the robots.

Travis, Haley, Daniel, Jaclyn, and Cassie managed to look politely interested until Cassie started flipping her phone open and shut. Strangely, Marcus seemed to be taking notes. Well, I thought he was. The notebook turned out to contain a drawing of a knight spearing an enormous cockroach with a lance.

Vaughn was watching music videos on one of the computers, the sound muted. What he was supposed to be doing was checking the cameras to see if Future Knight had managed to track us here.

I noticed all of it, but sometimes I couldn't quite stop myself from talking about certain things. I finished saying, "but I think it'll work well if they don't overheat."

For a moment, no one said anything.

"Bugging the place sounds like a great idea," Daniel said, breaking the silence. "It'll save me some work. My dad wanted me to sit on the roof and listen for anything interesting. Thing is, I already have been and haven't turned up much."

"Alright," Travis said. "So after we collect the dirt, then what?"

"We hand it over to my dad," Daniel said.

"I was just thinking we should handle this ourselves," Travis said.

Daniel scowled. "This isn't something we can afford

to screw up."

"Long term, we need to be able to do this ourselves. Your dad can't be our training wheels." Travis sat up in his chair. I'm sure he didn't intend to be intimidating, but between his height and his muscles, it was like looking at a bear.

Daniel didn't even hesitate. "What do you have against my dad?"

"Whoa," Jaclyn said. "Time out. I did not put off homework to come here and watch you two argue."

Cassie almost simultaneously said, "Maybe Daniel's dad could come here and—"

The doorbell rang.

The monitor showed Future Knight standing next to a bearded man in a red, medieval themed costume— Red Bolt. In short, while my grandfather had managed to hide his identity for more than forty years of active service, I'd only managed to hide mine for about a month and half.

Vaughn said, "It's them."

I could have pointed out that Vaughn would have seen them earlier if he hadn't been paying more attention to Shakira's dancing, but I didn't.

Vaughn sent the picture to the wall screen and we could see them from three different angles. They rang the doorbell again.

With a wave toward the elevator Travis said, "Nick, get up there before they knock down the door. Haley, go with him. The rest of us should suit up and take whatever tunnel will get us up there fastest."

From Haley's expression, I guessed she might be thinking the same thing I was, that being: "Who gave you the right to tell me what to do?"

I wasn't going to argue with him though. We didn't have the time.

* * *

The elevator from Grandpa's house to HQ barely fit two people. If you happened to be Travis, it fit one. Haley, despite being his sister, was a head shorter than I was, and so we both fit—though the close quarters made me more than a little aware of her.

Sometime between the years when we'd played together as little kids and now, she'd become good looking—not 'cars stop on the streets' good looking, but more 'cute'.

She had shoulder length black hair, a sprinkling of freckles under her eyes, and dimples.

"He gets so bossy sometimes," Haley muttered as the door clanked shut.

The elevator rolled upward, stopping with a jerk in Grandpa's workroom. Then the elevator's walls sank into the floor.

The doorbell rang yet again. A voice I didn't recognize said, "Prithee, Sir Knight, let us smash through the door."

"Oh jeez, Red," Future Knight said, "can you save the shtick for the civilians?"

Grandpa's workroom was in the back of the house so we had to run through the kitchen and into the living room in the dark. I turned on the lamp next to the couch and flicked on the porch light.

Then I opened the door and found myself eye-to-faceplate with Future Knight once again.

"So we meet again, Nick. Where's the rest of the choir?"

"In the basement playing ping-pong," I said. "I'm sure they'll come up soon."

I could only hope.

"Great," he said. "Mind if we come in? I'm sure you don't want a couple of superheroes standing on your porch."

"No," I said, "why don't you just stay on the porch? I'm sure this won't take long."

I couldn't see Future Knight's face, but behind him, Red Bolt looked annoyed.

Keeping his voice friendly (as friendly as a computer-processed voice could be), he said, "Okay, sounds good. I'll make it short for you and your lady friend.

"You're young, so I don't expect that you think about this much, but the only reason the government is as hands-off as it is about superheroes is that we police our own. Now you've just attacked a member of the government. You may have Mindstryke and the Rhino telling the papers that you're nice, but over on our side of the state, we've decided that you need some supervision.

"I'm empowered to offer you this on behalf of the Michigan Heroes Alliance—you take one of us on your team as an adviser and we'll do what we can to make this all go away. If not, I'm empowered to take you in and give you to the cops."

Under any other circumstances, I would have loved to have someone with experience on the team, but like this?

"No," I said. "We're not taking on any mentors and you're not taking me anywhere."

"Use your head, Nick. You're outmatched. I'm in

armor. You're not. I've got Red Bolt behind me. You've got a little girl."

Next to me Haley said, "A little girl?"

Ignoring her, he continued, "You'd be going two on two with us and all you'd get out of it is a criminal record. Think about it."

From outside, I heard a rush of wind followed by the scraping sound Jaclyn made whenever she skidded to a stop.

Red Bolt glanced back to where Jaclyn was standing on the sidewalk, arms crossed over her chest. He didn't look scared, but he should have. Jaclyn was a lot stronger than she looked.

"Three on two," I said.

Future Knight didn't wait to find out what would happen next. He dove into the house, pinning me to the ground.

The stealth suit took most of it, but hitting the wooden floor with my back still hurt. Worse, he'd grabbed both my arms, making it impossible to take a swing at him.

I could still use the sonic weapons on my forearms, though. Straining to aim, I brought my fingers down on the palm pad and pressed.

Grandpa's design did a wonderful job of narrowcasting the sound. I could feel the speakers grow warm under my arms, but heard nothing more than a high pitched whine.

Future Knight's faceplate shattered without breaking, still in one piece, but so full of cracks that it was completely opaque.

It didn't stay unbroken for long.

Haley yanked him off me, grabbing his left arm

with her right. He let go of me and swung wildly at her, but never connected. I saw a flash of black and white as she punched through the face mask.

He went limp.

Lowering him to the floor, her dull, gray claws adjusted, turning into hands, her milky white nails becoming short and pink.

I pulled myself up.

Just then, Jaclyn stepped through the front door carrying Red Bolt's unconscious body.

"Where's everyone else?" I asked.

"I don't know." She dropped Red Bolt next to Future Knight. "Call downstairs. They might still be putting on their costumes."

She stared at the two limp bodies and took a breath.

"I had no idea it would so easy," she said. "One punch and he was down."

She looked at Red Bolt, then at us. A pause. "Do you think he's okay?"

"He's still breathing," I said, "and I don't see any blood."

"Too bad we don't have anyone who'd know," she said. "So, are you going to be safe with 'Mirrorman' while I bring Red Bolt downstairs?"

"As safe as we are anywhere," I said.

* * *

The rest of the team arrived shortly after that and we returned to HQ. Jaclyn and Daniel laid Future Knight and Red Bolt face up on the carpet. Daniel remained standing between them. The rest of us sat down at the main table.

Except for Haley and I, everyone was still in

costume.

Haley sat next to me. "Are you okay?"

"I'm great," I said. "The suit took most of it when he jumped me, and you got him off me before he punched me. How about you?"

"Me?" She gave a half smile. "I'm good."

But it was only a half-smile.

"Good," Travis said, "you're great. I've never heard of the guy, but the armor looks tough. Good idea to go for the faceplate, Haley."

"That was Nick's idea. He broke it. I just punched through."

"Well, there's lots to be said for teamwork too," he said. "Which reminds me: good job Jaclyn."

"It's nice to be included," she said, in a tone so dry it hinted that she'd only barely been included.

That may have just been my imagination. Travis didn't seem to notice it. He turned to Daniel and said, "Hey Danny-boy, what've we got?"

"Nothing good," Daniel said. "They know who Nick is and they've got ideas about Vaughn and Cassie. Plus they're not the only ones out here. There's another team after Nick. I'm getting the impression that they're a bunch of nobodies, but Vengeance is here and he's after Vaughn."

"Holy shit," Vaughn said. "He's going to kill me over a mail box?"

Almost at the same time, Cassie said, "That doesn't make any sense."

"It doesn't have to," Daniel said. "The guy's crazy."

Marcus, slumped in a chair, looked up from his sketchpad. "I heard he collects ears."

"I don't think that's true," I said.

Travis said, "Daniel, did they tell anybody where they were going before they came here?"

"No." Daniel turned away from the bodies, giving Travis his full attention.

"Great. Then just wipe their memories. One problem solved."

"I can't do that. That's not right."

"Not right?" Travis said. "Letting these guys have our names isn't right either."

"I'm not letting them," Daniel replied. "They figured it out for themselves. Future Knight has something in there that detects when people are lying to him. He caught something when he was talking to Nick and then Kayla blew it open."

"Wait," Cassie said, "what did Kayla tell him?"

"Nothing," Daniel said, "she just figured out who you were and lied about it. That's enough."

Travis nodded. "Okay, Daniel. Why is it wrong?"

"Because it's their brains. They're trying to do the right thing. If I just erase today, I might erase a lot more than that. The brain's not a computer. Everything connects to other things and I don't want to turn these guys into vegetables by mistake."

Travis raised his eyebrow. "Is that likely?"

I couldn't help but think that erasing a day from Future Knight's memory sounded a lot easier than what Daniel had done to my head. I didn't say so, though.

Daniel shot a glance at me and frowned. "No. They'll probably be okay. But this isn't just a question of whether I wipe a day from these guys' minds. It's a question of whether we're allowed to do it in the first place. Your memories are who you are. I'd be permanently changing them."

"I'm not going to argue with that," Travis said. "But right now these guys are going to turn us all in first chance they get, right?"

I didn't need telepathy to read the answer on Daniel's face.

"Okay," he sighed, "I'll do it."

He walked back between the two unconscious men, sitting next to Future Knight.

"That'll buy us some time," Travis told me. "Maybe your bots will have the time to get something good."

"I hope so," I said.

"Me too, because if they don't, we need a backup plan. You should see if your friend at the FBI has anything."

"Yeah," I said.

Almost everybody left after that. Daniel floated the bodies down the coast a few miles, escorted by Jaclyn. Cassie and Vaughn left together, followed by Marcus, Travis and Haley.

I left a voicemail asking Isaac to call me. He hadn't been all that happy with me the last time we'd talked, but it had sounded like he wanted to help.

I stood up from the computer, thinking that I should shut everything down for the night. Isaac would call me at home if he wanted to. Then I began mentally running through the lights I should turn off and tunnel doors I should lock.

Adrift in my head, I did a double take as I realized that Haley stood only a few feet away from me.

"Sorry," she said, "I didn't mean to... *scare* you."

"I'm not scared," I said. "I just thought you were already gone. I thought everybody was gone. I was going to turn things off."

"I wanted to ask you something," she said, "so I came back."

"Sure," I said, "go ahead."

"You've seen me when I change," she said. "It doesn't creep you out, does it? The claws and the fangs?"

"I didn't notice you had fangs." I looked at her mouth. It seemed normal—except now it was quirked in an expression that might have been annoyance.

"I don't *right now*," she said.

"Sorry. No, I'm not bothered. I mean, it's what you do, right?"

"What I do," she said, "is turn into some kind of weird, half-human thing."

"It must be nice to have powers all the time, though. As it is, I'd need to have someone following me in a van if I wanted to change quickly."

"I don't want to change at all." She paused. "Well, that's not true. I like it while I'm changed. It's just that I look like a refugee from a horror movie."

I felt like I should say something. Someone who was actually good with people could have pulled out a line that would help her see things in a new and positive light. My dad would.

Unfortunately, nothing came to mind, and all of a sudden I realized that she was looking at me as if she expected me to say something.

What I felt like I should have said was, "You don't really look like a refugee from a horror movie." Problem was, she did. I just couldn't think of which one.

"Well," I said, "at least you can turn back, right?"

Chapter Eight

11:50pm, Friday night.

I was sitting in Grandpa's house, waiting for Haley to show up. It was after my curfew, but that was a moot point since I'd snuck out of my window anyway. When you're about to go bug the mayor's house, office and car, curfews didn't seem important.

I was sitting on Grandpa's old brown couch. Haley had said she'd arrive somewhere between eleven and twelve, but I was beginning to wonder if she was coming at all.

Inviting her along had seemed like a good idea for a couple of different reasons. First, she was Night Wolf's granddaughter, and outside of Ghostwoman, he'd been the best at sneaking around. Second, as dense as I sometimes could be about people, it had occurred to me that she might like me. She'd gone out of her way to speak to me after the meeting a couple nights ago. *Way* out of her way, actually. I'd had to borrow my mom's car to drive her home.

That was when I'd had the semi-brilliant idea of inviting her along for the bugging. It wouldn't be a date because it was "work," but at the same time it would allow us to hang out and give me the chance to figure out what was going on. She'd seemed enthusiastic at the time.

I waited, flipping through the channels on the TV, grateful that the opening monologues were over on Letterman, Leno, and Kimmel. It was easier to feel like I wasn't dragging my grandfather's name through the mud when I wasn't' hearing people joke about it.

12:10am, Saturday morning.

Maybe, I thought to myself, she wasn't coming. I'd blundered pretty seriously when I'd tried to check for fangs. Obviously she was sensitive about that. For that matter, the bit where I'd assured her that at least she could change back? That statement implied that her change was creepy, which was what she was worried about in the first place. In reality, she was cute either way. It's just that when she monstered out, she was cute with murderous claws and an inhuman skin tone.

Not that I would ever used the phrase "monstered out."

I think.

She arrived at 12:16am (or so said my cell phone), dropped off by a fortyish blond woman in a rusty Honda Civic.

I opened the door as she walked up. She waved at the car and turned to me. "Hi, Nick!"

She was wearing a black skirt and red t-shirt that said "Leo's Italian Dining and Pizza Takeout." She'd put her hair in a ponytail.

"Hey. Who was that?"

"Terry. She's another waitress at Leo's. I nearly got stuck closing tonight. That's why I'm late."

Haley's (and Travis' and Marcus') family owned a small chain of Italian restaurants, a couple of dine-in and a few take-out pizza places. Everyone in the family did their time as staff.

"Do you mind if I shower before we get in costumes? I reek of pizza and grease."

I hadn't noticed, but whatever. She was the one with better-than-human senses. We had to go downstairs to HQ for her to shower, because there hadn't been any soap in the actual house since Grandpa had died.

While she showered, I slipped on the stealth suit, went into the hangar to ready something else I thought we might need. When you weren't trying to hide the stealth suit under your clothes, you could use some additional accessories. There was a more powerful rocket pack that couldn't fit in a backpack, and a utility belt full of tools. Also pants, a jacket, a helmet, and gloves—all in black—that gave extra strength, protection, and warmth. Warmth came in particularly handy at night in October. Grandpa had mostly used the stealth suit when he'd needed to break into buildings.

Soon after, Haley came out of the bathroom in costume, all gray with a black wolf on her chest.

It felt awkward in a way that it hadn't when we'd gone out on patrol. Part of it was simply that back then I'd thought about her as Travis' younger sister—

someone who, to be honest, Daniel, Travis and I had tried to ditch as quickly as possible as kids. The other part of it was simply that your average superhero bodysuit is form-fitting for purely practical reasons (it makes it harder to get a grip on your clothes, for example), but for a teenage boy, well, even the most modest bodysuit is distracting. Hers didn't show much of anything, but still.

After a moment of mentally flailing for words, I said, "Half of us still haven't come up with names, how about you?"

Her expression was somewhere between amusement and annoyance as she said, "No, but I should. Did you see the paper after we fought Man-machine?"

The Grand Lake Sentinel's headline had been "ROCKET AND SIDEKICK DEFEAT MAN-MACHINE."

We left in Night Wolf's car. She drove. I had pulled it out of mothballs at Travis' suggestion, but she had as much right to it as he did. More than I did, at least. After the last debacle, Isaac had arranged three separate license plates for it, none of which had any connection to the Heroes League.

Bugging the mayor's office went smoothly. Hayley scaled City Hall and let the roachbots in through a boarded up window.

His house turned out to be another matter.

Back in the 1800's, local lumber barons had built houses on a hill near downtown. Mayor Bouman had bought one a couple of years before he ran for office. It was a Victorian (like a lot of houses in Grand Lake proper) with two turrets and a large lawn.

A police car was parked in front of it. Above the house flew a woman who appeared to be on fire.

Haley drove past. I looked out the window (which was now tinted dark enough that no one could see inside).

"This doesn't look easy," I said.

"Be optimistic," she said. "We'll think of something."

If love was blind, were teenage crushes unrealistically hopeful?

*   *   *

We parked the car two blocks from the mayor's house, and pressed the button that changed the car's color to yellow and the license plate to Illinois. Haley changed. I noticed the fangs this time. They didn't look incredibly long—just very white and very sharp.

We ran through several backyards, jumping a couple fences in the dark. Even in the stealth suit, I could leap six feet fences in a single bound.

Stopping behind the hedge that marked the beginning of the mayor's property, we reviewed the plan—such as it was.

"How close do I have to get?"

"Theoretically, I could let them out here," I whispered, "but I want to minimize how much they move because—"

"Because you don't want them to overheat," she said. "I caught that." Had she smiled at me when she'd said that? It was hard to tell in the dark.

"But that still doesn't tell me how close," she said.

"I don't know. They've got to find a crack to go through. They might have a good shot at going through the eaves and into the attic."

I handed her the bag of roachbots.

"I could do that," she said. Then, "Think I could make it up a turret?"

"Not a good idea," I said. "You'd almost be level with the flaming flying lady. You don't want to be seen."

"The flaming flying lady?" She sounded amused.

"I don't know her name. Anyway, I'll activate the bots now so all you'll have to do is let them out somewhere they can get a grip."

She leaned toward a gap in the bushes. "Wish me luck," she said, and dived through.

I got on my knees and pushed into the gap.

She covered the distance between the hedge and the house in a few leaps, making it to the wall just before the 'flaming flying lady' came to check out the side of the house.

Not wanting to risk drawing attention by making the bushes move, I remained still and continued to watch.

Some people with fire powers appeared to be engulfed permanently in flames. The flaming lady looked relatively normal, except that she just happened to be burning, small fires running the length of her body. She wore red robes, trimmed with gold—the kind of robes you'd see on ancient Greek pottery.

As she curved around the house, staying at the roof-height, she nearly flew over the hedge. Fortunately I was all but hugging the bushes by then and she didn't see me.

That's when I recognized her. I still didn't know her name, but I knew her group—The Elementals. Sometime last summer, back when I thought Cassie might be dying, we'd followed the press coverage of how some unknown US superteam had broken up a terrorist cell in Greece. Two boys and two girls; they'd obviously had no experience and from interviews it had sounded like they were all college students.

I hadn't seen anything in *Double V* about them since.

I wondered if it would be possible to get her attention and convince her that she'd cast her lot with the bad guys this time around, but I decided not to chance it.

Haley, meanwhile, stayed still, hanging on the wall about six feet off the ground and surprisingly close to being invisible.

After a few tense seconds, the flaming woman moved to the other side of the house.

The moment she was out of sight, Haley started climbing, managing to get up to the second story, then swinging sideways, and up the nearest turret. She let the bots out on a windowsill, then jumped to the ground, landing in a run, crossing the yard in seconds. All in complete silence.

"Success," she said as she slipped through the hedge.

I did what I could to extricate myself without breaking any branches, hearing them scrape my jacket despite my best efforts to be silent.

I checked the robots' controller. "Yep. They're in." They couldn't get through the window, but they'd crawled up the wall into a crack in the eaves.

"The turret's got a nice view," she said.

"I bet," I replied. Then I glanced at the controller again. The bots were beginning to spread throughout the house. Time to go.

We walked back to the car in silence, but it felt

more relaxed. We didn't try to hide, but we didn't do anything particularly obvious either. We stayed in people's backyards, and didn't walk on the street.

The only hint that we might not have been the only people around came when we were almost at the car. We were standing next to the corner of a house, making one last check before returning to the car.

"Did you just hear something?" Haley asked.

"No," I said.

"Yes," growled a voice from behind us.

I turned, expecting to see one of the Elementals. We'd just seen fire. That left air, earth, and water as possibilities. But the bearded man behind us was not linked to any element unless 'camouflage' had been added to the list. An automatic rifle that looked larger and heavier than normal hung on his back. His belt held devices I didn't even recognize.

"I am Vengeance," he said.

Cheesy? Just a little, but it seemed a lot less cheesy when you knew his reputation. He didn't have any powers worth mentioning, but he'd taken out powered people by the score.

"Tell the new Red Lightning we need to talk," he said.

Deciding that what I told Vaughn would be more of a warning than a message, I said, "Sure."

"I've got questions for him," he said.

"I'll let him know," I said. "Did you... want to meet him for lunch or something?"

He laughed. "I'll find him."

In the light of the streetlight, my eyes drifted toward something hanging from a cord around his neck. It didn't look like an ear—not a whole one at any rate.

Maybe an earlobe at most, but definitely a shrunken, dried bit of something.

"One more thing," he said. "Stay away from the mayor. Leave him to the big boys."

Next to me, Haley said, "Isn't that a little condescending?"

"Nah, it's just true. Get a few years in and you might be ready for this. For now, stay out."

He disappeared into the dark.

We stood there for a little while, staring into the darkness. Then we got into the car.

"What a jerk," Haley said. She didn't even put the key into the ignition.

I pulled off my helmet and put it on the floor. I didn't mind wearing it, but it got stuffy after a while.

"I know," I said. "I always heard he was crazy, not... I don't know. Whatever *that* was."

"Why did you even talk to him about Vaughn and all that?"

"I don't know. I was just hoping that he'd go away if I seemed cooperative."

We sat for a few more moments without saying anything.

"So, what do we do now?" Haley asked.

"I'm not sure," I said. Within my brain came the glimmering of a bad idea to ask Haley out on another non-date, to figure out if she'd say yes to an actual date—but she might not give any sign either way. Or worse, she might have already given quite a few and I'd missed them all.

"We've done what we planned," I continued. "I guess we should just go home. I don't know how you handled it, but I snuck out the window. I'll have to sneak back in."

"My parents think I'm heading to Sara's to stay overnight after work."

"Does she know that?" One parental call to Sara's could open up a big can of worms.

"She knows. If she gets a call, she'll tell them that I'm asleep. She thinks I'm secretly meeting a boy."

"That's believable," I said. "People really do that."

"They do," she said. Her expression struck me as somewhere between amusement and frustration.

That was the point at which I probably should have realized that she was trying to tell me something. But I didn't. I could only think how odd it was that even in the twenty-first century, the responsibility of asking someone out still often fell to the boy. She probably assumed that because I was older, I had some idea of what to do next, and she might even get offended if I didn't do anything.

"You know," she said, "It might be nice if we did something together. I'm not thinking of anything expensive. Coffee could be fun."

On the other hand, she might have a more realistic understanding of me than I'd thought.

* * *

Isaac caught up with me as I sat in League HQ the next afternoon. I'd slept in, but decided it might be fun to go in and look over the jet's manual.

The FBI symbol appeared on the League's wall screen the moment I'd flipped the first page. Thinking it would be good to know what, if anything, the FBI would be doing to help me out of this mess, I took the call. Then I saw Isaac's face.

"So, no support at all," I said.

"Nothing official," Isaac said. "I've been talking you up, but the boys upstairs get worried about bad press." He stood up and his face left the screen. The camera adjusted, zooming in. Given that I was watching him over the big screen in League HQ, it was more of a close up than I'd wanted. Imagine a twenty foot tall face, pores included

A bit of popcorn shell had gotten stuck in his gums.

"The good news," Isaac said, "is that no one associated with our Hero program is taking action against you. Between Mindstryke and me, the major groups won't interfere and all Mayor Bouman's got on his side are no-names."

"Which reminds me," I said, "do you know anything about a group calling themselves The Elementals?"

"The bare minimum. They operate out of Lansing. Probably Michigan State students. Apparently got their powers in Greece. Magic-based, I'm betting."

"That's more than I had," I said.

"Are they in this too?" Isaac shook his head as the camera mercifully pulled back. "Nick, you're going to have to watch it. They did a number on those guys in Greece last summer and that was back when they hardly knew anything. By now they might be competent."

He stepped back and sat on his desk, pushing away a pile of papers and a bag of microwaved popcorn to the right.

"I can't do anything for you officially," he said, "but remember this: your grandfather and the League were among the first superheroes. Even back in the 1950's, there were more powerful people, but the League was the best. People get a thrill at seeing the costume in action now, even though they know it can't be the same guy. Give them a good enough reason and they'll be behind you."

And I'd thought pep talks had ended the week before with cross country regionals.

Well anyway, I told myself, his heart was in the right place, but it was a good thing we didn't depend on the Feds for a whole lot.

*   *   *

I spent the next few days doing homework, reading, and listening through the recordings sent over by the roachbots. I talked to Haley on Tuesday night. We hadn't set a time to have coffee before then because Haley hadn't known her work schedule, but on Tuesday we set it for Thursday after school.

If you think that listening to someone else's day to day life sounds interesting, it's probably because you've never done it. The bots only recorded if someone was talking, but that still left a pile of uninteresting crap. I heard hours of the mayor's kids playing (and fighting), conversations with his wife about his day at work, and his actual day at work—including the schmoozing.

I fast forwarded through most of it, thinking that if I'd been smart, I'd have split monitoring up between the group. Better yet, I'd have come up with a way to have the computer transcribe the conversations and search for certain words.

On Wednesday afternoon, I trawled through the mayor's conversations so far.

I felt like I knew him a little better now. He liked his coffee with sugar, but no milk. He sometimes called his wife little endearments, and he managed to be home for supper with his family most nights, even if he did have to leave for a meeting afterwards.

Around 4:30pm, I found myself listening to a recording of him talking with his wife in the living room. The bots tagged the time as being 11:51pm Tuesday night.

"Tony says he's closing his sub shop," he said. "He tells me there's just not enough foot traffic downtown—"

That was the point at which I would have fast forwarded—except that his cell phone rang.

"Gotta get this, hon. I'll be in bed in a minute."

The roachbot lost the mayor's wife's reply as he stepped out of the living room and walked into the kitchen. The bot stationed there picked him up, but the reception wasn't perfect. It garbled Bouman's voice ever so slightly and didn't pick up the caller at all.

"—these guys are after me and you're giving me nothing. My only protection is people who'll throw me in jail the second they know what's going on."

It took a few minutes before I heard anything else. Then:

"How am I supposed to do that? I can't just send the police to raid some kid's house. Not when the trustee is a prosecutor. Think how *that* will look. If you want the machine, you'll have to send your own people or grab Red Lightning's grandson, and see if you can get him to talk."

Another wait...

"Well I don't know if he's used it. I'd bet yes, but how am I supposed to know?"

...followed by a deep breath.

"No. I didn't mean it that way. I'll do everything, and I mean everything in my power. Just tell the Cabal it won't be easy."

Finally, in a softer voice: "Much easier when we get it. I know, I *know*. I'll watch for Magnus' people too. I'll kill them if I have to."

I stopped the recording there, stood up, and walked away from the computer. We could use this. I'd have to obscure the bit about Red Lightning's grandson and the trustee being a prosecutor, as they pointed too clearly in Vaughn's and my direction for comfort.

But we could use this.

*   *   *

Aside from having the dirt that we'd been trying to get for weeks, I had another reason to be happy. I finally understood what was going on—at least on an abstract level.

It sounded like we had two groups—Magnus and the Cabal—going after Red Lightning's machine, or, more accurately, the knowledge that created Red Lightning's machine. Why were they even bothering?

It all had to do with powers in the end. From what scientists had discovered so far, it looked like very few people had powers or even the potential for powers. Among those who did, a few got lucky and had them practically from birth, while others experienced 'metahuman gene expression' at puberty. The rest needed some sort of trigger.

It was complicated by the fact that the same trigger wouldn't' work on everyone. Expose one guy to the bite of a radioactive giraffe and you'd get a superhero (Giraffeman? With super neck stretching powers?). Expose another and you'd get a nasty, infected wound.

The drink of gods and Red Lightning's potions had

to basically be the same thing—a temporary effective trigger that provided a low level version of a person's abilities. Beyond anything else, the hieroglyphic on Red Lightning's costume and Magnus' former employee's ring argued for a connection there.

My grandfather and Vaughn's had managed to create a machine that delivered a permanent version of Red Lightning's powers. If their trigger-finding process worked for even a *few* people, they'd created something that anybody using the drink of gods would want.

Plus, if you compared the rampaging gangs in Chicago earlier (that needed heroes from all over the country to control them) to Red Lightning's superpowered, drug addicted gangs back in the 1960's? Another connection. It couldn't be coincidental that the riots had taken out a bunch of Magnus' people. For that matter, that might have been the riots' whole point.

I felt like a detective—like I should be getting all the suspects into the parlor and informing them that it was Colonel Mustard in the conservatory with the candlestick.

Unfortunately, I was alone, in a basement the size of a basketball court with endless cardboard boxes containing forty years' worth of memorabilia.

I had a sense that I should be doing something. The problem was, what exactly? Release the conversation to the media? Call Daniel's dad as he probably expected?

Neither option was particularly heroic. I couldn't imagine my grandfather bringing down a politician with dirt—though who knows? I really didn't know half of the stuff the original Heroes League had been involved in. I also didn't quite feel like passing it off to Daniel's dad. Some part of me felt stubbornly like it was my life and my case and why shouldn't I take care of it myself?

Well, mostly because I had no idea what to do next, and also, it was suppertime. Mom generally had it ready between 5:30 and 6:00pm. It was now 5:12, so I walked home.

*   *   *

Mom had made stir fry, a meal that she liked because you could take just about any vegetables you happened to have in the refrigerator, combine them with meat, and have supper ready in about half an hour. Mom worked as dad's business manager/publicist and managed his website. Whatever she made had to fit into the time she had available.

Personally, I was a little sick of stir fry, but I wasn't in the mood to complain either, so I ate it.

After supper, I helped load the dishwasher and washed the wok. Then I headed upstairs to Dad's study. I caught him while he was arranging books and papers around the desk. He was working on another book— something about troubled teens, undoubtedly.

I decided to give him some practical experience.

"Dad?"

Dad looked up from moving the books and papers into comfortable reach.

"Nick," he said, "how're things going?"

I found myself thinking about just how much easier this would be if I could actually explain anything to him. As it was, I'd have to cloak everything in generalities to the point where Dad's advice might end up being useless.

"Okay," I said. "I was just wondering if I could ask you a question."

"Shoot."

"I'm working on a project with some other kids and I've hit something I'm not comfortable with."

Dad nodded. "What kind of 'not comfortable'? Are you saying it makes you nervous or do you mean morally?"

"Well, I don't think it's wrong so much as 'less right' than some other options," I said.

"You'll have to think about how much less right it needs to be before you say something," he said.

We talked for a little while after that, but I don't remember the details. I went to my room and started on my homework, pausing occasionally to think.

Chapter Nine

I caught Vaughn on the way out of the lunchroom. We didn't have any classes together and we hadn't eaten together lately because Cassie had been spending a lot of time with Kayla. Repairing relations, I guessed.

Vaughn was with a couple of other guys—skaters. I didn't know if he did much skateboarding, but it fit with the "long hair and wears a lot of black" look. Neil leaned against the wall next to the door, tracing the tattooed dragon on his forearm while Dave spoke.

"...Someone called the cops and we ended up climbing the fence holding our skateboards. They caught Mike, but Neil and I got away."

"Have a second?" I asked.

Vaughn stepped away from them. "What's up?"

I gave him a quick summary of what I'd heard the

mayor say and my guesses about what it meant.

"So watch out for the mayor," I said. "Not that you aren't already."

"I'm still more worried about Vengeance," Vaughn said. He glanced back toward Neil and Dave. They were deep into their own conversation.

"He says he just wants to talk," I said.

"I'm not going to bet my ass on that."

"I'm just passing it along. Is there any way we could talk about the stuff you gave Magnus' people?"

"I've got nothing going on after school," he said.

"Uh... how about tonight?"

"What're you doing after school? I know you're not going to Cross Country Finals."

"No. I've just got an appointment." I may have hesitated just a little before the word appointment, but Vaughn didn't seem to notice. Whether or not I was dating Haley wasn't his business.

Plus, he'd probably tell everybody.

"Sure thing," Vaughn said. "You want to meet at Hardwick House around eight?"

"You mean the museum?"

"I mean the mansion my family lets the city use as a museum. I've got keys, but you might want to wear your armor."

"Why?"

"Partly traps and partly just in case there's a cave-in."

"...there are traps in the museum?"

"In my grandfather's secret lair, yeah." Vaughn grinned. "It's pretty cool. Not in the best of shape, but they had some kind of massive battle there back in the 60's so I should just be glad it's still standing."

"Okay, I'll go," I said. I guessed I'd be able to get away with a short jaunt without pissing off Daniel's dad.

Solid Grounds was within walking distance of my house, one of four businesses in a strip of brick buildings that had probably sold hardware or groceries back in the 1880's. They had kept the original tin ceiling, but painted it black and hung red neon lights near the top of the walls.

The music alternated unpredictably between jazz and indie rock.

Haley and I sat at a table next to the smoking section, a glassed in area almost half the size of the coffeehouse. We drank our coffee in silence.

She wasn't dressed in her waitress uniform this time. She was in jeans, and a green shirt. I couldn't name the style, but I'd seen a lot of girls wearing it. Glancing across the table, it occurred to me that I hadn't seen her without a mask very often. Her eyes were green, even when not slit like a cat's.

She caught my gaze and looked up from her coffee, giving me a faint smile.

"I was just thinking you looked different without a mask," I said, realizing even as I said it that different could mean anything and that I'd just missed a chance to compliment her hair, or clothes or something.

"Not as different as you look," she said, smiling a little more this time.

At least I hadn't fueled her worries about what she looked like when she transformed.

We talked about school for a little while after that. Then we finished our drinks and pulled on our coats, deciding to take a walk before dropping by my house and borrowing my mom's car.

It felt cold. November started on Friday. Thursday was Halloween. The trees were mostly bare of leaves, a few stragglers waiting to fall.

Her hand bumped mine as we walked down the sidewalk. The first time I didn't notice, but on the second I realized that she might want to hold hands and caught hers. She didn't pull away.

"Do you think this will cause any trouble," she said, "with the team?"

"I don't know. I don't think so. Oh, hey that reminds me..." I told her about what I'd heard from the bots, what I'd figured out, and that I'd be meeting Vaughn.

"Does everybody know?"

"Just you and Vaughn so far."

"I know you don't want to release the recording to the media, but you ought to tell all of us. Keeping it to yourself will just make people angry."

The wind blew her hair into her face. She let go to push it away, then took my hand again.

"You're probably right."

We walked quietly for a little while.

"Can I come along tonight? I heard stories from my grandfather, but I never got to go there. I always thought they destroyed it."

I snorted. "It doesn't sound like it's in great shape. Vaughn told me to wear armor because of the traps. I was halfway to asking him if I should bring a whip and fedora."

She laughed.

"You can come along if you want to," I said. "We're meeting there at eight. What kind of stories did you hear from your grandfather?"

"The same kind you heard, I bet. How at the end everybody ended up captive in the lair and how your grandfather freed them."

"My grandfather didn't talk about it much. I don't think he was particularly proud of the way he handled it."

"Oh. I can see that."

She gave my hand a squeeze.

*   *   *

Putting the suit on and checking its systems took a good ten minutes. I ran down the tunnel to the exit in the middle of the forest in Veterans' Memorial Park. It felt good to be in the full suit. The last time had been when Haley and I had fought Man-machine—almost a month ago by now.

The doors opened above me and I jumped, making it a good twenty feet before the rockets kicked in and took me the rest of the way into the sky. The trees went past in a blur of branches. I found myself looking down on the city lights almost before I realized it.

To avoid being seen, I planned to shoot up like a ballistic missile and then fall down, using the rockets to slow myself until I landed directly in front of Hardwick House. It seemed like a better idea than flying low across half the city and being visible through anybody's window.

But I was wrong.

Either my armor was more vulnerable to radar than I'd realized, or one of the heroes who'd been summoned to deal with me had fairly impressive night vision. Whatever the case, something grabbed my arms from behind at about 500 feet above the ground, pulling them together. I slowed my descent and then hovered.

Twisting my head, I saw a man in a blue costume with a mask covering the upper half of his face. A missile superimposed over a circle appeared both on his chest and on his forehead, which told me who he was. According to *Double V* (whose RSS feed I evidently spent too much time reading), his name was Tomahawk. His powers? Flight, strength, and all-around toughness. Until two years ago, he'd worked for the Mafia in the Northeast, particularly Boston. Then he'd turned into an informant, giving up names and evidence, and since then he'd been living on the right side of the law.

Normally I'd have cheered him on, but at that moment I couldn't help but wish he'd gone into the witness protection program instead.

Breaking the silence, I said, "Aren't you the guy in the lock commercial?"

"You looking for an autograph? 'Cause your timing's pretty bad."

"No, just curious."

"You know what you oughta be curious about? Where we're going next."

"Okay," I said. "Where are we going next?"

"We're going to meet with a couple guys and come to an understanding about this situation."

Honestly, it sounded like he was still *in* the mob.

Probably at that point I should have sent a distress signal to the rest of the group, but I didn't. I thought I could handle the situation without help. He struck me as one of those guys who relied solely on his powers and hadn't done any real training.

For example, grabbing a guy's arms and holding them together behind his back might work on the ground, but in the air it opened up a host of problems. In my case, the only reason he hadn't tipped me, causing me to fire off in some random direction, is because I was deliberately hovering in one spot.

Holding my arms straight behind me showed another lack of forethought on his part. The weaponized amplifiers on my forearms were pointed roughly at his groin.

I fired them off on high power.

Human soft tissue doesn't shatter like glass, but judging from his shout, it felt at least as bad as a kick in the crotch.

He let go.

I flew up about fifty feet and started shouting down at him. "I didn't just punch the mayor for the fun of it. He's a telepath! He tried to break into my mind!"

Tomahawk rushed me.

Turns out blasting someone in the groin isn't a great way to gain their trust.

From there it turned into one of those fights that the media love and insurance adjusters hate; the kind of fight I mostly associated with Los Angeles or New York City. You know what I mean—two powered lunatics buzzing through the downtown, pausing only to exchange blows or plow into a wall.

Downtown Grand Lake wasn't busy during late fall, but there were people downtown. They got off the street as soon as they saw us coming.

I tried to escape most of the time, keeping my corners tight, and trying to avoid hitting streetlights and power lines. Realizing after a little while that he flew a little faster than I did, I opted to stay low, guessing that as a hometown boy I'd be able to use my knowledge of the city to lose him.

Unfortunately, I had a lousy sense of direction, and even though the helmet has a GPS readout, it was hard to concentrate on it in the middle of a fight. I ended up whipping around the corner to find that the alley I'd hoped would lead me out of downtown actually dead-ended into the back of a three story brick building.

As quickly as we were moving, I didn't have the time to slow down before I hit the wall, but neither did he.

I flipped over, nearly blacking out at the force of a one hundred-eighty degree direction change. He flew over me, beginning to try to flip over himself.

I opened up on him with the sonics as he passed above me, this time choosing the setting that created a massive piercing scream.

I don't know whether the sonics distracted him or whether he just didn't have time to flip, but he hit the wall with his back, crashing through into the store behind.

I had too much momentum to stop myself as well, but I hit the wall below his newly created hole relatively softly—I didn't go through.

After lying on the ground for a moment, I stood up shakily. From the shouts and screams, I guessed that the store was open. When I managed to look in, I realized it was a lingerie shop. Tomahawk had smashed into some shelving after plowing through the wall and the contents lay scattered across half the room. No one else seemed to be hurt though.

I considered calling 911 in case he needed an

ambulance, but then it occurred to me that it might be safer to do so from a distance.

So I flew away, leaving him unconscious and covered in thongs.

* * *

Hardwick House sat on a hill near the middle of downtown. It began, not especially humbly, as an enormous mansion back when Percival Hardwick made his fortune as a lumber baron. His heirs added on to it in a peculiar mixture of styles. The first section used the thin spires and intricate woodwork of the Gothic style. A later addition to the house had added an eight story tower and the extensive stonework of the Medieval Revival style. The final section of the house had been added in the late 1920's—six flat-roofed stories, each story less wide than the story below. The final story ended in the shape of an Egyptian pyramid.

Impressively hideous, it absorbed almost half a city block when you included the grounds.

I circled it once before landing in the garden next to the tower. Aside from the grass and trees, everything appeared to be dead. Autumn in Grand Lake wasn't kind to flowers, turning the garden into a place of drying leaves and dirt.

Vaughn and Haley (both in costume) stood just on the other side of a walled section of the garden, hidden from the street. Behind them rose a huge wooden door that was large enough for a horse (or possibly two) to walk through.

The dark tower loomed above.

"Geez," Vaughn said, "what happened to you?"

I looked down. Between a couple punches

Tomahawk had gotten in during the chase and hitting the brick wall at the end, I'd picked up a few scratches on my armor.

"Some guy tried to grab me on the way over."

Haley gave my armor a closer look. "Are you okay?"

"I'm fine. I hit a wall, but he hit it harder."

"Was it a cape?" Vaughn asked.

"Ever heard of Tomahawk?"

"I guess we'd better get inside then," Vaughn said.

He had a point. The mayor's house was just a block away on the same hill. Who knew who was patrolling there tonight and how far their senses extended?

He unlocked the door, motioning for us to enter. Once inside Vaughn flicked on a weak light, illuminating a hallway that kept up the medieval theme with the wooden floor and stone walls, but ruined it by filling the place with clutter—old couches, chairs, beds, bookcases, lamps, and debris from more than one hundred years of occupancy.

"Wow," I said, "it reminds me of HQ."

"Wait till we get to the lair," Vaughn said.

Haley stood next to a Victorian bed. The headboard was almost twice her height and covered with detailed carvings that I couldn't make out.

"I love this bed," she said.

"We've got piles of crap like this all over," Vaughn said. "The best stuff is out in the visitors section.

"Oh, Haley," he said. "Would you mind getting the lights? They're just down the hall, but we'll run out of light before we ever see the switch."

"Sure." Haley threaded her way through the furniture and disappeared.

Once she was gone, Vaughn said, "I don't mind

that she's here, but you could have told me."

"Sorry. She asked this afternoon and I didn't see anything wrong with it."

"There isn't, but she just appeared out of nowhere. Scared the shit out of me."

The lights went on and we walked down the curving hall, making a path over and through the furniture. Vaughn climbed over a couch and turned to me. "Hey, are you guys going out?"

"Uh... I don't know. We went out for coffee today, but that was the first time we've ever done anything."

"Did you clear it with Travis?"

"I didn't know I had to."

"I'm not saying you do. He just seems like the kind of guy who'd care, you know?"

"Even if he does care, it's none of his business," Haley said. I looked up. She hung on the wall above a series of bookcases and dressers.

"Right," Vaughn said, "got it."

He clambered across four chairs, past a Victrola and small 1950's era television. Then he stepped around the bookcases. I followed, glad to be standing on the actual floor again. Haley crawled to the section of wall above us and then dropped.

Stopping next to the light switches, Vaughn turned to both of us and said, "This is where things get interesting." He pushed in two of the stones and a previously hidden door fell open next to the switches, revealing a stairway that appeared to follow the curve of the tower deep into the ground. It was all concrete with no lights. I held on to the railing.

The door shut behind us as we descended.

"Did I just hear it lock?" Haley asked.

"Yeah," Vaughn said. "Don't worry about it. We can get out."

After another few seconds walking downward in the dark, Haley said, "What's that hissing sound?"

I didn't hear anything.

"Hissing?" Vaughn said, "That's the security system. It's probably trying to blow in poison gas, but no one's ever refilled the canister, so no biggie."

We walked further down the stairs. After another minute, Haley said, "I've reached the bottom."

"Great. Don't go any farther, okay? Nick should probably go first from now on."

"Why?" I didn't quite manage to keep the suspicion out of my voice.

"Machine guns, man. The hall's got a couple. They won't hurt you, so you can punch through the wall and, you know, trash them."

"Couldn't you have just turned them off?" I asked.

"I don't know how," he said. "I've never come this way."

"Why are *we* going this way then?"

In a casual tone, Vaughn said, "The tunnel I used to go through collapsed during the rainstorms we got near the end of August. This is the only other one I know about."

I couldn't see anything. Was I supposed to go down there and locate the gun by the flash from its muzzle? If I was lucky, the gun was fixed and capable of firing in only one direction. If I was unlucky, it would have the ability to track targets. My armor did well against bullets, but I didn't feel much of an urge to test its limits.

"Haley, can you see anything?"

"Just a hallway. The door's maybe fifty feet away

from us. No, wait. I think I see a hole in the wall. Two. One on each side. They're at waist level in the middle. I wonder if I could just crawl across the wall? Do you think I could?"

"I don't know. It depends on what triggers the guns. Vaughn?"

"Fuck," Vaughn said. "How am I supposed to know how the guns work?"

It felt like I was in the worst Dungeons and Dragons game ever—no equipment and no one with any skills relevant to the situation.

Finding the guns by the light generated from being shot at sounded more and more like a good idea.

"Okay. I guess I've got a plan. You guys back up the stairs a bit and I'll take care of it."

"I'll come along," Haley said adamantly.

"You don't have armor," I said.

Vaughn said, "Yeah, no matter what happens, Nick's not going to get hurt."

"I'm fast enough to dodge bullets," Haley said, "and my costume's a standard League suit."

Which meant that my grandfather had designed the material. It was probably made from the same stuff as the stealth suit.

"Just let me go first," I said. "That way they'll be firing at me. The armor can take it better than your costume."

"Great," she said. "Let's go."

"First" is a surprisingly fuzzy concept in English. It could mean waiting until I got ten feet ahead and then starting to walk. It could also mean following just a couple feet behind me. For Haley, it apparently meant that she could crawl along the wall the instant I set off.

Bearing in mind that I couldn't see much of anything, I couldn't know for sure.

I walked down the hallway blindly, wondering when I'd be hit and from which direction. The answer turned out to be "from the left and right simultaneously and at an angle." Bullets could knock me over if I wasn't expecting them, but in this case I was. It caught me mid-step and I rocked back, put my foot behind me, and holding myself in place. When the bullets didn't stop, I jumped forward, aiming for the flashes of light, and started punching the wall.

It broke under the force of my blows. Chunks of concrete hit my helmet, chest, and legs. My hand finally landed a glancing blow on the barrel of the gun, bending it a little, but not enough to stop the gunfire. Following the barrel back with my hand, I felt the body of the device. Pulling it to my chest, I yanked it free of its mounting and through what was left of the wall.

It stopped firing. I dumped it on the floor, listening to it crash against the ground.

It struck me that I'd just broken down a wall and yanked free a weapon that had been mounted to concrete. That was wild. I'd known that Grandpa could do that kind of thing and I'd known how strong the suit was, but I'd never had any reason to test it myself.

Then I realized that the other gun had stopped firing as well.

Something grabbed my arm. From the click of claws on my armor, I guessed who it might be.

"I didn't know I could break concrete," Haley said. "Did you see me punch through that wall?"

"I can't see anything," I said.

She laughed. "Of course you can't. Why didn't you

bring a flashlight?"

"When Vaughn said Hardwick House, I assumed there'd be lighting. What I'm wondering is why Vaughn didn't say anything."

Vaughn said, "I never take this way. The other tunnel had lights."

"Well anyway, let's go." I started walking.

Haley grabbed my arm again. "Wrong way," she said, turning me. "The door's over there."

Haley had to help Vaughn through the rubble too, but within moments we were all standing by the door. Vaughn gave Haley a series of numbers and she typed them into a keypad. The door clicked open.

Then the lights turned on and we saw the cave.

It looked like a cathedral, but a cathedral to what god? Concrete supports arched upward, holding a ceiling made entirely of stone. Across from us, the wall showed a mural of Red Lightning's symbol—jagged lightning under a golden arch with hieroglyphics. Like everything else, the mural had been blackened by fire.

Cells covered the wall on the right, reaching from the floor to the ceiling, everything in them completely visible through the bars. Everyone in the original League had been imprisoned here near the end.

Directly in front of us lay the remains of the last battle—warped metal machines, the skeletons of Red Lightning's henchman, and a silver dome, now ragged-edged and cracked in two, rising in the middle of it all.

"Looks pretty bad, doesn't it?" Vaughn said. "You'd never believe it, but my grandfather's personal stuff never burned."

"It must be the only thing that didn't," I said.

A layer of dark soot covered everything, mixed

with shrapnel that crunched when I stepped on it.

"Nah," Vaughn said. "The side tunnels didn't burn. That's where I found the stuff that I handed over. Let's go."

We turned left, moving away from the cells while avoiding the worst of the destruction in the middle of the room. I stared at the dome, thinking it might be interesting to go inside or possibly try to find Grandpa's old cell.

"Did you want to go into the dome?" Haley asked. "I'd like to."

"A little," I admitted, "but this is really more important."

"You want to hit it on the way out?" Vaughn asked.

"Sure," I said.

"Say," Vaughn said, "did you ever hear why the dome blew up?"

I'd asked my grandfather once—sort of.

He'd been explaining how he'd made some component solve two different problems. Then he'd stopped talking.

When I'd asked him what was wrong, he'd said, "Solving two problems works better in engineering than in life." He'd paused. "When Red Lightning captured all of us, he wanted me to construct a machine that increased his powers. I had to occupy Red Lightning's people and I had to free the team. I set the device to amplify his powers past any hope of control."

That was the most he'd ever told me about it.

"My grandfather sabotaged it," I said, wondering how many details I should share.

"My grandfather," Haley said, "said he couldn't tell whether Red Lightning or the machine inside had exploded. He just suddenly saw Red Lightning erupt out of the dome, surrounded by fire and lightning, and then everything began to burn."

Vaughn muttered, "Lousy way to die."

Haley glanced toward me, then toward Vaughn. "After everything he put everyone else through, he deserved it."

"I know," Vaughn said. "I'm not going to argue. I didn't even know him. I was just thinking that I'm glad I'm not going to be talking about this with my mom. She's freaked out enough already."

We exited the main area, walking between two huge vats. They had to be twenty feet tall. Smaller vats and tables covered with shattered test tubes were nearby.

Unlocking a steel door, Vaughn led us into another hallway. From the main area outside, I would never have expected the hall to look the way it did. It could have been transported from someplace in Europe— like maybe the Palace of Versailles. Paintings covered the arched ceiling and walls. Gold paint covered the woodwork. Well, I assumed it was paint. It may have been gold.

A closer look at the pictures made me realize that even if the Classical style fit, the subject matter did not. The pictures showed men in suits or workman's clothing, women in dresses, and children playing. All of them were white (except for the servants). They went about their daily business, working, cooking, cleaning, all of them smiling. It might have passed for a series of paintings about daily life in the 50's and 60's except that every picture included one man or woman wearing a red, Roman toga.

At the end of the hall, the final painting showed

a man sitting in a chair. Golden light surrounded his head and people were bowing before him. He bore a resemblance to pictures I'd seen of Vaughn's grandfather.

"These paintings are really weird," Haley said.

"No kidding." I stared up at the ceiling.

"Oh yeah," Vaughn said. "I shot up in here once. You would not believe the stuff that went on in my head."

We followed him into a room. Except for the bookshelves and desk, it looked like the hall. Red Lightning appeared to share reading tastes with Martin Magnus. The bookshelves held books in languages I didn't recognize, books on translating ancient languages, and a long line of handwritten journals (organized by date).

"This is where I got the stuff I gave to Magnus' people," he said. "I didn't give them much. You're welcome to the rest."

"I'll need to come back with a bag or something."

Haley picked the first journal off the shelf and started flipping through it. "If we were in Harry Potter," she said, "I'd end up possessed by this book."

"Which would make me what?" Vaughn asked. "Malfoy?"

"Have you read the journals?" I asked Vaughn. "Do you have any idea why he did any of it?"

"Not really. I've read bits. They're all pretty normal up till about two years before he got zapped with the Power Impregnator. After that they just get batshit insane."

"So there's no reason?" I said. "He just goes crazy? That's dumb."

"Ever read 'Breakfast of Champions' by Kurt Vonnegut?" Vaughn asked. "There's a character in there that goes crazy and starts killing people. Vonnegut blames it on bad chemicals in his brain. In the book, it's funny."

"That doesn't sound very funny," Haley said.

"But see," Vaughn said, "it's Vonnegut. He's funny as hell."

CHAPTER TEN

I'd decided to take the day off from costumes, but the day didn't want to cooperate with me.

School went okay. I saw Vaughn and Cassie in the halls and said "hi" but that was about it.

The day didn't fall apart till I got home.

I arrived before my parents, pulled the mail out of the mail box and grabbed the paper off the front porch. I unrolled it to find myself on the front page under the headline: "ROCKET AND TOMAHAWK BRAWL DOWNTOWN." A smaller headline below it said: "Mayor Calls for More Assistance."

Tomahawk turned out to be okay. No permanent physical damage.

Emotional? Maybe.

A reporter had made it to the lingerie shop while

he was still unconscious and photographed him lying covered in thongs. The photograph dominated the page. Next to it were three smaller photos of the fight. I'd never noticed anyone taking pictures, but on the other hand, I'd been more concerned with getting away.

I didn't bother to read the article. I walked around to the door by the garage, unlocked it and stepped inside. I put my coat into the closet, left my shoes by the door and dropped the mail and newspaper on the kitchen counter. Then I went upstairs to my room.

Sitting down on the bed, I realized that I didn't know what I was going to do next. I didn't feel like doing homework. I could go into HQ and work on the jet. Maybe do repairs on the suit? I dismissed the thought. Who knew who might be in? I'd get roped into a conversation about last night—or worse, about the mayor.

If I wanted to release what he'd said about killing people and the bits that made it sound as if he was controlled by mysterious forces, now was the time.

It still didn't feel right.

Specifically, I meant that it felt somehow morally wrong. I couldn't put it into words. When I tried to, it sounded stupid. It felt like I was blackmailing the guy and damaging his reputation. On the other hand, this was someone who really deserved to have his reputation damaged.

I tried to think about something else, but couldn't.

The best reason for not publicizing the recording was that it might make it harder to catch the actual forces behind him. On the other hand, making their existence obvious might force them into the open where more experienced people could take over.

Of course, I wasn't completely sure I *wanted* them to take over.

I lay down on the bed. I could almost have gone to sleep. After being shot, punched and slammed into a brick wall, I did feel a little sore.

I wondered what Haley was doing. Probably working. It was why we'd gone out yesterday. I couldn't imagine that Italian restaurants were particularly popular on Halloween, but I guessed that they still had to be staffed.

Should I call her? I thought about it. Obviously I shouldn't while she was working, but I'd heard that girls worried if they didn't get called back.

Of course, bearing in mind that I got all of my information about dating from novels and the internet, that may have been wrong.

I sat up again. I decided to go downstairs to the computer and find out if she had a Facebook page. But before I even left my room, my cell phone rang. I pulled it out of my pocket, checked who it was.

Travis.

I answered the phone.

In a bass voice that rumbled through the speaker, he said, "Heya Nick, you home?"

"Um... yeah."

"Great. I'm driving down your street. We've got to talk."

"I'll be here."

He hung up.

By the time I got downstairs, he was already knocking on the front door. I opened it and let him in. He was huge. I was almost a foot taller than Haley. He was almost a foot taller than me. Haley wasn't much more than five feet tall and she could throw cars. I had a bad feeling Travis could rip me in two whether or not I wore armor.

Still, he didn't seem angry.

"We've got to talk, Nick. How about over here?" He pointed toward the living room. Then he went and sat down on the couch.

Contrary to its name, the living room was more the 'preserved in amber' room. As in you could see the tracks from the vacuum cleaner (all running in the same direction) on the white carpet. Imagine pictures of Rachel and myself on the walls, a black, grand piano in one corner, and a picture window without the slightest hint of dust or cat hair on the wide windowsill.

Picture books sat on the coffee table in two distinct piles, one of foreign countries, the other of national parks.

Travis picked one up and flipped through its pages. "Ever been to Denali?" he asked.

"No," I said. "I haven't been to Egypt either." That was the book on top of the other pile.

"The pictures don't do it justice. You've got to go there and smell the place."

I walked into the room, aware with every step that I was leaving footprints, and sat down in the chair across from him. The cushion felt stiff.

"So Nick, can we take the mayor down on what you've got?"

"I don't know. It's not going to make him look good, but it's not exactly a confession. How did you find out about it?"

"I called Cassie. She drove Vaughn home from school." He leaned forward. "The story I got was all jumbled. The mayor's part of some huge conspiracy and he's going to kill people from another conspiracy and somehow it's got something to do with Red Lightning? What's the real scoop?"

"That's actually pretty close to all I've got. Except I think that Red Lightning must have gotten his abilities from those guys somehow."

He went silent for a moment. "Okay. Bottom line, what exactly is on that recording?"

"Well," I said, "the bottom line is he's obviously taking orders from somebody and he threatens to kill people."

"That's what we need, Nick."

"Okay," I said. "I'll take a look at the recording tonight and put something together for the local news."

"Thanks, Nick," Travis said. "Once we get this asshole off our backs, we can get back to fighting crime instead of other heroes. Which reminds me, how did you end up fighting Tomahawk anyway?"

I told him.

"Red Lightning's lair? That's unbelievable. You've got to take me down there." Travis put down the Denali book, placing it diagonally next to its rightful pile.

Fighting an urge to pick the book up and put it back, I said, "No reason you can't go. Just talk to Vaughn. He let me and Haley in."

"Haley?" Travis looked surprised.

"Yeah. She came along."

"That's good," Travis said. "That's what I was hoping for when I pushed her into the group. Ever since the press went after that wrestler and she quit gymnastics, all she's done is mope around the house."

Evidently she hadn't told him about the two of us

going out for coffee. Not that it really was any of his business, but I wasn't going to mention it if she hadn't.

"Did I ever tell you I had a match with that guy in high school? I pinned him." He grinned. "I wonder what he's doing now?"

"If he's lucky, he's in California," I said. "Don't they have a statewide, powered high school sports league there?"

"Last I heard they were having financial troubles," Travis said. "Well, anyway, I better get moving. Nice to see you, Nick. Let me know when you're ready."

He left.

I looked down at the picture book, put it back on top of the correct pile. On the floor, I could see the imprint of our shoes, small, regular indentations on either side of the coffee table.

I could have pulled out the sweeper and removed them, but I didn't. Instead I walked upstairs, recognizing that as gestures of rebellion went, this one was fairly pathetic.

*   *   *

Despite constant interruptions by children shouting "trick or treat" at the front door, I made my way through my homework quickly—largely because I only had math.

By the time I walked to Grandpa's house around nine, the kids were off the streets. Trick or treating was over for the year, but I still saw some pumpkins on porches, their eyes and mouths aglow with candlelight.

Using the computers in League HQ to cut the mayor's conversation took a little work. I burned a CD of it, then listened to it. As I did, I wondered how much an ordinary person would get out of it.

I listened to it again.

All I'd said to Travis was true, but the mayor didn't lay it out in as many words as I would have liked.

I listened to it yet another time. Then I did something I knew Travis wouldn't like. I called Daniel's dad.

He walked out of the tunnels minutes later in a navy blue costume similar to a uniform, the Greek letter "psi" visible on the left side of his chest. The costume looked more professional than the standard skintight thing, but personally, it reminded me more of Babylon 5's Psi Corp than anything else. For those of you who never watched the TV show, the Psi Corp was evil.

"Hi Nick," he said, walking over to the main table in the middle of the room and sitting down. "What have you got?"

I didn't bother to explain. I played the CD, figuring he'd grab it straight from my head anyway.

When it finished, he said, "That's not bad. What else do you have?"

"Nothing," I said.

"Then don't use it," he said. "Do you know why I'm saying that?"

"Because it's not clear enough?"

"It's not clear," he agreed, "but that's not it. At the right moment, what you've got there could be devastating, but you need more of it. As a vigilante, you've got two tools—violence and public opinion. You've got to put just as much work into the latter as the former. You don't need one snippet like that. You need five. If you can't find more, you have to look for other things like irregularities with campaign contributions or hints that he might be embezzling money. The key point is that you need to have a story, and then you use the press to put it into people's heads."

He said it totally calmly, much like the way Daniel usually talked, even though he was explaining how to destroy a politician's career.

"Oh," I said. It seemed obvious when he put it that way.

"I make the initial accusation," he continued, "then release supporting details, and when they're beginning to respond, I hit them with something totally new. The way you win is to pound and pound at them until they resign or make a mistake—and then you jump on that."

After he started giving examples, I realized that the police chief's resignation a couple years ago hadn't been as much of a surprise to him as to the rest of the city. It also occurred to me that he was basically teaching me how to run a very negative political campaign.

"Is there any other kind?" he asked. "Call me back when you've got more evidence. In the meantime, I'm heading home. The Midwest Defenders' telepath quit, so I've been in Chicago twice today already."

Seconds later, I sat alone in HQ, reflecting on the fact that I never wanted Daniel's dad as an enemy.

Then I went into the computer to check on the roachbots. According to the monitoring program, I had more than nine hours of audio to listen to and less than an hour before my curfew. I decided to go home.

During the walk, my cell phone rang. I answered it despite not recognizing the number.

Opening the phone, I heard the word, "Hello," delivered in an unrecognizable voice and accent, followed by, "I'm Martin Magnus."

"Uh, hi?"

I stood on a corner a couple blocks from my house. The street was dark and music came from the house behind me. With all the windows shut, I couldn't tell what kind except that it definitely included a bass drum. Cars lined the street in front of it. A man in a devil costume walked up to the front door and stepped inside.

I felt naked. My armor sat back in HQ and I wasn't wearing the full stealth suit—just the part that could fit under clothes.

"Once, my followers would have led you to my house and I would have shown you my wealth, treated you to my food, and shown you my gardens. In these times, I call you from my hiding place."

"That's okay," I began, "I'm just fine with—"

"Be *silent.*"

I stopped.

"Once, I had an army, men and women such as your friends who loved me as a god. Even now I have a few such followers, but too few. I decay, as do we all, and do not command the power I once did."

He paused, but this time I didn't say anything.

"You and your friends are at the beginning of your ascendancy. Surely you will achieve power and influence if you wish to, but you are young. You require guidance."

"Believe me," I said, "I'm getting a lot of guidance lately, and I can't say any of us want to control anything."

"But you want out from under your mayor's thumb? You don't wish to fight off his gang of men forever? You are the enemy of my enemy, and one he fears. We should make an alliance."

"With me?"

I was barely paying attention to him. I crossed the street, walking a little faster. I knew that the people who had tried to catch us during the cross country season worked for Magnus. They had had our pictures. Now he had my cell phone number.

He had to know where I lived.

"Yes. You, and your friends."

"So if we had this alliance," I said, "what exactly would we do for each other?"

"You have the power to act, to make war. My troops are damaged, destroyed, but I have resources, connections with those who have the power to control his wealth, to curtail his power."

"So you're saying you'd close his bank account?"

I could see my house now.

"After a fashion. And you will fight him, beat him, leave him on the ground with the blood running down his face."

He wasn't making it easy to pretend he was one of the good guys.

"I don't think I can make a decision on something like this without talking to the rest of the group," I said. "Maybe you could call me back tomorrow?"

"Very good," he said. "We will meet and our foes will fear us and run before our slaughter."

He also wasn't making it easy to pretend he was sane.

"Or you could just call me," I said. "We don't have to slaughter anything."

He hung up.

Abandoning any pretense of calm, I ran to the side door, unlocked it and ran inside.

I don't know what I was expecting to find. My parents dead on the floor? Magnus' men force-feeding them the drink of the gods?

Instead I burst in to find the kitchen warm, and still smelling of spaghetti sauce and garlic bread. Past the kitchen, I could see my dad sitting on the couch in the family room and hear the TV announcer babbling about football.

Mom was probably already in bed.

Dad stood up and stepped into the doorway between the kitchen and the family room. "Something wrong, Nick?"

"No," I said, "I just thought I might be late."

"Late? It's only ten. What were you doing?"

"Just playing video games at Grandpa's—I mean, at my house."

"Your house." Dad's expression stiffened for just a moment. "What your grandfather was thinking, I'll never know."

* * *

Sitting on my bed later, I tried to think through my next move.

I didn't intend to consider anything Magnus thought he had to offer even for a minute. It sounded like he wasn't going to be of any help in a fight and I couldn't see how cutting off access to the mayor's money would do any good. I would have blown him off immediately except that I had been freaked out that he'd called me on my cell phone.

Not that I still wasn't a little freaked out.

We needed to protect ourselves and our families, but how to do it wasn't clear. We couldn't watch our parents all day. Simply having Daniel strengthen everyone's "block" like he'd done for me wouldn't do it either.

I thought about it while getting my pajamas on. Then I got into bed, still running through possibilities.

I couldn't get to sleep.

I got up, pulled my cell phone off my dresser, and turned it on. I called Daniel, knowing that he generally turned off his phone when he went to bed.

It rang.

"Hi Nick," Daniel answered. "You're up late."

"I know," I said. "I'm trying to figure something out."

"What?"

For what seemed like the millionth time, I went through what I'd heard the mayor say, the fight with Tomahawk, how Haley, Vaughn and I had snuck into Red Lightning's lair, and how Travis and Daniel's dad had given completely contradictory advice about what to do with the recording.

I ended by describing the walk home and the call with Martin Magnus, ending with: "Magnus knows who we are. His people had the pictures. I think the mayor must know who I am too. We need to do something to protect ourselves before one of them takes us out."

I was sure I'd gone on for at least twenty minutes.

"I knew a bit of that," Daniel said. "My dad told me about the recording, and of course, the fight with Tomahawk was in the news, but I didn't know anything about Red Lightning's lair. Why didn't you tell me you were going over there?"

"I don't know. Everything happened so fast, I didn't

really have time to think about it."

"How did Haley end up going?"

"We were talking after school and I mentioned it. I mean seriously, things were busy and I never had the chance to call you."

"Well, okay," he said. "On a slightly different subject, my dad told me that I should remind you not to go out in armor again."

"I was surprised he didn't say anything when we talked."

"He was tired," Daniel said, "and besides, he thought making Tomahawk look silly was a great move even if you didn't do it intentionally. Did you read the paper?"

"I looked at the headlines," I said.

"You've got to read the article. More than half the people they interviewed were on your side."

"Not that it'll do us any good against Magnus or the Cabal or whoever any of these people are."

"It's popular support. That's worth something."

"Even if it's public support for my grandfather," I said.

We talked a little longer and then I went to bed again.

This time, I slept.

* * *

Daniel came by after school the next day and we went down to HQ.

I sat in the lab and assembled more roachbots. With some minor modifications, they would make great burglar alarms. I probably should have asked people if they wanted their houses watched, but decided it would be better if I had the roachbots available before

I asked instead of asking and then making people wait.

Seated on a stool in the lab with hundreds of little metal parts on the counter, I carefully fit the pieces together. It felt good. Repetitive work was like that sometimes.

Daniel went through the past couple days' recordings. I could hear them playing over the speakers in the main room. When I glanced out the doorway, I could see hazy images of the mayor's office, his house and sometimes his car. I probably should have gone with higher quality cameras.

The mayor and his guests talked about the usual boring crap—business zoning, details about contractors for road repair, and issues they planned to bring up to the city council.

A Girl Scout visited the mayor's office. Daniel fast-forwarded and the screen blurred into static. I would have, too. It was hard to imagine the mayor working against us by placing mental suggestions into the minds of girl scouts. What were they going to do? Sell us poisoned cookies?

Returning my attention to the parts in front of me, I went back to roachbot assembly.

Daniel interrupted me after about an hour.

"Nick," Daniel said, "come in here and take a look at this."

I put down the tools and the bot I had been working on and stepped into the main room. The big screens showed pictures of the mayor's office from several different angles.

I was a firm believer in redundant robots.

The window behind the desk had been fixed, but I barely noticed that. Superheroes filled the office—Red

Bolt and Future Knight, Tomahawk and all four of the Elementals.

They stood in circles, talking to each other, drinking coffee, sometimes laughing—all except Tomahawk. He looked angry.

The moment the mayor stood up, they stopped talking. He walked around his desk, gazing deeply into the eyes of one before moving on to the next. After he had stopped next to each of them, they started talking again as if nothing had happened.

"What did I just see?" I checked the time at the bottom of the videos. It showed 11:13:43 AM today.

"He's not strong enough to control them all at once, but he is strong enough to insert commands into their subconscious. I'm pretty sure that's it."

Daniel said this with about the same level of emotion he might show the weather.

"What do you think they're about to do?"

"I don't know," Daniel said, "but whatever it is, they've had a good five hours to get started."

I now understood why the mayor had slipped under everybody's radar for so long. We had a video right here of him planting commands into the brains of an entire team of heroes, while simultaneously having no evidence to prove it.

The fact that everybody had stopped and started talking on his cue pointed toward telepathy, but not inarguably. The evidence was purely circumstantial.

"Purely circumstantial is okay," Daniel said. "People get convicted on circumstantial evidence all the time. I don't know what my dad would say about this particular piece of evidence, but—"

"He'd say I needed to get five more."

Daniel laughed. "I got that lecture too. Remember when I was releasing everything I could find about the mayor to the press?"

"Yeah. What happened with that?"

"I ran out of good stuff to release."

I looked up at the screen again. "Do you think we should alert everybody?"

"I don't know. I'd send them a yellow, not a red."

"I suppose there's no reason to summon everybody here," I said.

I went into the computer and set everybody's homing devices to blink yellow. Hopefully people were wearing them. I'd passed them out the first time we got together as a team—more than enough time for everyone to have forgotten about them.

With any luck, we'd be getting calls in the next few minutes.

"Think anyone's still wearing them?" I asked Daniel.

He held out his right hand. The dark gemstone on his ring flickered yellow.

The phone rang.

Daniel pointed to the phone. "It's for you."

I picked it up and pressed line four, answering with, "Hi."

Haley said, "Hi Nick, I'm at work. Is something going on?"

"I don't know yet. The mayor's got some kind of control over all the out-of-town supers, and he's sent them out, but I don't know why."

"I don't see any of them here," she said, "but I'll look. Oh, my parents don't want me taking phone calls at work, but calling around now is okay. We're usually really slow before five."

And that, Daniel thought at me, *is a hint that she'd like you to call her at work occasionally.*

I'd have mustered up some righteous indignation against his assumption that I'd missed the hint, but I had.

Marcus called next, followed by Travis, Cassie, and Jaclyn. We were only missing Vaughn.

"Vaughn doesn't have one," Daniel reminded me. "He didn't make it the night we passed them out."

"Oh, yeah," I said.

"We should call Cassie," Daniel said. "They hang out sometimes."

"Wouldn't Cassie have mentioned it if he were with her?"

"Probably," Daniel said. "But she might know where he is."

The phone rang again.

"It's not Vaughn," Daniel said.

"Who is it?"

"I don't know. Just not Vaughn."

If I had the ability to sense the future, I'd want it to be a little more precise.

I picked up the phone. "Hello?"

"Nick?"

It was my mom.

"Don't come home. Don't go out. There were two..." she paused "...superheroes here asking about you. Nick, are you..." she paused again. "Forget that question. Just don't come home right now."

"Mom?"

She hung up.

It had to be the block. We grandchildren had the

weak version, something that prevented us from talking about things we shouldn't. Our parents had something more extensive, possibly more sophisticated. I didn't know anything about the details, but it sounded like she was on the edge of knowing something, but just... couldn't.

"My dad hated it," Daniel said. "He still does."

Then I thought about what she'd actually said. Two supers had been at my house.

"Red," Daniel said. "Set everybody's devices to red."

CHAPTER ELEVEN

I punched the distress call.

Above us, scattered lights began to slowly blink red.

I looked up. "I didn't know that happened."

"Me neither," Daniel said. "It looks like we've got a lot of dead bulbs."

We got another round of phone calls—except we got one less. In addition to Vaughn, Jaclyn didn't call back.

"Is there any way to triangulate where she is from her..." Daniel stopped for a second. "What do you call these things?"

"I call them homing devices, but it's not really the best name. Anyway, the only way to track them is if someone sets up a distress call—and she hasn't."

I stared at the screen in front of me, flipping

through the cameras at the tunnel entrances. I didn't see her.

The phrase "picking us off one by one" started to run through my head.

"Can you stop that?" Daniel asked. "It's hard enough concentrating as is."

Having a best friend who could read my mind had seemed like a lot more fun when we were little kids.

I ignored him and kept on flipping from camera to camera, finally moving the whole display to the big screen so that I could watch them all at once.

Next to me, Daniel closed his eyes. "The largest probability of danger comes from the downtown office," he said.

"What," I said. "Is the old League mainframe going to wake up and take over the world?"

"I don't need sarcasm right now."

"It's just that almost nothing in the downtown office actually works," I said.

"I don't get details," Daniel said. "You know that."

Something started beeping.

Leaving the camera display on the big screen, I checked the dashboard of the security program. Jaclyn and her grandfather had just been scanned at the downtown office.

Looking up at the main screen, I could see them running down the tunnel holding hands, Jaclyn leading, her grandfather carrying his cane. Bizarrely, both of them were in costume. It had to have been a long time for him. He started having problems with macular degeneration fifteen years ago. Near blindness and the ability to run at high speed didn't work well together.

"Is it really them?" Daniel stared up at their picture.

"The retinal scans check out," I said, "and they're moving at upwards of two hundred miles per hour."

Off to the side, the door to the hangar opened and Jaclyn and her grandfather walked out.

It really is *them*, Daniel told me.

"They're behind us," Jaclyn warned. "Not right behind us, but too close."

I turned back to the console and changed the security settings to high, wishing that I'd set a higher priority on checking out the security systems.

Steel doors clanked into place in the tunnels.

"There," Daniel said.

I looked up at the screen. Two of the Elementals stood in front of the downtown office. The guy was tall and skinny. The girl had dark hair in a pageboy haircut, and 60's style cats eye glasses that clashed with her costume. Both wore clothing from classical Greece— which had to be pretty cold in November.

Then the guy sank into the ground, coming up again inside the offices. As he did, I could see a shadowy, but bulkier form around him. The girl dissolved into a gust of wind, the door shaking as she poured through the cracks.

"Crap," I said. HQ's defenses wouldn't do much against them.

"They appeared in the middle of my living room," Jaclyn said, "told me I was terrorist, and that they were going to bring me in."

It didn't take telepathy to catch her anger.

"The mayor's been messing with their heads," Daniel said.

"Oh. Takes one to know one."

"What was that supposed to mean?" Daniel turned toward her.

"*Nothing*. He's a telepath too. That's all. Relax," she said.

Jaclyn's grandfather cleared his throat. We all turned toward him. Looking at him, I'd never have guessed he was in his nineties. I'd have guessed sixties, and, even then I'd have thought he looked young for his age. Blindness aside, he was in good physical shape. He had wrinkles and gray hair, but you could still see the muscles under his costume.

"Focus," he said. "Who can take them out?"

"I'm the only one," Daniel said. "They'll phase out of anybody else's way."

"Wrong," Jaclyn said. "Anyone can hit the guy. He doesn't phase out. He just phases into the ground."

"Good," her grandfather said, "here's your plan. When they get closer, Jaclyn, you go into the tunnel and distract them until Nick is finished getting his armor on, then lead them back here. Daniel, you take them out the first chance you get whether Nick's back or not."

"What if I don't get the armor on fast enough?" I asked.

"Hurry," he said, injecting enough urgency into the word that I didn't hesitate.

I ran for the lab.

As I left, I heard Jaclyn say, "What if they get past me?"

I didn't hear the answer.

*   *   *

By the time I returned, Jaclyn was already in the

tunnels. I ran down the side of the main room and through the door to the hangar. Jaclyn's grandfather stood next to it.

"She didn't want me too close to the action," he said.

Daniel (now in costume) stood next to the open tunnel entrance and racks of replacement parts. The League jet loomed behind him.

You and Jaclyn are supposed to keep them busy while I mindream them.

He looked scared.

I heard the rush of wind, running, and a very solid punch. This was followed by the sound of rock scraping concrete, and a bellow of pain. Jaclyn ran out, skidding to a stop and turning on a dime to stand next to me.

"I got a punch in," she said. "He's not happy."

Wind blew in of the tunnel, rattling parts in their boxes and tools hanging on the walls. In the middle of it, I could see the hazy shape of the girl. I wondered what effect the sonics would have on her. Would sound do nothing or would it disrupt whatever connected her to herself in that form?

I didn't want to kill her, so I decided not to think about it. She was Daniel's problem.

"She's kind of... mentally dispersed," he said, "but I can do this—"

The hazy form flattened as it hit an invisible wall, face, glasses and the back of her skull interpenetrating each other. She dissolved into a colored gas, reforming a few feet away as cloudy version of herself.

The guy ran out of the tunnel. The shadowy form around him seemed more detailed, all rocks and earth.

Both Jaclyn and I went for him, but Jaclyn got

there first, giving him a punch in the gut that he barely noticed. He hit her with two of his four hands, grazing her stomach with his own hand, but pummeling her in the face with the shadowy version of that hand so quickly I barely saw the punch. She fell, and didn't hit the floor only because she stepped backwards fast enough that she managed to get her feet under her, ending up behind me.

I considered charging him, but didn't. He struck me as someone who might be strong enough to start ripping off my armor.

I blasted him with the sonics instead.

He gritted his teeth as dirt and rocks shot outward from him, becoming solid as they landed on the floor. I didn't see any major damage. I tried to figure out my next move.

Just as I decided to risk hand-to-hand, Jaclyn came back into the fight. She hit him hard enough with her right fist that he flew backward five feet into the tunnel. She kept up with him, giving him another punch with her left that knocked him back again.

It reminded me of dribbling a soccer ball.

At least it did until he sank into the floor—which he did shortly after the second punch.

Jaclyn turned around, calling to me, "Do you see him?"

"Not yet."

He came up again in the middle of the hangar, just behind Night Wolf's car and to the side of the jet. His shadow form no longer looked like dirt and rocks. It looked like concrete and he now stood maybe a foot taller.

Above us, the girl with air powers was still dodging

Daniel's attempts to surround her with an air-tight telekinetic container.

Jaclyn's grandfather shouted out, "Work together!"

Honestly, what did he think we were doing?

Jaclyn blurred and then stood next to me. "I'll run at him and you can come from the side?"

"Sure," I said.

She shot at him, jumped over the car and started pounding him, dodging his attempts to punch back. Bits of concrete shot into the air from the impact of her blows and he backed up.

I started the rockets, flew in the direction of the jet, banked right, and dove toward the two of them. As I rushed toward him, a thought hit me. He had earth powers. What happened if he was no longer touching the earth?

I grabbed his legs and gained altitude—well, to the degree I could inside the hangar. Chunks of concrete crashed to the ground as I pulled myself upright and hovered, holding him upside down. I couldn't see any sign of a shadowy presence. In fact, he wasn't even trying to fight me anymore. He was shouting:

"Ann! I mean Air! Heeeey, Air! Help!" The guy was waving his arms and all but pissing himself.

Near the front of the hangar where she'd been fighting Daniel, Ann/Air turned toward me, drawing herself together to fly straight at me.

It took Daniel only an instant. She fell unconscious and floated to the ground. As soon as she was on the floor, the guy fell unconscious as well.

I felt like cheering. Even if he wasn't any more powerful than a normal man by then, I had still been worried that with all his moving around, I might have dropped him.

I flew down to where Daniel stood next to Ann's body. I lay the guy down next to her. Jaclyn had beaten me there, naturally.

"Did you hear him use her real name? God," she said, "I couldn't believe it. I knew better than that when I was ten."

"That shocked me too," Daniel said. "You never use someone's real name when they're in costume."

"Do you have a name yet?" I asked Jaclyn. "Or are we just supposed to call you Purple or something?"

Her costume *was* purple.

"He," Jaclyn said, pointing to her grandfather, "thinks I ought to call myself 'Little C'. *I* think that no one ever got his name straight after he changed it to 'C' from Hotfoot."

"It was a great name," her grandfather said. "It was a reference to the speed of light."

"It was a great example," she said, "of why people shouldn't name themselves after a piece of an equation."

The bodies floated up to waist height and Daniel said, "We probably ought to move them into the main room."

As we stepped through the doorway, I realized the phones in the main room were ringing.

"What now?" I said.

"Did you set security to high?" Jaclyn's grandfather asked. He'd turned his head to follow my voice, and looked as if he were talking to someone standing just to my left.

I admitted I had.

"Well, back in my time, high security meant that anyone who wasn't already in the base couldn't get in, even if they passed the scan."

Oops.

As I ran toward the table in the middle of the main room, I wondered just what else putting HQ into high security did. What if it sent an alert to other hero groups? I didn't feel like explaining all this to Guardian or the Midwest Defenders.

Glancing at the screen, I saw Travis, Haley, Marcus and Cassie crouched at the forest entrance, all in costume and looking nervous.

Picking up the phone, I said, "Hi."

Travis said, "We can't get in. What's going on in there?"

"Sorry, a couple of them got in and we got into a fight and I put it HQ on high security, but I didn't know it'd shut *you* ou—"

"Right," Travis said. "Just let us in."

I tapped the keyboard, making a few more errors than usual because of my gloves, but finally managing to move the security level to medium. The doors opened.

The forest entrance was a hole in the ground covered by doors of reinforced concrete. Grandpa had designed a system that kept the doors constantly covered by leaves and dirt, all of which fell in as the doors opened. Moments later, the four of them jumped in—well, except that Marcus, who turned his arms into wings and glided to the floor of the tunnel.

Within a few minutes, everyone stood in the main room in front of the video screen. Well, most of us were standing. Air and Earth slept on HQ's olive green carpet.

We filled the others in about the fight.

"What made you think to pick him up?" Jaclyn asked me.

"Something Daniel once said. He told me about a giant in Greek mythology who was impossible to defeat while he touched the ground."

"Antaeus," Daniel said. "He was a son of Gaea and Poseidon. Hercules picked him up and strangled him."

"That's kind of what I was thinking of," I said. "Except for the strangling."

"It's a great idea," Jaclyn said, "but if it didn't work, you'd have been holding him in the air while he tried to rip you apart."

"I know. I hadn't really planned that far ahead."

"But it *did* work," Haley said. "Good job."

Off to my left, I heard Travis ask Daniel, "So, did you get anything out of them?"

Daniel said, "Yeah. Everything I could. The mayor made them think we were being mind-controlled by some kind of telepathic terrorist."

Jaclyn laughed, "I wonder how he came up with that?"

"But can you prove it?" Travis asked. "If we brought in another telepath, could he see what you saw?"

"Oh yeah," Daniel said. "I didn't remove anything. I didn't mess anything up, and it's obviously not my style of work. Mayor Bouman's a self-taught telepath. You can't see it from the outside, but it's really crudely done. I'm stronger than he is and I've been trained, so my style would be considerably more precise."

Travis nodded. "Good. Glad we're covered there. So Nick, when were you going to release that recording?"

"Uh... I wasn't. I talked to Daniel's dad and he said to wait until we had more evidence."

"Well, why the fuck didn't you tell me earlier?" He sounded angry.

"I don't know," I said. "Too much stuff going on."

"Nick," he said, "when you agree to do something and then completely change your mind, you tell somebody."

"I'm sure he didn't mean to," Haley began.

"Hush," Jaclyn's grandfather said.

I'd forgotten he was even here.

He stood behind the group, his cane parallel to the floor as if he really didn't need it. With his costume on, the orange suit with a white "C" fading into his chest, I could imagine him thirty years younger.

"You have one man missing. Your enemy has sent powered heroes out to find you. Now isn't the time to assign blame. Now is the time to get to them first."

"What about proof?" I said. "Don't we have to have something on them?"

"You're not policemen, you're vigilantes. The mayor's not asking if he has the right to do what he's doing. He's attacking you. Worry about what's going to happen afterward, afterward. Right now, you need to take him down."

Kids don't really know adults. What I remembered of Jaclyn's grandfather from the picnics was a man who'd spent a lot of time laughing, telling funny stories, and coaxing me into racing Jaclyn. I think I only ever won one race. He gave me a forty-nine foot head start out of fifty feet, and even then it was a near thing.

As a crime fighter though, he had the old-school "fight the criminals and run from the cops" approach.

Maybe I should have expected it. The Heroes League had pretty much defined old-school, as well as brought about its demise. When you get popular, you don't have to run from the cops unless you want to avoid signing autographs.

"Now I don't know exactly what *we* would have done," he said, "except that Captain Commando would already be out there. He never did wait for anything."

He paused and thought for a moment. "It seems to me that Daniel should be able to find them all if his powers are anything like his grandfather's."

"I'm weaker than he was," Daniel said.

"Ah, your grandfather wasn't any great shakes at the beginning. You'll do fine. Mind you, if all of you come after them at once, they'll run away. I'd say find them and then let one of you become visible. After that, the rest of you come out of the shadows."

* * *

Twenty minutes later, we were all standing in the woods while Daniel scanned the area. All of us except for Jaclyn's grandfather—someone had to stay in HQ in case Vaughn showed up. Also, I didn't think he wanted anyone to have to protect him in a fight.

"I'm not getting much of anybody," Daniel said.

"You ought to be," Travis said. "We gave them the slip around here just before Nick finally let us in."

I wondered whether the irritation in his voice was directed at me or Daniel.

"They must have moved," Daniel said, flashing me a mental picture of Travis with his mask stuffed in his mouth.

No question as to who Daniel was irritated with.

"No, wait," Daniel said. "I've got all five of them. Red Bolt, Future Knight and Water are over on the edge of the park. Tomahawk and Fire are in the air above the park, looking for people."

"Hey," Cassie said, "we can split up and attack them simultaneously. Everyone who can fly goes up and the rest of us attack the people left on the ground."

"Right," Travis said. "Only let's use the ambush strategy C suggested. Also, Mystic, hang back unless the fliers are losing. If we lose you, we lose any chance to communicate between the two groups."

So that was how I found myself flying into combat with Marcus, the person I knew least on the team, while Daniel stayed on the ground.

I flew through a bunch of big evergreens and into the twilight sky. Marcus hung onto my leg, having transformed into a reptilian thing that reminded me of a pterodactyl, except that pterodactyls had never had tentacles. I had no way of knowing for sure, but I also seriously doubted they'd had the same grayish skin as Travis and Haley's hands after their transformations.

"Hope you don't mind," he said. "I'd never keep up with you if I had to flap my wings."

"No problem," I said.

Real pterodactyls probably never talked, either.

We saw Tomahawk and Fire at approximately the same time they saw us.

They had just passed the big swing set on the edge of the playground and were beginning to fly over the forest. Unlike when she'd been patrolling the mayor's house, Fire now appeared to be a woman-shaped flame.

Tomahawk looked just the same as the last time I'd seen him, except much, *much* angrier.

He made a beeline for me, screaming something.

He said he's going to rip you limb from limb and he

really means it, Daniel sent, but I could barely make it out. We were probably on the edge of his range.

I don't know whether I mentioned this before, but Tomahawk could really haul, and it was obvious he intended to ram me.

"Let go!" I shouted to Marcus.

"Sure. That guy looks insane," he said. He let go and transformed into a more dragon-like form, diving away.

I opened up the rocket pack to full power and swerved right. Tomahawk shot past me, trying to turn but failing. He ended up a quarter of a mile behind me before he managed to slow down, above the houses next to the park. If Grandpa had ever put aerial defenses into HQ, he wouldn't be far from their reach. I had to check on that sometime.

In the meantime, my best shot would be to get him over Daniel (or the Mystic while in costume) and let Daniel take the guy's head apart, but if I couldn't, I'd have to punch him until he went down.

I tried to get Daniel's attention mentally, but couldn't raise him.

Meanwhile, Tomahawk had turned around and started to rush toward me again.

I started to fly upwards, but then it occurred to me that the last time I'd defeated him by putting myself into situations where agility and planning mattered more than speed. He'd be able to take care of a change in height easily. What I had to do was get him over the forest where Daniel was hiding.

Adjusting my route, I flew straight towards him, passing over the forest and reaching the edge of the park before I turned right to lead him over Daniel's position.

Unfortunately, I'd misjudged how close I could get to him while still staying ahead. I felt him grab my leg and yank even as I began to fly over trees again.

It took less than a second for him to fly under me, flip around to face me, and grab my throat with both hands.

His face told me everything I needed to know about his intentions. Screaming incoherently at me, he squeezed the armor around my neck. It didn't break, but I could feel it move under his fingers. Cords of muscles now visible in his forearms, he strained to put as much force into the squeeze as he could.

For that moment, my armor held.

My martial arts instructor had always made a big deal about asking his students to think about what they were willing to do in a fight. Were they willing to maim somebody? Were they willing to kill somebody? If they weren't, they shouldn't practice moves that could maim or kill.

I decided early in my training that in a choice between life and death, I was willing to risk doing both.

Moving my hand in front of his face, I raked my armored fingertips across his eyes, following it up with the hardest punch I could manage to his solar plexus. His eyes shut reflexively and his grip loosened. My punch made him gasp and sent him soaring away from me and downwards.

We had passed over Daniel's position in the forest and were now flying above the dark waters of Lake Michigan. Even though I didn't want to risk being grabbed from behind again, I swung back toward the shore. I didn't know about Tomahawk's outfit, but the

Rocket suit didn't work well in water.

The fact that Daniel hadn't tried to help, or even sent me a message saying why, had worried me. I flew over what had been Daniel's position a second time.

Nothing.

I decided to check behind me. Predictably, Tomahawk was flying towards me at full speed. He was no longer shouting, but he definitely still looked angry.

I turned left and dove towards the open area next to the forest with the picnic tables and the playground. It seemed like the best place for a fight. In early November it was too cold and too dark for any kids to be out.

It amazed me that Tomahawk had managed to stay enraged this whole time, never stopping to think or try any better tactics other than catching me and trying to hurt me.

Well, the mayor had probably messed with his mind too.

I landed in the picnic area and turned to face him.

Less than one hundred feet behind me, he dove and closed the distance, hand pulled back, ready to punch.

Well, at least I hadn't blinded him.

His fist blurred toward me. I grabbed his wrist with my right hand, twisting my body as I placed my left hand behind his bicep, throwing him toward the ground.

He hit hard, headfirst, slamming into the grass, then tumbling a few more feet.

I ran to keep up with him. For a moment he lay still on the grass, but then he pushed himself up and growled.

My instructor would have kicked him while he was getting up (or even before), but I didn't. I waited for him to find his footing. Then he charged me, hitting me in the chest with his right fist.

I gave him a sonic blast with my right arm, and punched him in the face with my left.

He stopped, dazed.

I punched him in the face again with my right, not holding anything back.

He fell backwards and hit the ground.

Stepping towards him, I studied his chest to make sure that he was still breathing.

He was.

Of course, I had no way to tell if he would end up with brain damage, but given how much it had taken to bring him to this point, I had reason to hope he would be tough enough to avoid it.

Still, I wasn't completely sure what to do with him. I didn't have Daniel around to put him under indefinitely so I had to choose between leaving him and carrying him with me.

I don't know how long I stood there, trying to think, but then I looked up. Over by the edge of the forest, I saw a red beam lance across the sky.

It had to be a laser. Didn't Future Knight carry some kind of rifle? And who was he shooting?

Screw Tomahawk, I decided.

I ran towards the woods.

CHAPTER TWELVE

My grandfather's property (and all of the neighbors' properties on his side of the block) ran up to the edge of Veterans Memorial Park. I followed the chain link fence that separated private property from city property.

I slowed down as I got closer to where I'd seen the beam. No point in running into somebody's line of fire.

Three houses away from my grandfather's house, I heard Daniel in my head.

Nick. Stop.

I did.

Me: *Where are you?*

Daniel: *In the trees with Haley and Marcus.*

Me: *Where's everyone else?*

Daniel: *Stuck to the street in front of the house.*

Me: *What?*

Daniel: *Future Knight has some kind of gun that can shoot sticky stuff.*

Me: *That Jaclyn or Travis can't break?*

Daniel: *Not without ripping the skin off their legs.*

Me: *Ugh. So, now what?*

Daniel: *We're at a bit of an impasse. We've got Red Bolt, but they can't get close without me slamming them back. I can't get them because Water is* literally *water right now and Future Knight has some kind of anti-telepathy thing in his suit.*

Me: *How'd the mayor get into his head then?*

Daniel: *I guess it must not be on all the time.*

Me: *Well, depending on how much power it draws, I could see that.*

I stood over the fence of the Nicholson's backyard. As a little kid, I had played with their son Jon whenever I'd been visiting my grandparents. I glanced toward the house, wondering what the family was doing.

The answer? Staring at me. I could see four figures crowding the patio door. Mr Nicholson held a phone to his ear.

Daniel: *Whatever we're going to do, we'll have to do it before the police come.*

Me: *Yeah. Can we bring everybody in to discuss things?*

Daniel: *I'd rather just bring in those that can move. I'm getting kind of tired—oh, wait a second. Let me deal with this.*

Two figures stepped past the brown, two-story house on the other side of Grandpa's. The first— seven feet of walking human-shaped water—splashed toward the woods. Behind it came Future Knight, laser rifle in his hands, a wide-barreled pistol hanging at his side that reminded me of a musket. His silver armor glistened in the porch light.

Suddenly Future Knight started running towards the woods, sweeping the rifle's red beam like a flashlight. Then, as if attracted by an unseen force, Future Knight and Water flew together with a splash, killing the beam. Just as quickly, they shot backwards, disappearing between the houses.

Me: *That was pretty cool.*

Daniel: *Yeah, but they're trying to wear me out. I've done that about three times now.*

Me: *Why didn't you just hold them in the air or something?*

Daniel: *The water elemental guy is strong enough to break my hold. I've got to keep contact brief. Anyway, here's everybody...*

I felt Haley's presence, along with a brief happiness and a strong sense of anxiety. Then Marcus came into the link. He radiated amusement.

Marcus: *Hey Nick, I caught Fire by myself. Turned into a ball—with only a mouth—and snuffed her like a candle.*

Me: *Good idea. Where's she now?*

Marcus: *Daniel put her to sleep and floated her into HQ.*

Haley (almost simultaneously): *We don't have time to talk. They've got everybody else.*

Daniel and I (simultaneously): *Right.*

Me: *Well, I might be able to take out Future Knight... and if you guys can distract Water for a while maybe Cassie can cut herself free or something.*

Daniel: *She already tried once and he just gooped*

her again while she was doing it. I had to talk her out of cutting off her foot.

Haley: *Are you serious?*

Daniel: *It would grow back.*

Marcus: *I can just see her hopping after Future Knight on one leg like that knight in Monty Python and the Holy Grail.*

Me: *Wow. It would be exactly like that.* It's just a flesh wound!

Daniel: *Um... guys? Not now.*

Haley: *Let's go—*

Future Knight's computer-generated and amplified voice cut off her thought. "Attention Heroes League! I've called the police and the Midwest Defenders for assistance. Surrender now and it'll be easier for you."

Daniel: *Yeah, right. My dad's practically in the Defenders right now. If they come, they won't be helping these guys.*

Haley: *Let's go.*

Me: *I'm going.*

The rockets roared.

Only as I passed over the house did I realize that we didn't have much of a plan. I was going to attack Future Knight and they were going to do *what* to the water elemental guy?

Too late to stop now.

In the streetlights' illumination, I could see Travis, Jaclyn, and Cassie standing in the street. All of them were up to their knees in white stuff that reminded me of shaving cream or possibly meringue.

Future Knight stood on the sidewalk, talking to Water.

Not good.

I didn't want to end up within arm's reach of either of them.

I dove toward Future Knight, taking the most direct route that allowed me to avoid power lines and low hanging branches, bobbing and weaving in the air to make it just a little harder if he tried to shoot me.

I hit him at more than two hundred miles per hour, grabbing him with both arms and dragging him across the sidewalk, sparks flying. Then I cut the power and we both hit the concrete, tumbling over each other more times than I could count. We finally ending up lying on our backs about ten feet apart.

We made it to our feet at almost the same time. He began to draw his wide barreled pistol.

I jumped for him, catching him before the gun's barrel had left the holster.

I aimed my jump for just behind where he stood, making him stumble backward when I landed. Grabbing his right arm with both hands, I moved my right hand toward the gun and we struggled for control, somehow firing the gun into midair.

A long line of a white substance shot out—kind of like of Silly String, only thicker and not green. I didn't see where it landed.

He punched me twice in the side. It didn't hurt much.

I got a grip on the gun, and pulled. I had it. Then I threw it away as hard as I could, paying no attention to where it went until I heard a crash.

I'd broken the picture window of a house a few doors down from my grandfather's. Great.

During my moment of distraction, he punched me again.

Deciding to end it quickly, I threw a punch at his face. The faceplate had been a weak point last time.

He caught my fist, twisted it, and sent me tumbling toward the ground.

He pulled his sword out from its sheath. The edge of the blade glowed white. I raised my arm and did what I should have done before: I aimed for the face and blasted him with the sonics.

Unfortunately, I didn't hit the faceplate. The sword shivered during the blast, but didn't break. Still, he stopped to check it, which was enough time for me to give the rockets some fuel and slide halfway across the street.

I flew upwards as he ran towards me, sword still in hand. On the off chance that it could actually pierce my armor, I kept some distance—but not so much distance that he would try the rifle on me.

I landed next to a flowerbed on a lawn about ten feet behind Future Knight. As he turned around, I activated the sonics on both arms, hoping that at least one of them would hit the faceplate.

This time I was rewarded with the familiar spider web of cracks. I only needed to punch through and knock him out. Unfortunately, he still held the sword as if he believed it could actually hurt me.

I decided not to chance the possibility. Grabbing a rock from the flowerbed, I threw it at him.

I missed. It flew past him, crashing through the garage door of the same house where I'd broken the window with the pistol.

"Still afraid of me?" he asked. "The first Rocket would have taken me out by now. Don't you feel like there's something wrong?"

He started walking toward me, but not with the same confidence he'd had earlier.

My second rock knocked him over.

I jumped forward as he fell, eyes on the sword and the arm that held it. I dove onto him, grabbing his arm and pushing it to the street. It felt like trying to pull the pistol out of his hand before, with one difference. This time I knew my suit was stronger than his.

Pulling his fingers apart, I grabbed the sword, the white glow disappearing as I handled it. I tossed it a short distance. It landed point first, clattering onto the road.

"Are you going to kill me now? Don't do it. You'll kill an innocent man. You don't know the whole story. You've been brainwashed by the—"

I punched through the faceplate, knocking him unconscious. How many other memories had the mayor modified? How many other people would I have to hurt?

Then I stood up.

Not far from where the others were stuck to the street, Daniel, Haley, and Marcus were fighting Water and doing about as well as they could while fighting a puddle.

Haley stood in the middle of the road, directly in front of the elemental. Marcus stood just behind her, having shifted into a vaguely demonic shape complete with bat wings and wide blades for hands. Daniel stood on the sidewalk.

Haley slashed Water's middle, leaving ripples but no wound. She ducked a punch then flipped backward, allowing Daniel to take a shot.

Daniel concentrated and a hole appeared in Water's

chest, water splashing out on both sides, only to splash back in and fill the hole.

Travis began to shout, "Good one," as the hole appeared, but stopped as everything came back together.

Cassie shouted, "Nice try!"

Daniel frowned.

I ran down the street toward them, trying to think of what exactly I was going to do when I got there.

The elemental must have interpreted my run as the beginning of an attack. He jumped into the air (over Jaclyn who tried to grab his legs), landed directly in front of me, and hit me with a large liquid fist.

I fell backwards, smacking the street with my butt.

He pulled his arm back for another blow, but never hit me.

With a flap of his wings, Marcus landed behind him and chopped off his arm near the shoulder. It lost its shape as it fell, splashing on the street.

Water began to turn around.

Marcus chopped off his other arm.

The elemental stopped moving, turning into a shapeless watery blob, reabsorbing the liquid that had been cut off.

Then it flowed into the nearest storm drain.

"Got him on the run," Marcus said, changing into a snake-like shape even as he dove after him.

"Marcus!" Haley ran to the storm drain and peered through the grate. "They're gone."

"I'm sure Marcus will be okay," I said, pushing myself up.

"I hope so," she said. "I could barely hurt it at all."

From the street, Travis shouted, "Hey, Daniel!

Future Knight's got to know how to get us out of this crap. Can you deep scan him?"

*   *   *

Two minutes later we'd gotten everybody out. Daniel had floated Future Knight's pistol out of the living room of the house I'd thrown it into. Then he'd flown off to collect Tomahawk's body.

The pistol turned out to have another setting that dissolved the stuff. A quick spray and the mounds of coiled white strings became pockmarked. Then the little pocks turned to visible holes. The holes grew until only little rings of white blobs remained.

"I feel heroic," Jaclyn said as the last of it disappeared. "I got to stand around and watch everyone else fight."

"How did you get caught?" I let the pistol fall to my side.

"I knocked out Red Bolt again, but Future Knight got me from behind. Yeah, I know, I did get to do *something*, but after that I was useless."

"Travis and I were both trying to fight Water," Cassie said. "Did you see how fast he was? I think he broke five of my ribs in one punch. I was going to try my sword on him but then Future Knight shot us from behind, too."

Travis had a black eye. "Who would think we'd get hurt fighting a walking pond?" He stopped, closed his eyes for a moment, and sniffed the air. "We'd better get out of here before the police come. I've been hearing sirens in the distance the whole time. In fact—hey, what's that?"

"It sounds like a truck," Haley said. "Wait... No, not quite. They're making it a little harder to hear."

She gestured toward a group of people gathering on one of the lawns.

I, of course, couldn't hear the people or any other noise.

"Do you have a direction?" I asked. "I could fly that way and look around."

Haley put her finger to her lips. "Shh."

I walked a short distance away and tuned the radio inside my helmet to the police band.

Haley looked at me and made a face.

"Sorry." I turned it down as low as I could.

"*(crackle)* ...the important thing is to protect Mayor Bouman. Nothing else matters. They're after him... *(crackle)* ...I'm at the house now. The fire's out. No sign of the Hangmen. When did you say the Guard would be here?"

The sound of a massive engine overwhelmed everything else. I recognized the sound even before it came around the corner.

The Larrymobile.

Well, that was my name for it. He called it the Rhinomobile. I'd never quite decided whether it was a modified tank or a dump truck.

If you were to imagine a huge lump of gray metal on treads with a couple of turrets, you'd basically have the Larrymobile. It contained sleeping quarters, a workroom for fixing his armor, and space for a lot of fuel, equipment, and ammunition.

Fuel and ammunition made a *great* combination.

The door opened and Larry jumped out in the Rhino suit, bulky gray armor that matched his ride.

"Hey, kids! I got here as soon as I could. I was in Lansing on business when the League distress call started going and I was like, 'Damn, never thought I'd see that again,' so I suited up. I'd have been here faster but I had to off-road to get past the National Guard."

CHAPTER THIRTEEN

Legion HQ was full. Three of the four Elementals plus Future Knight, Red Bolt, and Tomahawk were sleeping on the floor. All of the new League (except for Vaughn and Marcus) plus Jaclyn's grandfather, Larry, and Mindstryke were seated at the main table.

Mindstryke had shown up just after we'd all sat down. He looked tired.

"I had to settle my dad down. He thought it was 1965 and the original League was still fighting Red Lightning. I didn't know he still had one." He held a ring in his hand. The gem flickered.

"How's Grandpa?" Daniel asked.

"Okay, for now. He's with Mom."

Daniel looked down at the table.

Jaclyn's grandfather said, "I'm sorry."

Mindstryke shrugged. "There's nothing anyone can do about it. Let's just get on with this."

Jaclyn's grandfather nodded. "Alright. As I see it, we've got six people with their brains modified. Once we capture Mayor Bouman, any decent telepath should be able to clear the Rocket. Am I right, Mindstryke?"

Daniel's dad nodded.

"Good. So what's it like out there?"

"Chock-full of tanks and troops," Larry said.

"I didn't go past the tanks," Mindstryke said, "but the whole block around Bouman's house is crawling with cops."

"While you all were out," Jaclyn's grandfather said, "I was listening to the radio. From what I can tell, the mayor called in the police, the National Guard, and the Feds around the time he sent out these clowns." He waved in the direction of the supers sleeping on our carpet.

"He can't do that, can he? I didn't think a mayor could just call the National Guard or the Feds in," I said.

"He can't," Mindstryke said, "but he's had every opportunity to touch the minds of people who can."

"What I'm thinking," Jaclyn's grandfather said, "is that stealth would be best. Travis and Haley, you both have Chuck's abilities, correct?"

Travis said, "Yes, sir," while Haley said, "Right," in a chirpy voice that seemed out of place.

"Good. Then I think the two of them should sneak in, knock him out, and leave."

"Unless the mayor senses them and bores straight into their heads," Daniel said.

"That's the hole in the plan," Jaclyn's grandfather

said, amused.

That you could drive a truck through, Daniel sent to me.

In both of our minds, Daniel's dad said: Listen.

"Since stealth isn't an option," Jaclyn's grandfather said, straightening in his chair, "we'll have to take the direct route. Larry, could you take the Rhinomobile straight up to the door?"

Larry laughed. "I could drive it into the living room."

"That's not what I want you to do. I want you to drive straight up to the house and distract the police and the Guard. Fight them if you have to. Everyone who can't fly will be with you.

"Everyone who *can* fly will be going in through the second floor. Nick, you'll want to hang back while Daniel and his dad subdue the mayor. Someone will need to be watching for aerial attacks."

"Is that likely?" I asked.

"Anything's possible," he said. "The Hangmen are in town. They've already been beaten back from the mayor's house once today. When the Rhinomobile breaks through, it'll be a race between you and Vengeance's Hangmen. Be there first."

He moved his head to face everyone at the table, regarding us with his near-sightless eyes.

"One more thing: you may kill somebody today. We don't want you to, but sometimes it's unavoidable. We won't think anything less of you for it."

"No. It can be avoided," Daniel's dad said. "Always. And it should be. Whatever we might think, in the public's opinion you'll have killed an innocent man."

"Not in my experience," Jaclyn's grandfather said

Daniel's dad stood up. "We need to talk through a few things privately. Nick, is the lab unlocked?"

* * *

"Are you getting anything?" I asked Daniel.

We stood about twenty feet away from the main table, where everyone else was talking quietly.

"Almost," Daniel said. "I'll pull you in when I've got it."

The grownups hadn't been gone for long.

My vision blurred. Superimposed upon the League HQ's main room, I saw the lab with its collection of machines and spare Rocket suit parts. Larry, helmet off, was fiddling with the controls of one of Grandpa's more advanced fabrication machines. Mindstryke and C were facing each other next to the counter on the left side of the room.

I'd left a lot of tools and a spare right arm on the counter while doing maintenance on the suit earlier. I hoped they wouldn't touch anything.

"—I don't like this plan at all," Daniel's dad said. "You don't tell teenagers that it's okay to kill people. You don't send them up against trained soldiers. This isn't the League, remember."

Jaclyn's grandfather leaned against the counter. His arm pushed a wrench into the soldering iron. They slid together with a series of clinking noises.

"Whoops." He pulled his arm back. "If the boy's grandfather were alive, I'd have never heard the end of that."

The tools floated back to almost the same position they'd been in.

"Thank you." Jaclyn's grandfather said. Then: "Do

you remember what your father was doing at their age?"

"Yes—"

"He was lying about his age so the army would take him."

"We're not at war," Daniel's dad argued.

"We're always at war. The venue changes."

"I've heard that line before. It makes it far too easy to justify—"

"It's a good line, David. It's true."

"There's a difference between trying to stop Hitler and whatever's going on here. Equating the two allowed you guys to set up things like the mind block. I spent my childhood with half of my friends practically lobotomized, and you didn't even stop when they got married. You had my dad block their spouses, too."

Jaclyn's grandfather barely raised his voice in response. "I didn't do it. The League did it. *We* did it, and it's the only reason you're even around to complain. We weren't fighting good men. We were fighting killers, men who go after wives and children. The block meant our kids never noticed our hours, our strange disappearances, or any hints about what we were. It freed them to live *normal* lives. It freed us from worrying about them. It freed you to experiment with your powers and not worry if your friends would ask questions."

"I'd have rather had the questions."

"Not at the expense of your life. Or theirs."

Daniel's dad stood quietly. "Let's get back to the main topic," he said after a moment.

Then he turned toward us, concentrating. The room disappeared, leaving the two of us standing next to each other in HQ's main room.

"I didn't know he could do that," Daniel said.

*   *   *

The night felt colder than before. Daniel, his father and I stood in the forest. Clouds covered the stars. I wondered whether it would snow.

Larry and the rest would be arriving at the mayor's soon.

"So," Daniel's dad said, "the two of you were witnesses to our little disagreement. It's okay. I'm not angry."

"I shouldn't have been," Daniel said.

"I'm glad you know it. Live it next time."

A few seconds passed. A crow cawed.

"I can't believe it," he said. "More than thirty years later, C still makes me feel like I'm tagging along with my dad." Then he checked his watch. "Nine o'clock. Let's go."

We rose into the air, flying above the treetops, and crossing the blocks of residential houses on the outside of the city. The mayor's house stood near the top of a hill on the edge of downtown, near a few other Victorian houses built by the city's leading families of the period.

Tonight, the mayor's house stood out.

Soldiers stood on the lawn. Police cars, trucks and two tanks were on the street. They'd also blocked off the roads surrounding the house. Around the corner was a "box," one of the bulky trucks specifically designed for holding supers. I didn't know much about military tactics, but it didn't look quite right to me. What exactly did they plan to do with the tanks?

A block away, I heard Mindstryke's voice in my

head.

Let's land and talk.

We landed on the street in front of a cluster of old Victorian houses. I hoped we weren't too obvious.

"It seems like overkill," I said. "Calling in the National Guard and all of these police for us? It's not as if they know you and the Rhino are involved."

"Blame Vengeance," Daniel's dad said. "He and the Hangmen attacked the second the Elementals left. They're taking no chances."

"How did they fight him off?" I asked.

From what I could see through the mask, Daniel's dad looked thoughtful. "I don't know."

Next to me, Daniel seemed to be spacing out. Concentrating would be the kinder way to put it. His eyes pointed at nothing, his mouth hung partly open.

"Hey," Daniel said, "I've found Vaughn. Marcus, too. Actually, they found each other. I've told them where we are."

Moments later, they stepped out from behind the nearest house and into the porch light. Marcus looked almost like himself except for with feathered wings. Also, though I hadn't noticed it earlier, he was wearing a costume, and had been all night. Gray like Travis and Haley's, his costume flashed different shades of green when he moved. On the left side of his chest were the words "The Shift."

Vaughn limped next to him, his left arm hanging in a way that seemed off. Blood spattered the lower half of his face. A slit the width of a knife blade exposed skin and dried blood on the right side of his neck. To judge from the amount of dried blood on his costume, it surprised me that there could be any left inside him.

"What happened to you?" I asked.

"Vengeance," he said. "It looks worse than it is. He really did want to speak to me, but I didn't want to speak to him. Trouble was, the Hangmen don't take no for an answer."

"That's their reputation," I said.

"I heard the distress call," Vaughn said, "and I hauled ass toward HQ, except one of them managed to catch me with a noose—"

"They really use nooses?" Daniel said. "I thought they were just there for show."

"They really use them," Daniel's dad confirmed. He didn't sound happy.

"Anyway," Vaughn said, "they pulled me out of the air and they told me to wait—except I zapped one of them. Then the other two beat me unconscious and tied me up."

"Is that when you got stabbed?" I asked.

"No," Vaughn said. "Vengeance did that. Did you ever notice that big knife on this belt? I swear it's alive."

"Alive?" I asked. "You mean it talks or something?"

"No," he said. "Alive like Stormbringer in Moorcock's Elric series. You know, as in 'Blood and souls for Lord Arioch'?"

"I never read that one," I said.

"I'm lying on the ground, barely conscious," Vaughn said, "and suddenly Vengeance is right there, and, he says something like 'let's see if you're anything like the original Red Lightning,' and I'm trying to say I'm the Storm King, but there's this burning pain in my neck, and I'm screaming, and he's holding my mouth shut, and I can feel a presence and *it's judging me.*

"Everything — and I mean *really* everything —

I've ever done is swimming before my eyes. Drugs and school and fights with my parents. All of it. Finally it ends and he pulls out the knife, tells me I'm innocent and leaves me there."

"You're innocent?" I said. "What would he have done if he found you guilty? Killed you?"

Daniel's dad said, "Exactly. He'd have left him to die. The cut's completely healed, right?"

Vaughn said, "Yeah."

"If you'd been guilty," Daniel's dad said, "you'd have bled, and it wouldn't have stopped."

A police car drove down the street, but it passed us without stopping or turning on the sirens.

"They didn't see us," Daniel's dad said, "but we'd better get going anyway." Gesturing to Marcus, he said, "Could you take Vaughn back to HQ?"

Vaughn said, "I'm not going back," at almost the same time Marcus said, "Why should I take him back?"

Daniel's dad sighed. "We don't have time to argue about it. Come along, but stay outside when we go in. The last thing we need is the mayor rearranging your heads."

We took to the air.

I assumed that Daniel's dad would want us to stay low, but I was wrong. He led us up a couple hundred feet and had us hover.

I thought about pointing out that even though it was nighttime, we could still be seen, but then I saw the Rhinomobile moving up the hill, picking up speed.

The police had blocked off St John's Avenue with two police cars.

The Rhinomobile flattened them, while the officers who had been standing behind the cars dove for the sidewalk. Then it roared straight up the road toward the mayor's house.

Soldiers pulled out their rifles while one of the tanks rolled (slowly and somewhat jerkily) into the middle of the street. The Rhinomobile swung to the left and moved around it with ease.

A figure leapt from the top of the Rhinomobile, somersaulted a few times and pulled out a sword. The blade shone under the streetlights. Cassie charged the tank and cut the treads on one side before moving to the other.

The Rhinomobile crossed the lawn, crushing a lamp and shattering the gazebo, before stopping by the front door.

Pipes popped out of the ugly gray vehicle and black smoke billowed out on all sides, turning the front yard into a sea of fog.

Smoke. Larry never stops tinkering with that thing, Daniel's dad thought at us. *Let's move in.*

We descended toward the house. Daniel and his father floated down with no visible means of support as if they were riding an invisible elevator. The wind held Vaughn in the air, blowing his hair wildly as he rode it down. Marcus circled down, gliding like a hawk. I followed Daniel, my rocket pack set to give slightly less force than it would take to hover.

Okay, Daniel's dad thought at us, *Bouman's in the basement with his wife and kids. He's armed with some kind of gun, probably equipment confiscated by the police. I have no idea what it can do, so be careful, and keep the violence to a minimum. If we can manage to capture Bouman without beating him unconscious in front of his family, I'll be happy.*

A burst of thought from Daniel: *We're going to be attacked shortly... um... now.*

Men and women rose from below and surrounded us, but they didn't attack.

I didn't count how many, but it couldn't have been more than ten. About half of them wore dark blue Rocket suits.

Seriously.

When my grandfather left the army, he'd left behind the suits he'd used during World War II. The government had paid for them, right? They'd left them alone for a while, but then reverse-engineered them in the 1980's. Despite their efforts to update the design, Grandpa estimated the government version had to be twenty years behind his—and not just in terms of technology.

Most supers, hero or villain, made an effort to wear designs that looked inspiring. The government agents wore navy blue costumes (whether Rocket suits or not) with "FBI" written in big white letters across the chest.

I found it interesting to observe what they'd updated and what they'd kept from Grandpa's design. For example, back in the war, the Rocket suit hadn't had sonics, but it *had* had mountings to attach weapons under the arms. These suits had mountings (mostly used them for guns), but lacked the amplifier system that Grandpa had put into the original suit. Also, to judge from the shape of the helmets, they probably had night vision and better communication systems.

If they had radar, I'd be jealous.

On the bright side, the way things were going, we'd probably end up with at least one wrecked suit by the end of the night.

I just hoped it wouldn't be mine. They probably wouldn't miss a few pieces from one of their suits. The helmet for sure, maybe an arm to check if they also had control buttons in the palm.

Just as I was about to edge toward them (the leg joints were an interesting departure from Grandpa's design), their leader started to speak.

She was a forty-something woman with a brush cut. She wasn't wearing a Rocket suit, only the armored bodysuit common to government supers.

"Don't move! FBI!"

Easily cutting through the shouting below us, her voice included a humanly impossible cascade of tones, ranging from a deep bass to soprano.

"Mindstryke, tell the Rhino to call off his attack."

"Sorry, Agent Brown, but hell no. Bouman down there has telepathic hooks into too many minds. The sooner we deal with it, the better."

To the rest of us he sent: *When I give the word, drop and get into the house. I'll handle them.*

Agent Brown said, "Can you support that? I've got orders to bring in anyone threatening Bouman."

"I've got six unconscious heroes who have something wrong with their heads, but I don't have time for you to independently verify it."

Drop.

We dropped. They didn't follow.

I don't know whether Daniel's dad stopped them, or whether they were scared and didn't even try to get around him.

Aside from being the son of a member of the Heroes League, Daniel's dad was definitely on the A-list on his own merits. Daniel's telekinetic output reached one thousand pounds of force on a good day. His dad's output could be rated in tons—double digit tons.

I may have heard automatic weapons fire from above me as I went down, but if I did, it ended quickly.

Still, Mr Cohen didn't follow us down.

Daniel shattered one of the windows in the tower on the far end of the house. We all climbed inside.

Books lined the walls, almost all of them about law, government and public policy. The desk in the middle of the room displayed pictures of the mayor's wife and children. The screensaver of the laptop on desk showed even more pictures—mostly beach scenes.

"The mayor's in the basement," Daniel said. "The Rocket and I had better go."

"What are we supposed to do?" Vaughn turned toward him. "Stay here and surf the internet?"

"I don't know," Daniel said. "Just don't come down. Bouman's a telepath. If you get in range, we could end up fighting you."

"Then why is Nick going down? He's not a telepath."

"Use his codename," Daniel said. "Anyway, the Rocket's got protection."

"I thought you were going to fight the mayor, not have sex with him," Vaughn said.

"Oh, *funny*," Daniel said.

Marcus laughed. "Guys, guys, let's keep moving. Mystic, just tell us when you think we're too close. We'll stop, right uh... what are you calling yourself again?

"It was on the news," Vaughn said, sounding irritated. When no one else said anything, he muttered, "Call me Storm King."

"I'm 'The Shift'," Marcus said. "As in third shift. Or shape shift."

From outside came several bursts of automatic weapons fire.

"Let's go," I said.

*　*　*

Walking through the house seemed to take forever. We had to go down three stories before we reached the first floor.

We couldn't see out of the windows because the smoke reached higher than our heads. Wisps of it came through the edges of the windowsill and from underneath the front door.

From what I could tell, the mayor lived very well. I couldn't really tell expensive decorations from cheap, but the house looked expensive. It had larger rooms than I would have expected in an older house, but then again it was an old mansion. The wooden floors showed no signs of wear and the furniture was heavy on wood and leather. Paintings hung on the walls, mostly depicting local scenes—the old lighthouse in Grand Lake's harbor, Hardwick House, City Hall, and the city skyline.

Behind the kitchen, we found the stairway to the basement.

"You'll want to stay back," Daniel advised Marcus and Vaughn. "He'll be able to sense you if you get much closer."

"Are you sure he doesn't sense us now?" Vaughn asked.

"Not completely," Daniel said. He peered at Vaughn. "At least he's not in your head. If you feel anything, get out of here."

"Right," Marcus said, grinning. "If I suddenly start

thinking the mayor's a nice guy, I'll try to remember that I'm wrong."

I heard a splash.

A human-shaped mass of water stepped out of the kitchen sink.

"Whoa," I said and asked Marcus, "Weren't you going after him?"

"I lost him," Marcus said. "In a sewer, all water looks the same."

The Elemental began to walk toward us.

Marcus stepped toward him and changed. Blades sprouted from his shoulders, chest, legs and hands.

"You're called Water, right?" Marcus said. "You and I, we both know what's going to happen next, don't we?"

His fingers lengthened into long, wide blades.

The Elemental hesitated and then stepped forward, readying his right hand for a punch.

Marcus moved faster than I could see. Using both arms to cut, he chopped through the right leg and the chest simultaneously. The body fell apart with a splash and a gurgling scream, turning into a big puddle in the middle of the kitchen.

"Snicker-snack," Marcus muttered.

The water reformed into a blond haired college-aged guy, who from his looks could have been a model. He took a long, gasping breath. "Oh my god, that hurt." He blinked. "You're the Heroes League, right? Until just a second ago, I thought you guys were mind controlled by terrorists."

"Part of the League," I said.

Almost simultaneously, Daniel said, "The mayor's a telepath. He planted that idea in your head, and I've just removed it."

He stood up, and I finally registered that he was wearing ancient Greek clothes like the rest of his team. "That bastard. We've been protecting the guy for a few weeks now, ever since all that shit about you guys hit the news."

He eyed Vaughn. "You're what? The new Red Lightning?"

"I call myself Storm King." Vaughn sounded irritated.

"So it was all fake? The news reports? Everything?"

"I wouldn't say fake," I said. "I really did punch the mayor, but he was trying to break into my mind at the time. So they weren't fake so much as... selective."

"Jerks," Vaughn said.

Water turned toward me (as if I had any kind of authority). "What happened to the rest of my team?"

"They're sleeping," I said. "The Mystic left them back at our headquarters. I don't think that any are badly hurt."

"Good. Then let's go downstairs and get this guy."

"It's just going to have to be the Mystic and me—" I began.

"Once I change, I'm immune," he said.

"He's right," Daniel said. "A telepath's got to catch him in his normal form while he's vulnerable."

"Uh... how about changing right now?" I said.

His body bulged, grew, then turned transparent. Beneath him, the wooden floor creaked and sagged. He began walking toward door to the basement.

"Wait," Vaughn said, "what are we supposed to be doing while you're down there?"

"I don't know," I said. "Mindstryke and C said we'd

probably have to race Vengeance to get to the mayor first. So, stop him, I guess."

"Oh yeah," Vaughn said, "because I did so well the first time."

Marcus said, "Don't worry about us, go get the mayor."

Daniel and I followed the avatar of the element of water through the door and down the stairs. We stepped into a room half the size of the first floor.

During the 1960's, some prior occupant of the house had finished the basement. Wooden paneling covered the walls. A bar stood in the far corner of the room, complete with stools.

On the floor in front of the bar, two boys moved Thomas the Tank Engine around a circle of tracks on the white carpet. Neither was older than seven.

A tall woman with long brown hair grabbed their hands and pulled them away from the toys. "I told you to come here," she said, dragging them to the wall next to her.

The taller one waved toward Water and shouted, "Hi," straining against his mother's grip to run across the room.

Water said, "Hi, Alex."

Mayor Bouman stood next to the bar, his hand on a lumpy object I didn't recognize.

"Why are you leading them here? Attack them!" He pulled the lumpy object off the bar. It could only be described as a raygun. I'd seen villains from the 50's holding ones like it in my grandfather's files and old issues of Double V.

The avatar of the element of water said, "You *douchebag*."

White light burst from the gun.

The beam struck the floor in front of us and the carpet caught fire. Water slid forward and became a puddle, smothering it. Then he reverted into human-shaped water.

"Come any closer to me or my family and I'll blast you," Bouman said.

"Oh, come on," Daniel said. "This has nothing to do with your family. That has got to be one of the stupidest rationalizations I have ever heard. You've been manipulating people for ages and now you're afraid to face the music. That's the only reason you're holding the gun."

I didn't know what negotiating tactics police forces taught their members for dealing with armed suspects, but I imagined that throwing the person's motives in their face wasn't one of them.

To Daniel's credit, at least he didn't move any closer.

Outside I heard a muffled explosion and then weapon fire.

The smaller of the two boys started crying. His mother pulled him closer.

"Manipulating people? I manipulated people into a higher millage for the schools and more money for street repair. I manipulated people into providing food for lower income students. What have you done?"

Mayor Bouman seemed to forget about the gun and it drooped as he talked.

Daniel didn't say anything. His face wore a blank expression

"Mayor," Water said, "give it up, guy. It's over. You can't get into our heads, and you're never going to blow away all three of us."

Bouman then remembered the gun. He pointed it at Daniel, but failed to pull the trigger.

It wasn't that he didn't try. He did, but his finger wouldn't move. He pulled it away from the trigger, bent it without a problem. Then put it back against the trigger of the gun.

Got him, Daniel sent to me. *He didn't realize until just now that I'd passed through his shield. Not that it was much of a shield.*

Mayor Bouman dropped the gun and stared at Daniel.

Then he grabbed the taller of his sons' arm and told his wife, "Sheryl, go!"

A hallway on the right side of the room ran even deeper into the basement.

He pulled the taller boy along while his wife carried the other. She opened the door, fumbled for the light switch, and ran through. Mayor Bouman followed her.

Almost.

Daniel said, "No."

The mayor froze in place.

Daniel said, "I'm sorry, Alex," and the boy floated through the door, landing next his mother. It shut behind him.

From behind the door came the boy's voice, "Mom! Daddy's back there!"

"Daddy will take care of himself. Come on."

When their voices faded away, Daniel said, "Well, now what do we do with him?"

"My team always turned them in to the police," Water said.

"It's nice when the police are on your side," I said. "Hey Mystic, didn't your dad have a plan?"

"Probably," Daniel said, "but he's not in range right now. We should just take the guy away, but I'd like to find out something first."

I'm going into his head to find out who's behind all this. It'll just take a second, Daniel said. *Do you want to come along?*

I did.

I have never known how to explain what it feels like to enter somebody else's mind. Maybe it would be easier if I could do it myself, but it was always filtered through Daniel, so whatever I felt was his interpretation.

In this case, I felt despair surround me, small voices muttering on the edges of my consciousness. "It's over. They'll know everything."

Daniel sorted through forty years of another man's memories. I saw flashes of Bouman's childhood—camping trips, days at the beach, a high school valedictorian speech...

He lost his first run to be mayor, ending twenty thousand dollars in debt. That night, he found himself alone in the hotel conference room he'd rented for the victory party. He didn't know the man talking to him, but I did. I'd seen his face in the information the FBI had sent me—Martin Magnus.

Magnus couldn't have been more than five and a half feet tall, and looked about thirty even though the government's documentation said he had to be at least fifty. He wore a blue suit.

"A plague on the fools," Magnus said. "People want to be ruled. With our help, you could learn to rule them."

This looks interesting, Daniel thought, *but we don't*

have time to follow it all the way through. I'm going to make him free associate.

Scattered memories of passing years—Martin Magnus conducting a ceremony in a dark room, and handing Bouman a cup. Letters and couriers appearing in the dead of night carrying secret messages, using an expanding telepathic awareness to enter the mind of one official after another, the mayor's inspection of a gun wielding assassin's now irreparably damaged mind...

A recent memory—a red-haired man in a black suit and sunglasses sat in the mayor's study upstairs. I could feel a mixture of anticipation and fear as the mayor looked across the desk.

"You haven't heard anything from Magnus?" the man said.

"Not since he left the Cabal, or I'd have reported it."

"He has wanted to know how the League made Red Lightning's powers permanent for years."

"Don't we all," the mayor said.

"We've got leads. During the Chicago operation, we found some interesting things in Magnus' offices. They managed to get Red Lightning's grandson to pass on some stuff he owned and it's authentic. It includes some revised formulas for the drink of the gods which improve on the original. Think about that for a second."

"That should cause a shake-up. Senior leadership has always said it couldn't be done."

"Almost all of the senior leadership is more than a thousand years old. They're long overdue for a surprise. We've also got pictures of the kid's friends, who have to be other League grandchildren. We don't know their names yet, but that's your job. Find out who they are and do anything you have to do to find the League's records."

"Are you talking about killing them?"

"I'm saying do whatever works."

The mayor sat in the study for an hour after the man left. Could he justify it? They were only kids. Kids with freakish abilities, but kids nonetheless.

On the other hand, if he failed (or refused) his own boys would grow up without a father. Besides, he could do so much more good if his powers were permanent. The needs of the city outweighed the needs of the few.

Daniel jerked us out of the mayor's head and back into reality.

The mayor's body tumbled to the floor.

"We could be in there for hours," Daniel said. "There's just too much to go through."

"Couldn't you record his memories or something? Then you could carry it along." I asked.

"That's not recommended," Daniel said. "Take too much into your brain and you end up with a fused personality—or worse, a kind of possession."

While we'd been distracted, Water had changed back to normal form. He leaned over the mayor. "Yeah, one of this guy is enough. If you're planning on getting him out of here, we should go soon. It's getting worse out there."

Now that he'd said it, I realized that he was right. I heard more shouting, machine guns, police sirens, and shattering glass than I had earlier.

"Where's the mayor's family?" I asked.

"Out the window on the far end of the basement," Water said. "I heard them while you guys were poking around inside."

"I've got him," Daniel said. "Let's get out of here."

The mayor floated into the air, flattening out as if he were on a bed, and moved up the stairs. We followed him.

I found myself walking behind Water. "With all the bullets flying around, I'm surprised you changed back."

"I get sick of it," he said. "There's a lot to like, but it's nice to breathe sometimes. Besides, I can change quickly."

We walked into the kitchen. Marcus was standing next to the stainless steel refrigerator. "You got him? Great. We've got to get out of here. I think I heard someone upstairs."

"I still think you're hearing things," Vaughn said. He stood next to the granite counter, using his right hand to spread mayonnaise on wheat bread. He was using his left hand to steady the mayo jar—but didn't seem to put much force into it. It probably still hurt.

"You're making a sandwich?" I said.

"I didn't have supper," Vaughn said. He put two slices of roast beef and a slice of Swiss cheese on the bread.

"I didn't take anything," Marcus said, "but they've got completely untouched shrimp Pad Thai and some kind of coconut milk based curry in the fridge. The kind with beef, green curry paste and those small eggplants?"

I hadn't had supper either. My stomach growled.

We really needed to get out of there. Maybe we could get pizza or hit the Chinese buffet down on Washington Avenue later.

"Could you guys stop thinking about food?" Daniel said. "Between that and all the people outside, I can barely sense—crap—"

He stared up at the ceiling as boards, plaster, and the chandelier rained down on the dining room table.

Vengeance jumped through the hole, using the edge to swing over the debris, and landed to the side of the table.

The Hangmen stumbled through after him, three hooded men with grayish skin. They landed in a clump, breaking the table. A jagged sliver of wood punctured the leg of one of them. It didn't bleed and the Hangman didn't seem overly concerned. He just pulled it out.

The walking dead are like that, I guess.

According to Double V, the Hangmen were dead people given the chance to live a second time. I didn't remember the article being clear as to why.

I understood how the writer might have missed that detail. The Hangmen didn't seem particularly talkative. In fact, they didn't say anything at all as they got off the remains of the table and onto the now heavily scratched wooden floor.

Vengeance stood in front of them, knife hanging from his belt, rifle on his back.

"Time to hand him over, kids," he said. "You did some nice work grabbing him, but this is too big for you."

Vaughn put down the sandwich he'd been about to eat, moving his hands behind the counter and out of sight—for Vengeance at least.

Sparks ran across both hands, but not any higher.

"How big is it?" Vaughn asked.

"Hey, it's Red Lightning Jr," Vengeance said. "No hard feelings about the stabbing. I had to make sure. But back to your question, hanging on to that man is like holding dynamite."

"Not too big for the Rhino and Mindstryke," Daniel said. "We're not acting alone."

Vengeance laughed. "I've been on this for weeks now. Trust me, you can't even imagine how big this is and it's not going to be solved by beer or mind reading."

He stepped forward.

Behind him, the Hangmen had spread out. They stood in a line behind Vengeance, each of the three holding a noose. Another couple feet and they would be standing in the kitchen.

"The Rhino's done a lot more than beer commercials," I said.

Ignoring me, he said, "Time's a wasting. Hand him over."

"What are you going to do with him?" I said.

"He's going to stab him," Daniel said. "If it judges the mayor unworthy, the knife will absorb his essence and kill him."

Next to me, Water said, "He'd deserve it after what he did to us. Don't look at me like that. He does."

"He deserves the judicial system," Daniel said. "Everyone does."

"So he can hire a lawyer and get off?" Vengeance said. "The law never touches his kind. Best thing you can do is hand them over to a judge that only wants justice."

Vengeance took another step forward. Behind him, the Hangmen moved a step closer to the entrance of the kitchen.

Now Vengeance stood across the counter from Vaughn, about ten feet in front of where Water, Marcus and I stood next to the refrigerator. Daniel and the still-floating mayor were on the other side of the kitchen, next to a small table.

It struck me that I couldn't hear anything happening outside.

He turned toward Daniel. "I've heard a lot of crap about the system over the years, but if it worked, we wouldn't be here. The first League went on and on about making the system work, but how'd they start? They burned down some mobster's warehouse and they weren't nice about it. It was war. They didn't go soft till they killed one of their own. Fucking fools. If they'd killed him earlier, that would have saved some lives. Me, I'd have opened him up the second I knew."

Daniel began, "I don't believe you. If there's one thing that came out of Red Lightning, it ought to be that we need rules of conduct—"

Vaughn interrupted him. "Vengeance," he said. "Hey, dude."

He pulled his hands out from below the counter. I could barely see his skin beneath the electricity arcing between them.

Vengeance began to move, but I didn't see where because of the lightning strike. The thunderclap rattled the windows—the ones that hadn't been shattered, anyway.

During the blast, I could only see white, so it took me a moment to realize that Vaughn had missed. The strike had blackened the wall, broken two windows, and set the drapes on fire.

As my eyes adjusted to normal light, Vengeance leaped off the floor toward Daniel, landing on him. Daniel fell backwards, hitting the wall.

The Hangmen closed the gap with more speed than

I would have expected. One jumped over the counter to struggle with Vaughn, both of them falling to the floor while bright arcs of electricity lit up half of the room. Then came a cracking noise and the electricity stopped.

The remaining two Hangmen went for Marcus, Water and I, running toward us, throwing their nooses ahead.

The rope caught Marcus mid-shift into a kind of panther. The noose snaked through the air, the rope end growing in length while the noose constricting around his neck. He didn't fight it. He just fell, his limbs unmoving.

The other noose widened, and before I could do anything, it closed around my neck. I couldn't feel it, of course. It only touched my armor.

In all likelihood, that had to be the reason I could still move.

The Hangman who had caught Marcus swung the rope end of the noose toward Water. He froze as it touched his neck, the rope tying itself into a second noose. However quickly he'd thought he could change, Water ended up in human form.

They'd taken us all out.

Well, all of us except me, but I'd decided to pretend otherwise. With any luck I'd get some useful information and maybe the chance to surprise them.

Out of the corner of my eye, I saw Vengeance pull himself up off Daniel and turn towards the Hangmen.

"Kids," he sighed. "Do you suppose any of their parents know what they're doing? Anyway, will one of you boys put out the fire? I gotta give this man the test before we're interrupted."

Behind Vengeance, the fire on the drapes continued to burn. A line of flame ran up the left side of one drape, the smoke rising toward the ceiling.

A fire alarm began to beep.

Vengeance pulled his knife out of its sheath.

I stopped pretending.

Grabbing the rope, I yanked the Hangman toward me, punching him in the face.

It did nothing.

He grabbed my arm and punched me back before I had the time to react. It didn't hurt.

Instead of trying to pull my arm away, I stepped toward him, grabbed his belt with my left hand and pulled him into the air above my head. Then I threw him as hard as I could.

He flew out the entrance to the kitchen into the dining room, hitting the wall and smashing the frame of a picture of a clipper ship, finally falling to the floor. The picture fell on top of him, revealing cracks and broken plaster on the wall behind where it had been hung.

I would have worried about hurting him had he not been already dead. Seriously, what more could I do?

Unfortunately, the other two Hangmen decided to take advantage of my distraction. The one who'd used his noose on Marcus and Water dove for my chest while the one who'd had taken out Vaughn ran toward me, hitting me with his shoulder.

Without the suit, I would have surely dislocated something, or at the very least ended up on the floor with the two of them on top of me.

With the suit, I remained standing.

I moved my hand against the belly of one of them

and pushed upward and away, launching him across the room. He hit the far wall of the kitchen, landing on the wooden bench built into the wall next to the table.

I threw the other out the entrance, watching him land on the remains of the dining room table and the chandelier.

I turned toward Vengeance to find him watching me. I couldn't quite read the look on his face, but I might have seen a little fear. Everyone else in the group looked like teenagers, but the style of the Rocket suit hadn't changed since the 1950's.

Almost anybody could be inside, for all he knew — possibly even someone competent. If that was what he thought, I decided not to disillusion him.

I stepped over Marcus, preparing to blast Vengeance with the sonics if he tried to stab the mayor.

He didn't.

The window behind the table spanned half the wall. He turned around, stepped around the table and onto the bench, smashed it with his knife, knocking down a couple of the bigger pieces, and stepped through. I assumed that his camouflage must offer some protection against glass.

I didn't chase him.

A survey of the room showed I had other priorities. The fire had spread from one drape to the rest. Worse, one drape had burned through, a piece falling onto the pile of newspapers on the far end of the bench.

One of the Hangmen lay next to the pile.

A part of me wanted to pull him away from the fire. Another part remembered the Double V article. It didn't matter what I did. The house could burn to ashes—actually, it could probably be thrown into the sun—and the next morning those guys would get up, dust themselves off and start walking home.

Well, maybe not from the sun.

I could only think of that as a good thing though, because looking at the angles of the bodies, I had to have broken their necks.

Or backs.

I looked away.

If they had been normal people, I would have killed them. On the other hand, if they had been normal people, I'd have never thrown them like that.

I stood there for a moment, unsure if I should look for a fire extinguisher or just pull everyone out. The mayor had to have an extinguisher somewhere. Hadn't the city done a major push to get people to buy fire extinguishers and alarms just a couple of years ago?

It would be extremely ironic if he didn't have one.

I finally made up my mind when I noticed Daniel lying on the floor next to the mayor.

I stepped over the mayor, picked up Daniel, stepped onto the bench, and jumped through the window. I landed in the remains of a flowerbed.

Making sure I couldn't see any glass shards, I put Daniel on the ground and climbed back in to get the others.

As I stepped back onto the bench, I heard Haley's voice from behind me.

"Ni—I mean, Rocket, you're going back in there?"

"Everyone else is," I shouted back. "Everyone else is in here, I mean."

The mayor lay on the floor. I stepped over him again and did what I should have done earlier: I pulled the noose off Marcus' head. It resisted at first, but I didn't stop pulling.

Once it was off, he started and pulled himself back into a fully human.

"I don't know where I was," he said, "but I was somewhere else. All around me, I could feel this strange humming—"

Haley jumped through the window, landed on the table and hopped down on the other side of the mayor. She looked around at the bodies, the Hangmen, and the growing blaze.

"Oh my gosh," she said, "is that a gas stove?"

*   *   *

The house only blew up a little—at least in comparison to an atomic bomb. It didn't have a mushroom cloud, just gouts of flame pouring out the kitchen windows and doors. Judging from what it looked like afterward, it must have blasted out a couple pieces of wall too, but I was too distracted by the flames and smoke to notice.

We had already gotten out. The explosion destroyed the kitchen, part of the dining room, and set most of the back of the house on fire. Even through my armor I could feel the heat.

I'd hit the ground when it blew with everyone else, realizing belatedly that I probably hadn't had to.

As Marcus, Haley, Water and I got to our feet, the Rhinomobile pulled around the side of the house. Daniel stayed on the ground in front of me, still not feeling well enough to stand. Vaughn and the mayor lay near Daniel's feet.

The Rhinomobile stopped just short of us. A fire hose led down the lawn from the back of vehicle to a fire hydrant.

Over the loudspeakers, Larry shouted, "Anybody still in there? If you need help, give a shout. Otherwise I'm hosing this place down."

The side of the Rhinomobile opened and Larry walked out onto the ledge above a tread carrying another hose. He jumped down and ran to the back of the Rhinomobile to attach it.

Daniel said, "There's no one left inside. No one living, anyway."

"Got it," Larry said, and opened up with the hose. It didn't take long before he'd put out the worst of fire.

We all rode back in the Rhinomobile. No one bothered to chase us. In fact, cars pulled off to the side of the road to let us go past. They probably didn't want to get run over.

I stood in the opening between the sleeping area and the... I don't know what to call it. The cockpit? The cab? Whatever you call the place people sit in to drive a vehicle that doesn't fly.

Larry drove, of course. Marcus sat in the bucket seat next to him, asking questions about the dashboard. It had a lot of buttons.

"That's for the oil slick," Larry said.

Marcus pointed to another button. "That one?"

"Engages the flamethrowers," Larry said. "I like to set the oil slick on fire."

"Is that why you've got a fire hose?" I asked.

"Nah," Larry said. "I've got a fire hose because every time I go somewhere, something starts burning."

CHAPTER FOURTEEN

Larry parked the Rhinomobile inside the hangar and we all walked out together. Larry carried the mayor. I found myself walking in next to Vaughn and Haley.

Travis, Jaclyn, Cassie, Marcus, Water, and Daniel followed us. Jaclyn was telling everyone about how she'd disarmed the police.

"Half of them were standing in a row," she said. "It's like they were saying, 'Jaclyn, could you please take my gun?'"

Everyone laughed, Travis particularly loudly.

"Like both arms," Vaughn said to Haley and me over the noise. "They hurt. Not unbearable pain or anything, but it's stayed there and won't go away."

He tried to roll up his right sleeve, but barely got

it halfway. What we could see of his bicep looked red and swollen. The forearm of his left arm—the arm he'd used to roll up the sleeve—didn't looked any better. He lost his grip on the sleeve three times while rolling it up.

"Fuck," he muttered. "I give up."

Haley said, "You need a doctor. Nick, the League used to have an arrangement with somebody. Do you remember who?"

"If they did," I said, "the doctor's probably eighty-something. Or dead."

She frowned.

I pressed the button that opened the door between the hangar and the main room of HQ.

If the room had felt full before we left, it felt twice as full now. Aside from the bodies still on the floor, Daniel's dad and C were sitting at the main table, talking to the Guardian and two women—Dreadnought and Flick—which meant we now had almost a third of the Midwest Defenders in residence.

Aside from the people who were physically there, the big wall screen held three more images: The Marvelous X, current president of the Michigan Heroes Alliance, and a man and a woman were wearing dark business suits.

Daniel's dad stood up from the table as the door rolled open and I heard Jaclyn's grandfather say, "They're back. Time to get started."

The people disappeared from the screen.

The Guardian and Flick followed Daniel's dad, the three of them meeting us halfway into the room.

The Guardian looked just as he had while chewing us out after we'd fought the Grey Giant: big and muscular in a silver costume. I pegged him as being in his early forties.

Flick looked a lot smaller, but only by comparison. She had blond hair and wore a powder blue costume. Her mask covered the upper half of her face.

"Aside from the explosion, it sounds like you kids did a good job," the Guardian said.

From our last encounter, I had a feeling that this would be the closest thing to a compliment that he'd ever give.

"Oh come on," Flick said, "it's not as if we've never blown up anything. They did great."

The Guardian stared at Vaughn. Between the blood covering his costume, the new scar on his neck, and the swollen redness of his arm (he still hadn't rolled down his right sleeve), he looked bad.

"Christ," the Guardian, "what happened to you? Let's get a look at this."

He pulled the sleeve up the rest of the way and then said, "Where else does it hurt?"

Vaughn held up his left arm, wincing as the Guardian rolled up the sleeve and inspected Vaughn's forearm.

"Kid," he said, "you've got two broken arms."

"He's a doctor in normal life," Flick said, watching them.

I'd guessed that from his gentle bedside manner.

Daniel's dad had already walked over to Daniel, so I asked Flick, "Not that I'm not happy to see all of you, but why are you here?"

"You know Mindstryke. You've been all over the news for weeks now. They've been showing pictures of your fight with Tomahawk, and the broken window in the mayor's office. Mindstryke thinks you'll need an appearance that will put you on TV, and maybe throw out a few memorable sound bites."

"Is there some way I could avoid being on TV?" I said.

"Are you nervous?" Haley asked. "Your grandfather was on TV all the time."

"Was he your grandfather?" Flick said. "I wondered about the connection. I remember seeing him on TV as a little kid. He always seemed so calm."

Flick didn't seem all that much older than us. I would have guessed mid to late twenties. At best she could have seen him at the tail end of his career, unless she'd seen some old news footage. During a history class, I once saw him in a World War II era newsreel.

"Grandpa handled questions from the press," I said. "He said no one else ever wanted to."

"Was that how it happened?" Haley asked. "My grandfather always said it was because he was better at it than anyone else."

"No," I said. "He just hated it less."

"I'm sure they won't make you if you don't want to," Flick said.

Off to my left I heard a crackle of energy and then a door-sized, reflective rectangle appeared next to Vaughn and the Guardian.

"Flick," the Guardian said. "Kid Lightning over here needs more medical attention than I can give him without supplies. I'm taking him to the Chicago HQ. Don't let them start without me."

He didn't even wait for a reply. He dragged Vaughn through, the reflective surface splashing bits of itself into the air before disappearing entirely.

Vaughn's voice cut off as they disappeared. "Hey, I'm called Storm Ki—"

"Wow," I said. "He doesn't hesitate."

"He doesn't," Flick said, "but when you get to know him better, he's a real sweetheart."

Maybe he was, I thought. Maybe deep inside Guardian loved people and fluffy bunnies, but it didn't stop him from being a total jerk on the outside.

"So," Flick said, "tell me about yourselves. How did you get involved in all of this?"

We spent the next hour talking with Flick and with each other. While we'd been out, Jaclyn's grandfather had ordered pizza because no one had had supper. Checking the time on one of the monitors at HQ's main table, I found that it was only 9:13pm. It felt like months had passed since we'd left.

In order to eat, I had to pull off my helmet and use the mask from the stealth suit. It left enough of my mouth uncovered to allow eating. I considered eating without the mask, but didn't. Dreadnought and Flick were heroes, but I didn't know them.

After an hour, Jaclyn's grandfather said, "Now I know Guardian's not back yet, but he's agreed to everything. For the benefit of the kids, let's talk about what we're going to do. Mindstryke?"

Daniel's dad stood up and addressed us.

"You've all seen the news reports about the mayor, the Rocket and Storm King. What that means is that when we turn the mayor in, we can't turn him in quietly to the police or the Feds. We've got to give them an image to compete with all the destruction. At 10:00pm, we'll land in front of the police station. Between C and I, we've contacted the local and national media. We'll also have a Fed telepath waiting for us at the station. He'll be going through the mayor's mind and the minds of all the heroes who had been misled into helping him.

"The Michigan Heroes Alliance will have their own telepath along as a witness. That way we've got a neutral party there. We're going to reestablish trust in the League by reminding them of the first League. What that means is C's going to be running alongside the Rhinomobile with Jaclyn and we're going to minimize how much anybody speaks to the press. We'll use the Rocket as a spokesman."

"What?" I said.

Daniel's dad said. "Don't be nervous about it. I'll tell you what to say."

"I'll be your puppet?" I said.

"No. I'll just be offering advice. Good advice. Nothing's going to say the Heroes League is back like the Rocket taking the microphone. If you could tweak the vocal output to give just a hint of those old recordings of your grandfather's voice, it would be even better."

"I don't want to be a fake."

"You won't be a fake. You'll be reassuring. They'll know you're not the original. You'll know. I'll know, but it doesn't matter. People don't make every decision based on logic. They base them on impressions. It's your choice whether those impressions work for you, or against you."

I opened my mouth to begin to object, but I heard static off to my left. Guardian and Vaughn stepped out of a gate. Both of Vaughn's arms hung in slings.

"Already at it?" Guardian said. "I asked you to wait."

Daniel's dad said, "We're just going over the basics.

Nothing you haven't already agreed to. The Rocket and I were just talking about how he fit in."

"Nice touch," the Guardian said. "It's 1953 all over again."

"I don't really want to," I said. "I don't like public speaking."

"Sometimes you just have to suck it up and do it. Besides, this doesn't have to be hard. Let him into your head and Mindstryke over there can flap your lips for you."

"No. There's no way I'm doing that," I said.

"That was a joke. I wasn't suggesting you let Mindstryke take over, but you need to listen to the guy. No one thinks about it when they start, but managing your image is a major piece of the job."

Guardian pulled a couple pieces of pepperoni pizza onto a plate.

Flick leaned in toward the table and smiled briefly. "He's right. Some of you have heard about what happened when I joined the Defenders. I think the most important thing I've learned in the past two years is how to handle myself in public."

I hadn't heard, but didn't get a chance to ask.

She looked over at Daniel's dad, and then to the Guardian. "You're not planning on having him speak very long, are you?"

Daniel's dad said, "Nothing long. Just a short explanation of why we have the mayor."

Cassie looked up from her own plate of pizza and said, "Nothing against the Rocket, but I've heard his explanation for why we needed to get the mayor and it's not short."

"I won't have to go over all that stuff with Magnus

for the press," I said.

"You'd better not," Cassie said. "And if you feel the urge to talk about how the roachbots work, resist that, too."

Water, standing on the far end of the table next to Marcus said, "Who's Magnus?"

Marcus said, "Don't worry about it." Turning to the rest of us, he said, "I'll tell him later."

Flick turned toward me. "Roachbots? As in cockroaches?"

* * *

Grand Lake's police department operated out of an old building downtown. From the 1920's up to the early 1970's, it used to be Fleischmann's department store, but the store moved to a mall in the suburbs. The building dated from the late 1800's, but any interesting architectural features had been removed by renovations in the 1980's. Now it looked like a tall, featureless, brick building.

Oddly, the 2002 renovation for the police department's relocation included adding in Victorian-style lights and circular signs with the word "Police" in large letters.

I ran in front of the Rhinomobile with Jaclyn and her grandfather. Marcus, Daniel and Daniel's father flew just above us. Everyone else rode inside.

Ahead of us, the police had blocked off traffic so we could take the Rhinomobile directly in front of the main entrance.

"Watch out for the curb," Jaclyn said.

"I've been stepping over curbs since before you were born," I heard her grandfather say.

News crews stood on both sides of me, but the police kept the path from the Rhinomobile to the entrance clear. In front of the door stood the FBI agents that had tried to catch us earlier—Agent Brown and her people, wearing copies of Grandpa's 40's era armor. The group included a new member, another guy in the standard navy blue FBI super uniform. This guy, however, had a silver helmet. So... Fed telepath? Check.

A skinny guy in a green karate uniform stood off to the side of them. I recognized him. It had to be PsyKick, the telepath from the Michigan Heroes Alliance. I'd always thought he had one of the cheesier codenames imaginable. It was like he sat down one day and asked himself, "I'm a martial artist and a telepath. What will I call myself? Ooooh. Psy... Kick! Isn't that clever?"

He glared at me.

Annoyed Michigan Heroes Alliance guy? Check.

Daniel landed next to me. *You need to think a little more quietly*, he suggested.

A silver rectangle appeared in front of us. Flick, Dreadnought and Guardian stepped out of it and the doorway disappeared.

If I'd had any worry that this would end up in a gigantic melee, their arrival would have ended it. Dreadnought and the Guardian had to be on the A-list of powered supers. Guardian had been turned into some kind of super-soldier by a race of energy beings. I didn't know Dreadnought's origin, but I knew that (appropriately, given her name) she could throw battleships.

Between the two of them, I was fairly sure the police and the Feds felt motivated to give us the benefit of the doubt.

Behind me, I could hear the door of the Rhinomobile open. I turned to watch the rest of the team jump out— Larry, Water, Travis, Haley, Cassie and Vaughn (slings and all).

After them, the bodies of the mayor and all six of the heroes who had fought us floated out.

Cameras flashed while reporters shouted questions.

Now, Nick, Daniel's dad told me.

So this was it, my moment in the spotlight.

"Attention, everybody! Hey!" I said, giving the sonics enough volume for me to shout over the crowd.

Everybody stopped talking and looked at me expectantly.

I suddenly wished I had three by five cards or had taken Daniel's dad up on his offer. What was I supposed to say again?

The mayor, Daniel said.

Thanks, I sent back.

Don't thank me. Talk.

"The mayor was a telepath," I said. "He left commands buried in people across the state and nation. We don't yet know all the people who were affected, but it definitely included government officials, police and the supers that we're bringing in now. We've got a bunch of telepaths here to probe him for information so... um... you can all expect to know more pretty soon... Okay?"

Leaving off the 'okay' would have sounded a little more professional.

I didn't really have a chance to think about it, though.

Nancy Gonzalez, the anchor for Channel 10, started shouting at me. "Can you tell us how the fire started?"

I tried to think about whether I should answer or not.

Haley took my hand. "Rocket, we're supposed to go in now."

From my other side, Larry, massive in his own powered armor, said, "She's right. Let's get on in."

*   *   *

Inside, the police department looked like most institutional buildings—beige walls, tile floor, cubicles—but with the obvious addition of men and women in blue, carrying guns.

We ended up inside a conference room. "We" in this case meant new and old Heroes League members, the Midwest Defenders, the FBI representatives, PsyKick, Larry, and a few police.

It was a big conference room—two, actually. They'd taken out the divider between the rooms as we walked in.

The tables had been pushed to the wall and the sleeping bodies placed in the middle of the room. All the rest of us stood around the edges while Daniel, his dad, the Fed with the psychic helmet, and PsyKick deep probed their minds.

We had nothing to do. Daniel's dad had asked us to be as quiet as possible before they'd started.

For a while, I watched the telepaths, but watching three men stand motionless while a fourth (PsyKick) sat and meditated wasn't interesting. After that I looked around, read the motivational posters, and decided that I felt more tired than motivated.

Next to me, Haley leaned against the wall, quietly

drumming her fingers against the wall.

The Fed wearing the silver helmet looked at her. Then he held up his left hand, pointed at it with his right, and shook his head.

Haley pulled her hand away from the wall and looked at me, wearing a mildly annoyed expression.

I shrugged.

She shook her head.

After a few more minutes, I had a bright idea. I adjusted the pitch of the speaker so that it went above the range of human hearing.

"Can you hear me?" I asked.

She moved so that her back faced the telepaths. "You sound like a hamster," she whispered.

"Best I could do," I said.

She glanced over her shoulder.

No one seemed to have noticed us.

"We ought to do something again," I said. "I don't know when, but it looks like this whole thing with the mayor is wrapping up. Do you have any nights off next weekend?"

"I don't know," she said. "Travis always seemed to get nights off when he was at home. I'll talk to my dad. Even if I don't, there's always weekdays."

"Assuming we both don't get grounded because of tonight," I said.

"I'm safe," she said. "Both of my parents are working till two."

"Lucky you," I said. "My dad's probably up reading and waiting for me. I'm surprised he hasn't tried to call me yet."

The readout above my helmet's eye holes showed the time as 10:23pm.

"You two are dating?" Travis said.

The last I'd seen, he had been standing across the room next to Jaclyn, Cassie, and Vaughn. I didn't even notice that he'd moved until he was standing beside us.

"None of your business," Haley said.

"Hey," Travis said. "I approve. I mean, the Rocket's a hell of an improvement over that guy you were dating last year." Turning toward me, he said, "We're talking *total* asshole."

"We didn't date very long," Haley said.

"You know how much of an asshole? She ended up scratching the guy. You know, with the poison dewclaw?"

"Travis," she whispered, but it was a loud whisper. Then she gave a quick kick to his foot.

"Like I said," Travis continued, "he was an asshole. Anyway, I'll leave you two."

Everyone in the room seemed to be staring at us as he walked away.

"Sorry," Haley said.

"Well," Daniel's dad said, "we were done anyway."

Guardian stepped away from the wall. "What have you got?"

"A lot. We should go over it in private." Daniel's dad turned to the agent next to him. "Sid, did the helmet record everything?"

Sid nodded. "Every last bit. The kids should consider themselves cleared of any charges. We might have questions for them later, but we know what was really going on now."

"Good." Daniel's dad turned to us. "You can go if you want. If you need a lift, the Rhino can take you back."

"Call me when you need me," Larry said.

"It'll be soon." Daniel's dad examined the bodies. "As long as Sid's recorded everything and PsyKick can testify that he's seen the same thing as everyone else, I'll dismantle Bouman's suggestions and wake these people up. PsyKick?"

"My mystic powers have revealed unto me the mayor's deceptive tactics as well."

Daniel's dad said, "I'll… take that as a yes."

Then he turned back to the bodies.

Daniel walked over to Haley and me.

Switching back to a normal voice, I said, "So what did they find? Anything we missed?"

"Some more, yeah. My dad had me show him what I found earlier and then he explored a little deeper, but he didn't pass anything back my way. They're going after Magnus and the Cabal, though. I could tell Dad was looking for the day-to-day operational stuff. You know, the way they communicate, the kind of resources they have, where they live, names of people involved…"

Out of the corner of my eye, I noticed Cassie and Vaughn joining us with Jaclyn, Travis and Marcus close behind them.

"We'll get in on it, right?" Cassie said.

Daniel shrugged. "I'd like to, but I get the feeling Dad's not too wild about it, and even if he were, I know that Guardian isn't. So I'd bet against it."

"That's not fair. We're the only reason they even know about it. I should go over there and…" She stopped and watched the middle of the room. Daniel's dad stepped back as Water helped Fire to her feet. She hung on to his shoulder. On the floor, Earth and Air blinked at the lights, looking confused.

Mindstryke turned toward me. "Rocket, you'll want to get out of the room before I wake Tomahawk here. Bouman wasn't powerful enough to get that much of a response without something to work with."

"Wait," I said, "so Tomahawk really hates me?"

"I wouldn't say that," Daniel's dad said, "but let's call him a sore loser."

* * *

I shut down HQ for the night around 11:23pm, knowing that my parents weren't going to be happy.

We had arrived back at 10:47pm. In theory, I could have been home on time if I'd skipped showering and let everyone else turn things off. Unfortunately, just taking off the armor and putting it away had taken 10 minutes. Short of asking Jaclyn to carry me back to the house at full speed, I couldn't see any way to get home on time.

Since I was already in the hole, I decided to take a shower. With only one locker room, this meant waiting while Jaclyn, Haley and Cassie used the showers. The guys stood out in the main room with Larry and showered after the girls were done.

Given the wait, I think I did fairly well.

Larry hung around while I turned off the lights.

I turned them off everywhere except for the hangar and the main room, skipping the hangar only because that was where the Rhinomobile was parked.

We stood next to the Rhinomobile, Larry leaning against the tread. It felt good to be in street clothes. The armor got stuffy after a few hours.

I said, "I'm tempted to tell my parents. It would make nights like this easier. I'm going to get grounded for nothing tonight, and I'm sure this won't be the last time. My parents' block won't work if you just tell them straight out, will it?"

Larry looked uncomfortable, and said, "Can you say it straight out?"

"I don't think I could when I was a little kid, but I think I can now. Daniel said blocks degrade over time."

Larry paused for a moment, took a breath and rested his hand on the top of the tread. "Nick, don't expect too much out of your parents. I've got a feeling their blocks will still work."

Larry pulled himself up and sat on the tread. "Back when the original League was active, Daniel's dad and I spent a lot of time together. As stupid as it sounds, we were basically sidekicks, him to his dad— the Mentalist—and me to the Rocket. David hated the whole idea of the block. I could see his point. It seemed like the Mentalist had been in the head of everybody we knew. David even dated Suzanne, Red Lightning's daughter, for a while there. Oh god, that made things interesting."

"Wait," I said. "You mean Vaughn's mom?"

"Well, yeah. She must have figured out that he was a hero three times before they broke up. Freaked out every time, and the Mentalist had to erase it every time. After the third time, David's dad just forbid him to date her anymore, and finally David actually listened.

"He wasn't happy about it though. As soon as he had the chance, he planned to take all the blocks down."

"Were they dating when the League was fighting Red Lightning?"

"Nah," Larry said. "They were both under ten during all that. I wasn't much older. I only met Giles once or twice before your grandfather blew him up."

"So why didn't Mindstryke take down all the blocks?"

Larry sighed. "I'm not totally clear on it myself, but however the Mentalist made them, the blocks got linked to other things. David said that if he took down the blocks, he risked some kind of general personality collapse."

"*Oh*," I said.

"But they'd probably be okay if the block fell apart naturally."

"Huh," I said. "I don't think Vaughn's mom has a block at all anymore."

"Yeah?" Larry said. "I don't know anything about that, but I wouldn't be surprised. Nothing they did to her head ever seemed to stick."

We sat in silence for a moment, both of us lost in our own thoughts. Then Larry stepped into the Rhinomobile and it rumbled off.

*   *   *

The walk home felt cold. Barely illuminated by the streetlights, I saw the remains of our fight on Grandpa's street—the white goo from Future Knight's gun, the broken garage door, the window. It could have been worse. If Vaughn had been in the fight, he'd have flung lightning around. Imagine the devastation from one of his misses.

I checked the messages on my cell phone. Isaac Lim left a message congratulating me and letting me know that his superiors were allowing him to contact us again. Martin Magnus had left a message that I should call him back.

I didn't plan to.

I walked through the door to my house around 11:45.

Dad sat at the kitchen table, a pile of books and notebooks next to his laptop. Mom had to be in bed by now.

He looked up as I stepped in. "Hi Nick, how'd it go?"

"How'd what go?" I said.

"Whatever you were doing at Daniel's house. His dad called around supper time to let us know you might be home late."

"He did?"

Dad pushed his chair back from the table and said, "He did. What were you doing?"

I hesitated. Should I try to tell him? Even if he didn't like it, I'd still feel better with him knowing.

"Well," I said, "that's an interesting question. I got together with Daniel and some friends and we kidnapped the mayor and turned him in to the police."

"Got together with friends? The DVD night thing?"

"Kind of," I said. "Except there wasn't a movie and we almost burned down the mayor's house."

"Good. I always thought you ought to get out more. You're never going to have this kind of free time again in your life. Look at me: it's Friday night and I'm working." He closed the laptop. "Well, not any more, I'm going to bed. You should, too."

I hung up my coat in the closet while he picked up the books and put the computer in its bag.

Obviously the block was still in full force. Crazy. I'd spent half the night stopping the mayor from mentally manipulating people, and freeing the people he had deluded with his mind control.

My own parents were stuck within the block until they worked their own way out.

"Good night, Dad," I said, and walked up the stairs to my room.

1953

Birth of the Heroes League

Even the snow in the parking lot passed his ankles. Joe Vander Sloot stepped out of the Chevy, shut the door, and walked across the almost empty lot to "Chuck's Pizza."

Giles' black Jaguar put the "almost" next to the "empty lot."

Joe shook his head. Only someone with the Hardwicks' money would put a car like that through a Michigan winter. Joe stopped next to it, brushed snow off the window, and out of curiosity checked which side the steering wheel was on. Despite being a made in Britain, the steering wheel turned out to be on the left. Joe wondered if they'd redesigned it for the US market or whether Giles had had his customized.

After a few moments, he walked away from the car. Ignoring the "Closed" sign in the window, he opened the door and walked inside.

Just as small on the inside as it appeared on the outside, "Chuck's Pizza" held four booths and a couple tables. To the right, Joe could see the kitchen on the other side of the counter. To the left, Giles and Chuck sat at the booth on the far side.

They were the only people in the restaurant.

Giles wore a pinstriped suit and looked heavier than Joe remembered. Chuck still looked small, but a muscular sort of small. He wore a grease stained apron over his clothes.

Unzipping his coat, Joe walked toward the table.

"Joe," Chuck said. "It's been an age. How are you? How's the wife?"

"Hi Chuck. Romy's fine. We're both fine." He sat down next to Giles.

Holding out his hand, Giles said, "Hi-di-ho."

Joe shook it. "Giles, I saw your car."

"You like it? The salesman told me they're popular in Hollywood these days. Humphrey Bogart's got one."

"I like it," Joe said.

Chuck leaned in. "I still don't believe it. You and her? She was on the other side."

Joe shrugged. "The war's over, Chuck. It's been over for eight years and it wasn't personal."

"War's over, yeah, but I don't think there's one of us she didn't take a shot at. Besides, you took up with her while it was still going."

"She came over to our side while it was still going." Joe's heart was racing. Were they really going to go over the same old arguments again?

"She was a spy," Chuck spoke with complete certainty. "You couldn't know what she had in mind."

"I've told you before—Isaac did. He passed her."

"Isaac made mistakes too. Remember the—"

Giles held up his hands. "Boys. Boys! Why rehash that old argument? The war's been over for years, and remember? We won. Let's talk about why we're here. Chuck?"

"Hey," Chuck said, "sorry about that. Seeing you guys again puts me back a few years. I didn't mean anything by it."

"It's alright," Joe said. "So, why are we here?"

"It's my father-in-law. He got involved with the Chicago Outfit. You know, the mob. Remember how 'Leonardo's' used to be a speakeasy? They got him liquor during Prohibition. He got extra food during rationing. Now he wants out, and as the guy who's going to take over after he retires, I agree. I don't want to be connected to those guys."

Joe nodded. "I wouldn't either. What are you planning to do?"

Chuck said, "Well, I thought I'd get a few of us together and put the fear of God in them. You know, what I'm doing in the neighborhood. Just bigger."

* * *

Two hours later, Joe sat in the sub-basement he'd excavated below his house. Nearly one hundred feet below the surface, all gray concrete, and filled with tools and machines, it wouldn't win awards for interior design.

Joe didn't know why he'd done it. A secret workroom had seemed like a good idea when he'd come back from the war. If nothing else, it worked as a fallout shelter. Of course, that hadn't been the real reason. Originally he'd intended to start up as the Rocket again—just like he had been before the war.

But he hadn't.

Some guy calling himself Man-machine had appeared while he was overseas. He ran around town in a huge suit of powered armor.

Joe didn't think that Grand Lake needed two armored protectors, and by the end of the war he had fewer illusions about what being a hero meant.

He'd decided to concentrate on his job. Being an engineer for an auto parts factory didn't inspire him, but it paid the bills.

He inspected the armor that stood in the corner. He had the suit he'd left three quarters finished when he'd gone to war. Dull, gray superstructure, and layered artificial muscles, it waited for action.

He'd left the version of the Rocket suit he'd created during the war with the army.

He sat on a stool and thought. If he did help Chuck, he'd have to finish it first. He had a few ideas he'd never gotten to try during the war and a few improvements.

Half an hour passed and he sat motionless, flipping from one possibility to another in his mind.

Romy floated through the ceiling, cigarette still in hand. Her feet appeared first, followed by the hem of her skirt and finally the rest of her body.

Joe didn't even look up.

She tapped the ashes into a metal bowl, eyed the suit, and in an amused tone said, "So, are you going to tell me what you're planning, or will I have to torture you first?"

* * *

He woke knowing that he had just drowned in the North Sea in full armor. He couldn't pull it all off before sinking. Half naked in the darkness, he had kicked and pushed. But had he really been swimming upwards? He couldn't tell.

Gasping for air, his mouth filled with water.

Bolting awake, at first not realizing where he was, he took a breath.

"Joe?" Romy's voice cracked, as if she were just waking from sleep as well.

"Sorry. Bad dream."

"Which one?"

"One of the drowning ones. The North Sea this time."

She sat up and laid a hand on his shoulder.

"It could have been worse. It didn't really happen. I've seen worse in real life," he said. The sheets and blankets lay on his lap. He suddenly realized how cold it was.

"I know," she said.

"I haven't seen any action since the end of the war, but I'm still dreaming about it," he said. "I don't plan to get back into it, but what have I been making downstairs? Some kind of bunker. I don't think all of it's even on our property any more. It's partly under the park."

He leaned back against the headboard of the bed.

"I told you about what Chuck and Giles are doing. I'm going to finish off the suit, help Chuck out, and then maybe it'll be over."

Romy said, "It doesn't have to be. You don't really

like your job. You've said yourself that you were at least making things that mattered during the war. Maybe there's a way to make a living off of being the Rocket."

"Well," he said, "maybe there is, but I can't think of one unless it's advertising. I could be the Rocket, sponsored by Camel."

"I'd try for Lucky Strikes," she said.

"Thinking they'll pay their share in cartons?"

"I can only hope," she said. "But I'm not joking about this. It seems like there are people in costume all over now. Man-machine here in town. The Marvelous X over in Lansing. Someone has to invent their devices. You're already doing it for Captain Commando and you did it all the time during the war."

"He's an old friend, and anyway, he breaks them practically the second they touch his hand."

"Then you'll have repeat business," she said.

"It's a good dream," he said. "I just don't see myself as much of a businessman. The best thing I can do is find a better job. Consulting isn't stable."

"It's better than being bored."

"I'd rather be bored than unemployed."

The alarm rang. He fumbled till he found it on the end table and shut it off. He reached over the alarm clock and turned on the lamp. She'd already pulled the covers back over herself.

Well, he thought, another day of helping General Motors conquer the world.

* * *

He stopped by Cannon's Hardware on the way home.

The snow wasn't any better than the night before,

but at least it had been plowed. Sand lay on a hardened layer of snow that covered the streets. The temperature was too low for salt to melt anything.

He parked in front of the store. It stood in a line of stores in two story buildings from the 1880's, one of Grand Lake's boom times. Neon lights spelled out "Cannon" on a sign that ran down from the roof to just above the first story. Kay's Sewing stood just to the right. He would have to stop there, too. Romy had asked him to pick up material.

He hadn't even known that she could sew.

He crossed the sidewalk. Cannon's kept it shoveled all the way to the concrete. By this time in the winter, most other businesses seemed to end up with a layer of snow that didn't seem worth removing somewhere around their stores.

He approved. If they kept the store like their sidewalk, he might stop here more often.

He walked in, pulled out his list and started going through the store. Half an hour later, he had almost everything he needed.

Pushing the cart up to the counter, he passed his list over to the cashier, a tall, blond teenager. Putting down a notebook, the boy looked it over and said, "We'll have to special order most of this. We don't keep these kinds of welding supplies in stock."

"And this," the boy said, pointing far down the list, "isn't really for residential use anyway. We try to focus on homeowner needs. We can special order it for you, but I've never seen it on the shelves, sir."

"As long as I get it by next week, it doesn't matter."

The boy pulled out a couple forms and some catalogs from under the counter. "I'll have to fill these out a second."

"That's no problem."

Joe looked over the counter while the kid wrote information out of the catalog onto the form. The notebook lay open next to the catalog. The headline of the newspaper clipping pasted to the page said, "Rocket Moves to Pacific Theater."

The picture showed him flying over the ocean toward an aircraft carrier.

Next to the article, someone had drawn his armor, labeling the parts, and making another purely speculative drawing about what might be under the surface. The handwriting and the drawing were both clean and precise.

The guesses, Joe thought, weren't bad.

"The Rocket's been gone for a while now," Joe said.

The kid looked up from the second form.

"Oh, I know, but he was great. He was from Grand Lake. Did you know that?" The kid flipped to the first page of the notebook which showed a yellowed clipping of the picture from some long lost article. It showed him running downtown in the first Rocket suit. He hadn't even added the rocket pack yet at that point. He couldn't have been much older than this kid when he'd done it either.

"I'd heard," Joe said. "Do you have pictures of the rest of them? He wasn't the only guy in that unit."

"No, just the Rocket. The rest of the guys always seemed to be sneaking around. The Rocket wasn't afraid of a full on fight."

"I don't think any of them were afraid of a fight, but tactically, the Rocket was the best choice. In war, you use people where they fit best."

"But you never saw them taking on tanks." The kid was getting red in the face.

Joe could actually think of times they had.

"Not in the paper," he said. "So am I all set?"

The kid didn't say anything for a second, but then said, "Yep. Do you need me to help carry it out to the car?"

"I'll be fine."

*   *   *

The butler opened the door and showed the two of them into Hardwick House.

Stepping into the small alcove next to the door, Joe noticed that Giles had had the place redecorated since he'd last been in. All the old Victorian furniture with its intricate carvings had been replaced by modern furniture with straight lines, uncarved wood, and basic shapes. Joe wondered where all the old stuff had gone, but didn't plan to ask. It really didn't matter.

Turning to the butler, he said, "Mitchell, if you don't mind, we'll find our own way in. They're at the top of the pyramid, right?"

The butler nodded.

As they followed the main hall from the older, Gothic mansion to the pyramid-shaped section on the far end, Joe sometimes poked his head into the rooms and pointed them out to Romy.

"The ballroom," he said.

A little later: "The library."

"That's the guest suite. I think Teddy Roosevelt slept there once."

Without the old furniture, the rooms looked less cluttered but somehow less impressive, Joe thought.

On the other hand, it wasn't as if he was ten anymore. He couldn't seriously expect Giles to have kept the house the same.

The elevator stood in a column in the middle of the first floor of the pyramid. They stepped inside and Joe pushed the button.

"A pyramid. A tower. A house that recalls the style of a cathedral," she said. "It's as if the owners are desperate to be old, but this house isn't even one hundred, is it?"

"It might be eighty," Joe said. "Still, it seemed impressive enough when I was a kid. Try to imagine playing hide and go seek in here. The basement is almost as large as the house."

"What do they use it for?"

"Not much. I think they started digging before they even asked why they wanted to dig."

They reached the top floor. The elevator opened and they stepped out into an open room with windows on all four sides. The top of Hardwick House's tower stood just across the roof to the west, blocking the downtown view. Beyond that, Grand Lake and Lake Michigan merged into the darkness.

Chuck and Giles sat at a table near the window.

They both stood up as Joe and Romy stepped out of the elevator. Giles said, "Good to see you both. Can I get either of you a drink?"

"I'll have a beer," Joe said.

Romy said, "What have you got?"

As Giles waved her over to the bar, Chuck moved beside Joe. "You told her?"

Joe said, "She asked."

"My wife asked, but I didn't bring her in. You don't tell people about this."

"You know Romy can keep a secret. She worked with us for almost half of the war."

Chuck glanced toward the bar. Joe followed his gaze. Romy and Giles were already walking back.

"Okay, she can help, but watch her."

Joe didn't reply.

"Well, let's start," Giles said. "Chuck and I have been going over the basics and we have come up with some ideas. We can't just tell the Chicago mob to keep away from Leonardo's because if we go after them later, they'll guess we're connected to his father-in-law. What we need to do is think big. We're going to tell them to get out of Grand Lake."

Romy handed Joe a glass of beer as they sat down at the table.

"We're just going to kick the mob out of the city?" Joe said. "That won't be easy."

"Easier than you'd expect," Chuck said. "The cops have to pay attention to evidence and proof and all that. We don't. I figure we go after one thing only— the profits. The mob wants to make money. If we want them out of here, we make it too much of a hassle to make a profit and they'll go."

"How?" Romy said. "How exactly will we go after their profits?"

"Lots of different ways," Chuck said. "First, my father-in-law has a general idea of who's paying protection money. I'm going to go in as Night Wolf and tell them not to pay anymore."

"That's one," Romy said.

"The other one," Giles said, "and this is the part I love, is that we start going after their property. They own some warehouses and some businesses. We burn down the warehouses and start giving their businesses hell. I'll use my influence to start investigations by the police, and make sure anything they need from the city bureaucracy moves at a snail's pace. I'll have my people buy up anything they need and sell it back to them at double the price."

Joe nodded. "I'd be lying if I said I didn't like parts of it, but off the top of my head, I see a few problems. The mob's going to strike back and the obvious target's going to be the other business owners. We need to make sure they don't take the brunt of it. Second, we're going to end up fighting the police or maybe even Man-machine when we start burning down buildings. Do you think we can get away with it?"

"Details," Giles said. "We'll sort it all out in the end."

"We're better off if we start sorting it out now," Joe said.

Romy took another sip out of her wine glass. "I think we've got the germ of something good here. Let's start one step further back. What sort of resources do they have?"

They talked until well past two in the morning.

* * *

Two weeks later, Joe stood in the McAllister's living room. Chuck sat on the couch. He wore a baggy flannel shirt.

"You can't see it," Chuck said, "but I got shot twice. Once in the gut, the other grazed me. I had my doc sew me up."

"How did it happen?"

"I'd just dropped by King's Smokes. The owner was on my list of people to contact. I talked to the guy and the whole time I could smell that he's scared as hell and just getting worse. So, I cut it short. On my way out, I climbed up the building across the street and when I looked back, I saw that he was on the phone. Before I got even a block over, people in one of the passing cars started shooting at me. Luckily my doctor's house wasn't far."

Joe nodded, then said, "Wait, did you change or does the doctor know about Night Wolf now?"

"The doc's one of my wife's cousins and he's known for a while. It's not the first time I've walked in there bleeding. I've stayed active, you know? I should give you his number. You might need it."

"If something gets past the Rocket suit, I'm not going to need a doctor. I'll need a morgue."

Chuck laughed a little and then grimaced. "Yeah. You've got a point there, but still, you never know."

"Yeah. You don't. I guess I'll take that number."

* * *

King's Smokes closed at seven at night. Joe landed the Rocket suit half a block down the street at six-thirty and walked down the sidewalk to the store.

A few cars moved slowly down the road. None of them stopped.

Joe guessed that the Rocket had been forgotten during the eight years between the end of the war and now. That, and it was dark by six in the winter. It could be that they just couldn't see him very well.

He opened the door to the smoke shop and walked in. Even through the helmet, he could smell the pipe tobacco. Boxes of cigars and tobacco covered the shelves. Behind the counter, a bald, mustached man smoked a pipe.

The pipe dropped from his hand when Joe walked through the door, his armor golden in the light.

"Hi," Joe said. He didn't quite sound like himself. Before leaving, he had experimented with the PA system in the helmet, modifying his voice to sound deeper.

"I'd like you to do something for me," he said. "Yesterday, Night Wolf came to visit. You called the mob and they came and shot him. I'd like you to do the same for me."

The man pulled his pipe off the floor, then, hands shaking, dropped it on the counter.

"I didn't call the mob. I don't know anyone in the mob. He didn't die, did he?"

"No. He didn't die, but he did see you calling somebody. Who were you calling?"

"My... wife. I was coming home late."

"I don't buy it." Joe's voice came out of the helmet speaker emotionless.

"It's true, goddamn it. What is it with you people? You're a bunch of thugs just like they are. Can't you leave things alone? I'm trying to run a business here."

Joe wondered when he'd stepped into a Raymond Chandler novel.

Stepping up to the counter, he said, "No. We can't just leave things alone. I don't see the point of being shot at all over the world only to get home and find mobsters in my own home town and people like you helping them."

He smacked the counter for emphasis. It made a loud booming noise, but didn't break.

Even as he did it, Joe felt like he was in two places—

like he was on the outside, watching himself. When had he gotten this angry? He needed to step back and calm down.

The man backed away from the counter, bumping the shelves behind him. A box of cigars fell to the floor.

"Look at it this way," Joe said. "You've been paying them protection money for years, right? If we're just a bunch of thugs, it's time to call them and get your money's worth."

"Okay. *Okay*, I'll call them, but can you get out of the store? I don't want to be near you if they come in shooting."

It almost made him want to stay. Anyone who snitched on people to the mob deserved to get his store shot up.

Giving the guy a final look, he said, "I'll walk outside. Just make that call quickly. I don't want to stand out there any longer than I have to."

The man didn't reply, but he did pick up the phone and start dialing.

Joe walked outside and let the door swing shut behind him. He walked a few steps away, waiting while the snow fell, appreciating the heater he had built into the suit.

He didn't wait long.

The car came around the corner, traveling quickly up the street.

Not a bad response time, he thought.

It stopped directly in front of him, maybe ten feet away. The passenger side door opened and a man stepped out. He wore a winter coat instead of a trench coat as Joe might have expected from the movies, but he did hold a gun in his hand.

From what Joe could see, the other three guys in the car also had guns.

Not that that mattered.

"Hey you," the mobster said, "get away from that store and stay away. Tell all your friends to stay away, too."

The mobster had a typical Midwestern accent. Joe couldn't hear even the slightest hint of Italian. It figured. He'd heard that the Chicago mob included more than just Sicilians.

He whistled, but it wasn't a tune. He started with one note, slowly heightening the pitch, using the suit's PA system to increase the volume to an unbearable level.

The mobster held his hands to his ears.

The car's windows shattered. The ones on the side nearest to him went first, followed by the front, rear and then the other side.

The man opened the door and jumped back into the car.

Joe closed the distance in one long step. Crouching, he grabbed the bottom of the car and pulled it upward, flipping it over onto its side.

The rear tires rotated uselessly.

"Tell your boss," Joe said, "that one way or another you guys are going to leave Grand Lake."

* * *

"So what happened after that?" Giles said.

They sat at the kitchen table at Joe's house, both of them holding bottles of beer. It wasn't as luxurious as the Hardwicks' mansion, but it was comfortable. The white refrigerator hummed in the background.

"The guy pulled out a gun and shot me."

Giles laughed.

"Yeah, I know," Joe said. "You know how I had the car on its side? I flipped it onto its top and started pushing it down the street. I'm not Reg, but I got the car up to the speed of traffic."

"How did they take that?"

"They didn't like it much. Chunks of packed snow and ice were coming in through the windows. You know, the big chunks that build up behind the wheels? You should have heard them cursing at me. After a couple blocks, I came to Harris Hill and pushed them down it."

"The hill where we used to go sledding when we were kids? How'd they take the big bump?"

"Not well. The car rolled."

Giles laughed for a while.

"I stayed until they got out," Joe said. "They were all walking and didn't look badly hurt. That made me feel a little better, but I still don't think I'd do it again."

"Why?"

"Well, with no windows, it would be all too easy to stick an arm out and crush it under the car."

"Ah, but they're all parasites," Giles said. "They don't make their own money. They steal other people's. I'd say they deserve whatever comes to them."

"I'd say you're right except they wouldn't have been hurt in the name of justice. They'd have been hurt because I was angry that they shot Chuck."

Giles shrugged. "The law will never catch up to them. I've spoken to the mayor and the chief of police. They don't have any evidence on these people. We're as close as it gets, mixed motives or not. I'd say they still got treated better than they deserved."

Joe mumbled, "Could be."

"Well," Giles said. "We've got their attention anyway. A couple of them stopped by while Chuck was at the restaurant today. They told him that he was to call them if any of us came by or if he had any clue as to who we might be."

"Did Chuck lie or just play dumb?"

"Oh, he played dumb. He turned on the charm and pretended he was just another scared little lap dog. I don't think they have any idea what's coming. Which reminds me, how's Romy doing?"

"I think she's got just about everything we need."

*   *   *

Joe stepped into Cannon's Hardware to check on a couple more things he'd ordered. Just like the last time he'd been there, he marveled at the care that someone had taken for the store. Everything that needed to be labeled had been, and the floors appeared to be spotless despite the constant stream of customers with dripping boots.

Either the store owner was a fanatic about cleanliness or the employees were extremely bored.

Judging from how the owner kept the sidewalk, Joe would bet on the former.

He walked up to the counter to find the same teenager as before. The Grand Lake Sentinel lay folded over on the counter. On the bottom half of the page, he saw a story entitled, "Armored Man Pushes Car Down Hill."

The notebook lay open to an empty page.

The kid stared at the paper.

"I can't believe he's alive. I figured he'd died in the war."

"Who," Joe said, "the Rocket? Why did you think that?"

"He didn't do anything after the war, but the other guys in his unit did. I just don't understand why he'd go after Mr Monroe's people."

"Did you know the guys in that car?"

"No, but the article says they work for Mr Monroe. The guy who owns the garbage collection business. He's a nice guy. When I was little he used to have my family and a bunch of others over for a Christmas party and play Santa for the kids. I don't get it."

"I'm sure that the Rocket's got a reason."

"It can't be a good one. This just makes no sense."

* * *

Joe stood in the sub-basement, completely suited up except for the helmet.

He attached the flamethrower under his left arm, a modified Browning automatic rifle under his right.

Crazy, he thought. Here he was back home and armed for war. If he kept on doing this, he would have to swap the attachments out for something less lethal. He'd far rather hand over a living criminal to the cops than a bullet-riddled, burning corpse.

He picked up the helmet and walked over to the tunnel that led up to the basement, shouting, "Romy, are you ready?"

A voice behind him said, "Long before you were."

He turned around to find no one in the room.

Then she appeared in front of the band saw, changing from transparent to solid. She wore a white costume with a mask that covered the upper half of her face. A semi-automatic pistol hung from her utility belt.

"You've got a new costume," he said.

"The old one had too many swastikas," she said.

"Do you really need the gun?"

"Says the man with a flamethrower and a machine gun?"

They laughed.

"And yes, I do," she said. "But if you've invented something better, I'll use it."

"I didn't think I'd need to," he said.

"Then you've got something to think about for next time."

"What makes you think there's going to be a next time?"

She smiled. "Normal people don't build underground laboratories."

* * *

It felt like he'd set half the city on fire.

It wasn't true, of course. He'd burned down a couple bars and a car dealership. Giles and Chuck had taken out a restaurant and the warehouse.

They'd gotten into a rhythm after the first two buildings. Romy would fly through to make sure that nobody was inside. He would break through the door and spray the inside with trails of the flamethrower's fuel. It didn't take much to start it burning after that.

Torching the car dealership had been a little like making popcorn. The ones that had exploded tended to blow up in clusters, with a couple more going off even after he'd thought they were finished.

They'd left Monroe's garbage collection business for last, planning to meet there.

The business wasn't much to look at, especially in the dark. Surrounded by old brick factories and warehouses, "Monroe's Garbage Collection and Removal" boasted a squat, brick building that was large enough to house garbage trucks, with space for administrative offices. It sat in the middle of a parking lot half filled with trucks. Lights on the building illuminated the parking lot and the chain link fence that crowded the edge of the sidewalk.

Joe and Romy stood on the roof of the factory across the street.

"Think they're on the way?" He said.

"They can't be far," she said.

Neither of them were looking at the building they'd come to burn.

South of them, near Grand Lake's harbor, a warehouse burned. Earlier the flames had reached past the roof, although they weren't visible now. The sound of sirens had ended not too long ago.

"The fire department's having a long night," Joe said. "I hope no one gets hurt."

"If Chuck's doing his job, there won't be any reason to get hurt."

Joe laughed. "No hard feelings about his sense of smell?"

"If anything I should thank him. Imagine what might have happened if he hadn't caught me."

Knowing the answer already, he said, "Have you ever thanked him?"

"No, and I don't think I will while he's still hinting I might turn you over to the SS."

"He's more up to date than that. I'm sure he thinks you'll turn me over to the Russians these days."

She laughed briefly. Very briefly.

The wind picked up, blowing small snowflakes across the roof.

"Cold?" Joe asked. "We could fly down to the street."

"No, but I think that if they don't get here soon we should start without them."

They waited another ten minutes. Joe watched in the direction of the harbor, hearing police sirens and wondering what that meant.

Romy's hand sank through the Rocket suit to touch him on the shoulder. "Let's finish it," she said.

"You're right. They can take care of themselves."

She faded, becoming transparent and rising a foot above the roof. "I'll go first."

He watched her fly toward the building, becoming invisible as she crossed the street.

Starting the rockets, he rose into the air and crossed the street, landing next to the building. He considered flying up to the roof to get a better view, but decided against it.

He walked around the side of the building, no longer able to see the road because of the garbage trucks blocking the view.

Someone had placed a wooden dog house next to the building. Joe checked inside, but couldn't see a dog. The mound of blankets, old towels, and shed fur inside argued that the dog had been there recently. Hopefully someone had taken it home. It was too cold to sleep outside, he thought.

Deciding that this was a good spot to stay out of

sight, he leaned against the wall and waited.

Romy stepped out next to him a few minutes later.

"There you are," she said. "I went through their files but didn't find anything new since Tuesday. It's all yours now."

"You didn't happen to see a dog?"

"The dog? No. It's always outside."

"It doesn't seem to be here now. I guess it's time to start the fire, but, could you check on what's keeping the other guys?"

Soundlessly, she flew away, disappearing through the brick wall across the street.

It didn't take long. He broke down the door and sprayed the offices inside with fuel. He left the repair bays alone. Then he took to the air and hit the garbage trucks and the building with fuel from above. The liquid splashed on the building's roof and ran down the side of the trucks.

Hovering over an empty section of the property, he raised his arm toward the building, set the flamethrower to burn, and clicked the button on his palm that started the stream.

He had sprayed a lot of fuel on the building's flat roof and it went up with a roar, creating a massive cloud of smoke. He wondered if anyone had heard.

The garbage trucks went randomly. One exploded. For the others, the fuel just burned, blackening parts of their metal bodies and cracking the windows.

He wondered if he should go back and finish them more thoroughly, maybe shoot a few bullets through the windows, but decided not to. The point had been made. He'd just done thousands of dollars of damage. It might have been covered under insurance, but what he could burn down once, he could burn down twice—assuming the documents Romy had been collecting all week didn't put Monroe and his people in jail.

A large, dark shape ran away from the trucks into the open area of the lot.

It stopped, turned to look back at the building and the trucks, then bounded to the chain link fence, pausing in front of a door. It had been chained shut.

Huh, Joe thought, the dog. Where had it been hiding?

He thought about carrying it over the fence, but discarded the thought. If he let it out, he'd either have to bring it home or let it wander the streets. If he left it, the firemen would get it back to its owner or bring it to a shelter.

He flew toward it, hovering some twenty feet away. He couldn't guess the breed, but suspected he wouldn't have been able to in broad daylight either. It looked like a mutt the size of a Great Dane.

It stared up at him, then turned its head to the street.

He heard footsteps. Big ones.

Joe followed the dog's gaze. Something huge and almost human-shaped ran up the street toward him. If he didn't know better, he would have guessed it was his suit's older brother.

Fifteen feet tall, the machine's chest and head easily cleared the fence. Joe looked it over. While, it had superficial similarities to his powered armor, it was an entirely new design.

The Rocket armor simply amplified his own strength. From the way the new machine moved and the loud whine as it approached, he guessed that multiple engines did the work. However jerky its movements, it moved quickly.

Dull gray, its limbs and torso seemed to be shaped almost entirely of rectangles. A massive gun hung under the right arm while a metal screen covered much of what would have been the face.

Joe had seen his picture in the paper, but now he was seeing Man-machine in the steel reinforced flesh.

Out of Man-machine's loudspeaker came the words: "LEAVE THE DOG ALONE! What are you going to do? Burn him like you did everything else?"

"What are you talking about?" Joe asked. "I'm not going to burn the dog. I only burned the building because the mob owned it."

"The mob? Mr Monroe's not part of the mob. He's a decent man."

"My definition of *decent* doesn't include protection rackets or money laundering."

"He doesn't do that. I've known him—I mean he's been in this town for years. Just ask around."

"I've been in this town for years. I didn't know anything about it until a couple weeks ago."

Man-machine adjusted his stance, lowering the gun arm.

Joe decided not to read anything into it, but hoped it meant his message was getting through. Just in case it wasn't, he edged ever so slowly right, moving away from the dog and between Man-machine and Monroe's building. If the guy did start firing at him, his misses would hit something that deserved the damage.

"Where are you going?" The gun arm went back up.

"Nowhere. Just moving a little. Thought I might get

away from the dog."

Joe stopped. No need to make the guy nervous. He had a huge gun hanging under that arm. Stupid. Could the guy have copied the features of the wartime Rocket suit without thinking about what he'd designed it for?

"So," Joe said, "what's with the gun? I've seen smaller weapons on tanks. Have you been facing some kind of armored menace I haven't heard about?"

"No... I just thought, the bigger, the better."

"I'd wondered. If you carry that thing around, you're going to use it on a civilian sooner or later."

"Well what about you? You're carrying a gun."

"I'm out to destroy buildings tonight. If I keep on doing this and I have to face people, I'll use something that takes them out without killing them. If you want, I'll pass on the design."

"I don't want your design! I know Mr Monroe. He's been a friend of my family for ages. I can't even tell you how much he's helped me—"

Joe stopped listening. It came together all at once. The overly certain attitude. The connection with Monroe. The powered armor with almost all the same features as his own. Could it be the kid from the hardware store? But where had he gotten the money to build this thing?

"Monroe paid for your materials, didn't he?" Joe said.

The gun arm came back up.

"Look, I'm not trying to make you angry here," Joe said. "I'm just thinking. How many mob related tips have you gotten from Monroe? If you think about it, you'd be a great weapon against rivals. Short of a bazooka, they'd have no way to stop you."

Man-machine didn't say anything. He seemed frozen in place.

"So what is it?" Joe asked. "Does he tell you that he's heard about a mob operation or do you receive anonymous tips?"

"You've no right to accuse him after what *you've* done."

Man-machine fired a burst from his gun. The bullets missed Joe, flying over Monroe's building to thud into the top floor of the factory behind him.

Joe gave the rocket pack fuel and shot upward.

The kid (if it was the kid) wasn't listening. Joe didn't care to find out what would happen if Man-machine hit him, but whoever it was in that armor had used deadly force just because he'd gotten angry.

That bothered him.

He rotated a little to the right, flipped over and shot downward, aiming to hit toward the back of Man-machine's left side.

Man-machine tried to twist and bring the gun around, but the armor couldn't twist quickly enough. Joe hit him in the side, knocking Man-machine over, but bouncing off him as Man-machine fell down.

The bounce carried him upwards.

He twisted left, making a quick circle over the burning building and the trucks to land on the street some thirty feet from where Man-machine struggled to stand up.

"Hey, I know you don't believe me, but hear me out. Read the paper tomorrow and then go out and hunt me down if you still want to."

Man-machine stood and shouted, "No. I don't believe you."

Then he jumped.

Joe stepped sideways, narrowly avoiding being landed on.

He threw a punch at Man-machine's leg, knocking him sideways, but not very far. To make matters worse, Man-machine's arm swung down from above, hitting him in the side with the bottom of his fist, knocking him down the street.

When he stopped tumbling, he pulled himself up.

Man-machine was already coming for him, boxy legs covering the distance far too quickly.

The dog, stuck behind the fence, barked at both of them.

Joe punched the button on his palm that fed fuel into the rocket pack, rising into the air. Hovering one hundred feet above the street, he thought through his options. He could fly away. It was a pointless fight. Whoever was in that armor hadn't thought about what it meant to use it. A punch or stray bullets from that thing could easily kill.

Man-machine needed to learn that.

The question, Joe asked himself, was whether he personally had any duty to teach.

Unfortunately, if he didn't do anything about it, who would? No one, unless Romy found the guys soon.

He could just wait, but who knew when Romy would be back? He could try to talk some sense into the kid, but it hadn't worked so far. At this point, Joe figured the best thing he could do was damage the kid's suit enough to the point that he couldn't fight.

Down below, Man-machine raised his gun arm and began to fire. None of the shots hit, but Joe cursed and started moving, thinking how much of an idiot he was to hover when his opponent had high-powered weaponry.

He aimed for the air above the factory, giving the rocket pack all the fuel it could take.

Man-machine fired at him continuously.

Stupid kid, Joe thought. Didn't he realize all those bullets had to come down somewhere?

Crossing the factory's roof, he shot toward its north side, where it met Elm Street. Then he came down on the other side, landing just around the corner.

Out of Man-machine's sight for a moment, he rechecked his own gun. It was ready, armed with armor-piercing rounds.

He leaned just enough to the side that one eye could see around the corner. Man-machine stood in the street in front of the factory, not seeming to know where to look. Sometimes he'd look up where the Rocket had disappeared, sometimes nervously in one direction or another down the street.

Joe stepped out from behind the wall and started firing—single shot, not automatic—at Man-machine's legs.

He fired carefully, using the sight inside the helmet. The first shot grazed the outside of the right leg. The second hit the leg solidly, making a hole in the middle of the upper part of the limb.

Man-machine pulled up his arm, beginning to aim the gun.

Joe jumped into the air, punching the button in his palm that gave the rocket pack fuel, weaving to make himself harder to hit as the rocket pack's thrust closed the distance between them.

He aimed for the middle of Man-machine's chest,

but at the last moment twisted to grab Man-machine's upper arm, hitting the right shoulder of Man-machine's powered armor with his left.

Man-machine toppled.

For a few frightening moments, the Rocket suit's thrust dragged them both down the street, bumping across the snow and bare sections of concrete and ice.

Snow sprayed up from the street, hitting Joe's helmet.

Flailing, Man-machine tried to get a grip on Joe's armored leg, but failed, unable to bend his arms far enough sideways.

Halfway down the street, Joe cut fuel to the rocket pack, then let go of Man-machine's arm, pushing off the street with both of his own arms. Man-machine slid past him.

Joe landed on his butt, but pulled himself to his feet while Man-machine struggled to coordinate both legs. The right leg wouldn't straighten out.

Deciding that it was time for the fight to end, Joe pulled up his gun arm and fired at the lower half of Man-machine's torso. Hole after hole appeared. After a moment, several began to leak fluid. Joe guessed it might be battery acid.

Man-machine's suit fell to the street and the limbs stopped moving.

Joe walked closer. "Are you okay in there?"

Silence.

"I don't know if you're hurt or just pretending, but I'm going to have to rip open your armor to make sure."

In a noise just short of an explosion, the armor cracked open. Steam filled the air above it as a man in a black mask and jumpsuit leaped out of the wreckage and began to run away.

Joe didn't give chase.

* * *

Holding the phone to his ear in the kitchen five nights later, Joe said, "Well, how was I supposed to know the kid was going to do that? He must have had more than one set of armor."

The Grand Lake Sentinel lay on the kitchen table with the headline, "Man-machine Destroys Monroe's House: Kills 2." Lower on the page, another headline read, "More Documents Link Monroe to Chicago Mob."

"The article says the deaths were accidental and I'd believe it. He didn't seem like a killer to me. I think he's just got a temper and an oversized sense of personal injury."

He listened a little longer. "Sure, Chuck, I'll be at the meeting."

A pause.

"Yes, Romy's coming."

Another pause.

"I've got to go. I need to drop by a couple places before they close.... Right. Good-bye."

He hung up the phone.

Romy stood in the doorway to the living room. "Are you sure about this?"

"I've got a duty to the animal," he said. "I should check on it."

"Well, the soup will be ready when you get back," she said. "Don't be long."

He pulled on his coat and hat, put his galoshes on over his shoes and walked out to the garage.

He stopped at Cannon's Hardware on the way. He walked to the back and grabbed a wrench. He'd needed one in that size for a while anyway. The store still looked clean, but the sidewalk outside hadn't been shoveled as well as it had been before. A thin layer of snow had been trampled into a flat, hard snow/ice mixture. Someone had put sand on top for traction.

Joe noticed sand and melting ice on the floor next to the front door as he walked up to the cash register.

The tall, middle-aged man behind the counter looked like an older version of the teenager.

"I expected to see your son," Joe said, putting the wrench on the counter.

"Yeah. He's out doing something. Hasn't been worth much of anything this last week."

Joe tried to think of a way to get a little more detail, but the man spoke again.

"Jerry's been all broke up. Came home last week with bruises all over his body. Wouldn't tell me how he got them. Then he saw the paper a couple days ago and blew up. He'd always liked Harry Monroe."

"The mobster?" Joe said.

"Yeah. I've been paying him protection money for years. I never explained it to the kid. I didn't want him to be afraid. Besides, Harry, he played it like we were all friends, and he was just visiting because of his garbage business."

The man picked up the wrench and read the price tag. "That'll be two dollars even."

Joe pulled out his wallet and paid.

Handing him the receipt, the man said, "I just hope he gets over it all soon."

"Ah," Joe said, "he'll get over it."

He waved as he left the store.

Starting up the cold car a moment later, he wondered if the kid would actually get over it. Losing two childhood heroes in a week, then accidentally killing two people? It seemed like a lot to "get over." Still, Joe had been through the war. He didn't even know how many people he'd killed. Hadn't he gotten over it?

He hoped so.

On the other hand, he'd spent the last couple of years digging a bunker and recreating his weaponry. What did that say?

He shook his head. Nothing he could do about it now.

Next stop, the dog pound.

Afterword

Stories don't come out of nowhere. This one in particular comes out of a community.

While people have been putting their fiction online since the beginning of the Internet, 2007 saw the beginning of a community of writers who deliberately published their fiction on blogs.

The Legion of Nothing was one of the earlier serials done in that style. This novel represents roughly the first year of Legion's posts. You can read the first draft of it there, but also the first drafts of upcoming books in the series.

Its address is http://legionofnothing.com.

There you'll find links to other serials as well as places you might find more online fiction.

The most important of them is http://webfictionguide.com.

While the reputation of fiction posted on the Internet is that it's probably awful, many are quite good. If you're looking for superhero serials, for example, I'd recommend looking up "Worm" and "The Last Skull."

You'll find many other stories worth checking out as well.

Acknowledgements

Thanks to the readers of the online version of this story (too many to list here), who found a massive number of typos and grammatical errors.

Thanks also to Anna Harte and Terra Whiteman, my editors, who found many more typos as well as suggesting other ways to improve the text.

MCM, Natasha, Tim, and others involved in creating the book's cover and layout also deserve my thanks.

Finally, I'd like to thank Ed Heil, whose penchant for entertaining himself by creating characters for role-playing games prompted me to create the first version of the Rocket. His drawing of the character played a greater role in the character's development than I probably realize.

About the Author

Jim Zoetewey grew up in Holland, Michigan, near where L Frank Baum wrote The Wizard of Oz and other books in that series. Admittedly, Baum moved away more than sixty years before Jim was even born, but it's still kind of cool.

Jim didn't attain his goal to never leave school, but did prolong his stay as long as possible. He majored in religion and sociology at Hope College, gaining enough credits to obtain minors in ancient civilizations and creative writing—had he thought to submit applications to the relevant departments. He attended Western Theological Seminary for two years. He followed that up by getting a masters degree in sociology at Western Michigan University.

Once out of school, he took up the most logical occupation for someone with his educational background—web developer and technical support. Simultaneously, he finished all but three credits of a masters in Information Systems, a degree that's actually relevant to his field.

He's still not done.

In the meantime, he's been writing stories about superheroes and posting them online. He's still not sure whether it's a good idea, but continues to do it anyway.

He's also not sure why he's writing this in the third person, but he's never seen an author bio written in first person and doesn't want to rock the boat.

More Books from 1889 Labs

Ascension

Vero Lau is just another teenage girl. Then she wakes up in the body of a robot. Her only hope for freedom is winning a tournament she hasn't trained for. Her teammates are scrap metal, her opponents seasoned battle robots. And if anyone finds out Vero's human, she's dead. "Hunger Games on robot steroids."

Codex Nekromantia

"Shaun of the Dead meets Hitchhiker's Guide." Life, love, necromancy, the fragile human condition when caught between the jaws of a very robust human condition, and wholesale zombie slaughter.

Typhoon

Kani is just another high school girl. Then her best friend is kidnapped. Forced into space piracy to pay the ransom, all Kani needs is to make one fatal mistake: tell them who she really is. "A thriller exploring betrayal, human struggle, strife and loss."

Gangster

From the dark, basement speakeasies of 1926 Chicago, to the decadent parties of the Hollywood elite, psychopathic Clara slices her way through various people across America in her quest for fame.

The Antithesis

Heaven and Hell like you've never seen them before. New Jury recruit Alezair Czynri lives in Purgatory and helps enforce the Code between angels and demons. But a storm lays just over the horizon... one that brings with it a war.

1889 Labs is an independent publisher dedicated to producing the best strange fiction conceivable by the human brain. Catering to a specific demographic of men and women between the ages of 3 and 97, we print everything from kids books to serious stories for adults. Our goal is to bring you on an amazing adventure onscreen and off. We hope you'll take us up on the offer.

For more information and our full list of books, visit http://1889.ca